"WHAT HAPPENED? ARE YOU HURT?"

She shook her head, trying to force her eyes to stop watering. Crying would only serve to make him feel worse. "I'm sure it's nothing." She pasted what she hoped was a convincing smile on her face. "I shouldn't have let the hammer slip. The finger's throbbing a bit but it'll be okay in just a minute."

"Don't be silly, I can see the pain in your face." He waved his hand in a give-it-here gesture. "Let me have a look."

She tentatively placed her hand in his.

He lightly cradled her hand, studying it with bent-head focus.

His touch was surprisingly gentle as he turned her hand to examine it. His own hands were callused and she saw the scar on his right thumb, the slight crook to his pinkie. These were the hands of a man, not a boy. A man, moreover, who didn't shy away from a hard day's work. But they were also the hands of an artist, a producer of beautiful creations. He was both a creator and a laborer, someone any woman would be lucky to have as her *mann*.

Praise for Winnie Griggs

Her Amish Springtime Miracle

"This beautiful story shows the sacrifice of two very different people who long to be together, and how they come to that conclusion through trials and challenges to find their happy ending. A touching story I won't soon forget!"

—*New York Times* bestselling author Lenora Worth

Her Amish Wedding Quilt

"Griggs builds a cozy world readers will happily settle into, and skillful characterization makes her hero and heroine leap off the page. Fans of Amish romance won't be able to resist this sweet treat."

—*Publishers Weekly*

"An amazing read…This is the first Amish-themed book that I seriously could not put down."

—Only by Grace Reviews

"A darling Amish tale with cute kittens, artistic quilt designs, fine furniture, a caring craftsman, a merry matchmaker, and Christmas cheer."

—The Avid Reader

Her
Amish
Patchwork
Family

Her Amish Patchwork Family

Winnie Griggs

A Hope's Haven Novel

FOREVER

New York Boston

Copyright © 2023 by Winnie Griggs

Cover art by Anna Kmet. Cover design by Daniela Medina. Cover images by Shutterstock.
Cover copyright © 2023 by Hachette Book Group, Inc.

Forever
Hachette Book Group
1290 Avenue of the Americas, New York, NY 10104
read-forever.com
twitter.com/readforeverpub

First Edition: April 2023

Forever is an imprint of Grand Central Publishing. The Forever name and logo are trademarks of Hachette Book Group, Inc.

The publisher is not responsible for websites (or their content) that are not owned by the publisher.

The Hachette Speakers Bureau provides a wide range of authors for speaking events. To find out more, go to www.hachettespeakersbureau.com or call (866) 376-6591.

ISBN: 9781538735848 (mass market), 9781538735862 (ebook)

Printed in the United States of America

OPM

10 9 8 7 6 5 4 3 2 1

*To my fabulous editor Junessa who not only
helps make my stories better but who is
always upbeat and supportive.*

*And as always, thank you to Renee, my
wonderful friend and brainstorming partner
who encourages and challenges me (in the
best way!) in equal measure.*

Her
Amish
Patchwork
Family

Chapter 1

Hope's Haven, Ohio
Late March

Martha Eicher leaned forward in her seat as the driver turned the hired car onto the familiar lane. It was *gut* to be back home, for sure and for certain.

When she'd left home to visit her cousin Brenda in Shipshewana right after Christmas she'd intended to be gone for only a few weeks, just long enough to help Brenda before and after the birth of her third child. But Brenda had developed complications and needed assistance much longer than expected. So what had started out as a three-week trip had ended up lasting almost three months.

Martha hadn't really minded—with both her younger *shveshtra* and her widowed *daed* recently married, it had felt *gut* to be so needed, and so in charge, again. But now she was looking forward to being back home—especially after the nearly five-hour drive it had taken to get here.

As soon as the car pulled to a stop in front of the house Skip, her *familye*'s English shepherd, came bounding out to greet her, barking as he ran circles around the vehicle.

Martha quickly climbed out and bent to accept the dog's enthusiastic greeting. Before she could straighten, the door to the house opened and her *daed* and Leah, his new *fraa*, stepped out with broad, welcoming smiles.

"*Gutentag.*" The sound of *Daed*'s booming voice let her know she was finally home again. "You made *gut* time."

Martha gave him a tight hug. "I was able to get an earlier-than-expected start. And Virginia here is a wonderful *gut* driver."

Leah stepped forward, holding her arms out for her own hug. "It's so *gut* to see you back home safe and sound. We missed you."

"Leah cooked your favorite meal," *Daed* said as he paid the driver and picked up the biggest of her two bags. "Chicken and dumplings."

"*Danke.* That sounds lovely." Actually, chicken and dumplings was her *shveshtah* Greta's favorite dish but *Daed* had never kept those little details straight. And at least Leah had tried.

Before she could take another step, an unfamiliar dog came bounding from around the house and began barking at her.

Martha took an involuntary step back just as her *daed* uttered an authoritative "Lady, *kum.*"

The animal immediately went to her *daed*'s side, tongue lolling and tail wagging.

"What have we here?" Martha studied the animal in

surprise. She hadn't been aware *Daed* was looking for a second dog—they'd gotten along with just Skip for quite a while. Lady was smaller than Skip and didn't look at all like a working dog, in fact she was the kind of dog *Daed* called a useless ball of fur and refused to tolerate. What was going on?

"Lady showed up here about two months ago and we couldn't find her owner. I think someone must have dumped her." *Daed* stroked his beard disapprovingly.

Leah spoke up. "She had a litter of pups about three weeks later. Five of the cutest little things you ever did see." She smiled at Martha. "After you get settled in I can show them to you if you like."

Leah had obviously wanted to keep the animal, which had no doubt influenced *Daed*'s current tolerance of the animal.

Daed waved her over. "Martha, you should make friends with Lady, since she lives here now."

With a nod, Martha approached the dog and squatted down, holding her hand out for the animal to sniff. If *Daed* was happy having Lady here, who was she to disapprove?

It took several minutes but the dog appeared to be naturally friendly and was soon accepting head scratches from Martha.

"*Kum*," Leah finally said. "I know you must be tired after your long drive. And Lady will still be here this afternoon. Let's get you and your things inside."

Martha stood, trying to ignore the little twinge of discomfort she felt at Leah's words. She knew her *shteef-mamm* meant well, but her phrasing had made Martha feel like she was a guest rather than a member of the household.

Then, as soon as they stepped through the front door, Martha paused, noting a number of changes since she'd last seen the place.

Several pieces of furniture had been moved around and an unfamiliar rocking chair had been added. It held a place of honor next to her *daed*'s recliner. The chair that formerly held that position, the one her own *mamm* had favored, now sat across the room. There was also a new clock on the wall, a side table she didn't recognize and some unfamiliar throw pillows scattered about.

It was disorienting to see the familiar furnishings out of place. "It appears you've made a few changes while I was gone." She was proud at how calm her voice sounded.

"*Jah.*" Leah's smile was tentative. "I brought in some of my things from my old home. I hope you don't mind."

"Of course she doesn't mind." *Daed* put a hand on Leah's arm, almost as if he thought he had to protect her. "This is your home too, ain't so?"

Martha smiled. "*Daed*'s right. This is as much your home now as it is ours. You must do as you wish here." She picked up the bag *Daed* had set down. "If you'll excuse me, I'll go upstairs to unpack and freshen up a bit before I join you for some of that chicken and dumplings you mentioned earlier."

As Martha headed to her room she noticed a number of other small changes that had been made since she left, changes that unmistakably put Leah's mark on the place.

She set her bags on her bed and took a deep

breath, trying to sort through her feelings. Leah had every right to arrange things to her liking. After all, she was *Daed*'s *fraa* and as such the lady of the house now. The thing was, she herself had been in charge of the household for twelve years, ever since her *mamm* had died. And old habits were hard to break.

When her *daed* married Leah right after Thanksgiving, Martha had known her role in the household would change, but she hadn't understood exactly how much it would change. After all, Leah had lived with them for several weeks last year when a tree fell on her house. If Martha had given it any thought at all, she'd figured the running of the household would go on as it had then.

But she realized now that had been a very naïve way to view things. It was only right and proper that Leah take on a primary role in managing the household along with her new role as *Daed*'s *fraa*.

And her own role was now that of dutiful *dochder*— it was a role she'd had before and one she could take on again. She just had to take a deep breath and pray for a humble spirit.

Once her things had been put away, Martha straightened and reminded herself that Leah was lady of the house now. Then she turned and went downstairs.

When she stepped inside the kitchen, she halted on the threshold. Her *daed* and Leah stood near the counter, speaking quietly. She couldn't hear what they were saying but there was a certain intimacy in their expressions and demeanor that made Martha feel as if she was intruding.

It seemed the two of them had gotten used to having the house to themselves in her absence.

In the future she'd have to remember to make a little noise before entering a room.

How many other things had changed in her absence?

Chapter 2

The next morning as soon as breakfast was over and the kitchen had been cleaned, Martha turned to Leah.

"I know I just got back home yesterday, but if you don't mind me leaving for a little while, I'd like to pay Joan a visit." Joan Lantz was her best friend and was due to get married next week. Not only was Martha looking forward to seeing her friend, but she felt the need to get away from her house for a little while.

"Of course." Leah gave her an understanding smile. "I'm sure the two of you have a lot to talk about with the wedding coming up so soon."

"*Danke*." And with that Martha was out the door.

She greeted Clover, the buggy horse she'd raised from a foal, with a handful of apple slices and a smile. "Did you miss me, girl, because I certainly missed you."

Once she had the horse hitched and was headed down the lane, she felt exhilarated. This, at least, hadn't changed. She could still find wonderful joy in the sense of freedom she got from driving alone in her buggy.

Joan's home was a short ten-minute ride and before long she found herself turning down the lane marked by a bent hickory at its head.

As soon as Martha stepped out of her buggy Joan came rushing out of the house and the two met in a joyful embrace.

"*Ach*, Martha, it's so *wunderbaar* to see you again. I enjoyed your letters but I've missed seeing you in person these past three months."

Martha smiled as her best friend stepped back but before she could respond, Joan's *daed* came out of the barn.

"It's *gut* to see you, Martha. My Joan has been fretting that you wouldn't make it home in time for her wedding."

Martha gave her friend a mock-frown. "She should have more faith in me. I'd never miss her wedding."

"So I told her." He waved them away. "Go. Catch up with each other. I'll take care of your horse."

"*Danke.*"

Martha fell into step beside Joan as the two strolled toward the Lantz family cherry orchard.

"When did you get home?" Joan asked.

Could she even call it home anymore? Martha drew her sweater more tightly around her. "Yesterday around noon."

"Well, I'm wonderful glad you've finally returned, that's for sure and certain. And with barely a week to spare! *Daed* was just teasing, but I really was beginning to worry you wouldn't be back in time."

Martha tried to let go of her worries and focus on her friend's upcoming nuptials. "I promised you I'd be back in time, didn't I?" She truly was very happy for Joan. The barely-there pinprick of emotion underlying that joy wasn't envy exactly. It was more of a longing to experience the same thing herself.

Pushing that uncomfortable thought aside, she gave her friend a let's-get-down-to-business smile. "How are the wedding preparations coming?"

"There's still a lot to take care of but I'm sure it will all come together in time." Joan hunched her shoulders against a sudden gust of wind. "My last day working with the *kinner* at Asher's was yesterday so that's freed up my time and attention."

Joan's cousin Shem and his wife had passed away a year ago and Shem's younger brother Asher, a bachelor who also had responsibility for his *grossmammi*, had taken in their four *kinner*, all preschoolers. Joan had moved in to help him out and had remained with them until now.

"Who did they finally settle on to take your place?"

"Debra Lynn Fisher. She's young but full of energy and thankfully she seems to be settling in quickly." Joan sighed. "I miss the *kinner* already, but I'm sure they'll do well with Debra Lynn."

Martha nodded. She'd only watched over Brenda's little ones for three months but she missed them now that she was home. It must be so much more difficult for Joan.

A moment later she looked over at Joan and realized her friend was studying her with a searching expression.

"What is it?"

Joan tapped her chin. "I was going to ask you the same thing."

Martha mentally winced. She'd forgotten how perceptive her friend could be. "What do you mean?"

Joan halted in her tracks, fixing her with a stern look. "Martha Elizabeth Eicher, I've known you since the first grade." Joan's tone would have shamed the strictest of schoolteachers. "I know there's something bothering you. I'd like to think it's just because you'll miss me when I move to Fredericksburg, but I know it's something more."

Martha picked a stick up from the ground and twirled it between her fingers. "Of course I'll miss you." Then she tried playing on Joan's sympathies. "But you'll be too busy with your new life to give me much thought."

"Nonsense and don't try to avoid my question."

Martha waved a hand. "I'm still tired from my trip, that's all."

Joan crossed her arms. "Shame on you for telling stories. How can I be happy on my wedding day if I know my best friend is unhappy?" She lifted her chin. "But if you don't feel you can trust me enough to tell me ..."

Martha sighed, knowing she'd been outmaneuvered. "It's not that I don't think you're trustworthy. It's that the truth doesn't present me in a very charitable light."

Joan raised a brow. "You forget, I've seen you at your worst."

If only that were true. But Martha sighed and gave in to her friend's not-too-gentle probing. "I came home to find a new dog has taken up residence and

Leah has fully taken over as woman of the house. Oh, she's been very sweet and makes room for me, but it's now more her house than mine. Which of course is only right as she's my *daed*'s new *fraa*. Then there's something else, I've come upon them on a couple of occasions when I felt I was intruding on them."

She tossed the stick. "My two younger *shveshtra* have gotten married and moved to their own homes. My *daed* has found a new *fraa*. And now—" She halted, not sure how to finish that statement.

But Joan finished it for her. "And now your best friend is getting married and moving away."

Martha nodded. "I am happy for you, for sure and for certain. It's just," she grimaced, "it's just that I don't know where my place is anymore."

"But *dechder* who are at home help their *mamm*s run the household all the time. It's what I did before I moved in with *Aenti* Dorcas and Asher. It's just the way of things and I'm sure Leah and your *daed* love having you around."

Did her friend really not understand? "*Jah*, and this is what shows how terrible I am. It's not the way of things for a *dochder* to have been in charge of the household and then to slip back to the role of helper. And besides, despite their ages, *Daed* and Leah are newlyweds. There are times when I feel like I'm intruding."

"Oh." Joan seemed a bit uncomfortable with that last. Was she thinking of her own upcoming newly-wed status?

Time to change the subject. "When does James arrive?" James Slabaugh, Joan's future *mann*, was a widower who lived in Fredericksburg with his three-year-old *dochder* Hilda. Most of James and Joan's courtship had happened by correspondence after their initial meeting at a friend's wedding.

Joan's look said she knew what Martha had done, but she went along with the conversational detour. "He and Hilda arrive on Saturday and will stay with my *bruder* Adam and his *familye*. The rest of James's *familye* and friends will come on Tuesday." Joan's expression shifted into something like worry. "I just hope the weather holds."

Martha nudged her hip against Joan's. "You and I have both attended weddings in rain and snow. It doesn't seem to dampen the bride and groom's joy any."

Then Martha linked arms with her friend. "Now, tell me what I can do to help with the preparations." Keeping busy was just what she needed to lift her mood.

Joan grinned. "I thought you'd never ask." And with that, Joan changed direction and headed toward the house where the two of them could go over the list of things remaining to be done.

Chapter 3

Asher wiped his hand on a shop rag as he stood and stretched his back and neck. Rowdy, the family dog who was part Lab, part collie and all energy, had kept him company for the past hour. But apparently he took Asher's stance as a signal that it was time to head outdoors, and took off at a run, which seemed to be the only speed the dog had.

"Deserter," he said to the animal's retreating form.

Then he frowned down at the forecart he'd been working on. The task he'd set for himself this morning was to start getting the equipment checked and ready for spring planting. And the first item on his list was the forecart. He'd meticulously inspected it from the shaft assembly to the hitch, tightening, greasing and lubricating parts as needed.

He'd also planned to change out the worn tires for the new ones he'd picked up at the farm supply store in town last week, but one of the bolts securing the left wheel was stubbornly frozen in place. He thought he remembered seeing a can of penetrating oil in the basement. If not, it meant another trip to town to purchase some. Which was not anything he really wanted to do. It would eat into his workshop time, something he tried to protect as much as possible.

This time of year, when the demands of the farm were not as high as they were in spring and summer, he spent as much time working on his orders for punched tin as he could. And it didn't hurt that it was the thing that centered him, made him feel creative and grounded.

His thoughts were interrupted by the sound of Rowdy's we've-got-company bark. He moved to the open doorway of the equipment shed, and sure enough a buggy was coming up the drive. Tossing his rag on the worktable next to the door, he headed toward the vehicle to greet his guest. It wasn't until the buggy was parked and the driver stepped out that he realized it was Daniel Mast, the person who was leasing the house that had originally belonged to Shem. Asher had purchased it shortly before Shem's death, allowing his brother to move here where there was more room for his growing family.

Why was Daniel here? The rent payment wasn't due until the end of the month. Hopefully there wasn't anything wrong up at the house.

Daniel spotted him and lifted a hand in greeting, then waited for him to draw close.

"*Gut matin*, Daniel."

"*Gut matin.* I hope I'm not interrupting anything."

"*Nee.* In fact I was just taking a break."

As they'd exchanged greetings, the two men had

drifted to the nearby paddock fence. When Daniel didn't speak up right away Asher did a bit of prompting. "So what brings you out here? No problems with the place, I hope."

"Not at all," Daniel rushed to assure him. "Just the opposite. Marylou and I still love living there. In fact I actually have a proposition for you concerning that very thing."

Interesting. Asher turned to lean his elbows on the top board of the fence. "What kind of proposition?"

"We'd like to purchase the house and land from you."

That set Asher back for a moment. He hadn't planned to sell the place any time soon. Perhaps not ever. Yes, Shem and Lydia were gone. And Asher himself was needed here on the family farm at the moment, but that didn't mean it would always be so.

He and *Oma*—his *daed*'s *mamm*—could always use the money it would bring, of course, especially now that there were so many mouths to feed. But it wasn't as if they would be in dire straits without it. The steady income from the rent payments was giving them the cushion they needed.

But at the back of Asher's mind was the memory that the house had been his for five glorious weeks last year. The only time in his life when he'd tasted the freedom of being completely on his own. Before Shem's death had pulled him back here again.

He understood Daniel's desire to have a place of his own, though, especially now that he and Marylou were married. No doubt they'd be expanding their *familye* soon.

"Of course I'd pay you a fair price," Daniel added quickly, as if he read Asher's silence as hesitation.

Asher straightened, pushing away from the fence. "Let me think on this and get back to you. There'll be time enough to talk price if I decide to sell."

Daniel nodded. "I understand. I just want you to know, Marylou and I want a place of our own. We'd like that place to be the home we're living in now. But if you decide not to sell, we'll probably start looking elsewhere soon."

Asher nodded. "I appreciate you letting me know. You'll have an answer before next month's rent is due."

"I'll understand whatever your decision." Daniel held out his hand. "I'll wait to hear back from you before we do anything." Then he returned to his buggy.

Asher watched Daniel's vehicle turn and move down the drive. The man was close to his own age but at the moment seemed so much more mature and certain of what he wanted out of life.

The sound of children's squeals caught Asher's attention and he looked up to see the triplets racing around near the garden, apparently engaged in a game of tag or keep-away.

Debra Lynn was nearby, keeping a close eye on them. Joan had chosen her replacement well.

He looked around for Lottie and spotted her sitting on the back porch, playing with her doll. Thank goodness she wasn't as rambunctious as her *brieder*. Three energetic, rambunctious *kinner* were enough for any one household.

He slowly moved toward the house. It had been almost a year since Shem and his *fraa* had died and he still had trouble believing that he'd be responsible for these little ones until they grew into adults. The transition from being their *onkel* to being their stand-in *daed* still didn't feel quite real.

Thank *Gotte* he had help. *Oma* of course. She'd done a *gut* job of helping raise him and his *brieder* after their *mamm* died eighteen years ago, but she was older now. One thing he'd realized after moving back here was that her mobility issues had gotten worse. There was no way she'd be able to care for these little ones on her own, not until the three-year-olds turned school age, and maybe not even then.

Joan had been *gut* for the *kinner* and for *Oma*, moving in here so she was available twenty-four hours a day. And the *kinner* had learned to depend on her presence, to consider her a part of this new family they were being woven into. Luckily there had been time to prepare them for Joan's exit, but it still hadn't been easy.

It was still too soon to see if Debra Lynn would develop that kind of relationship with them, but he had high hopes.

When he stepped inside the kitchen, he found *Oma* sitting at the table, peeling potatoes.

"Was that Daniel Mast I saw drive up?" she asked without looking up.

"*Jah.*"

"What did he want?"

"He'd like to buy the place they're renting."

She paused and finally met his gaze. "And what did you tell him?"

He moved to the sink and filled a water glass. "That I'd need some time to think about it."

She nodded and went back to peeling her potato.

He waited a moment for her to say more but she merely continued with her task. Finally, after taking a swallow, he spoke up again. "Do you have any thoughts on the matter?"

She waved the potato peeler. "That property is yours now, so what you do with it is up to you." She looked up again. "But is there some reason you want to hold on to it?"

He set the glass down, still not ready to dig into that subject. "I just don't want to rush into such a big decision without taking time to pray about it." And with that he headed for the basement to search for that can of penetrating oil he'd needed earlier.

Yes, he needed time to pray and think about it. But not right now.

Pushing those thoughts aside, he focused on finding the oil. He checked everywhere he could think of in the basement, but it seemed there was none to be found. It appeared he was making a trip to town after all.

He trudged back upstairs, then paused once he reached the kitchen again to speak to *Oma*. "I have to go to the hardware store. Is there anything you need from town?"

"*Nee*. But that box on the other end of the table contains my best serving pieces. I told Joan she could borrow them for the wedding. Would you drop it off when you go by?"

"Of course." His afternoon was already shot anyway.

Forty-five minutes later Asher lifted the heavy box of serving pieces out of the buggy, grateful *Oma* had cushioned them well.

When he reached the side door of Joan's parents'

home, he used his elbow to knock. A moment later Joan opened the door for him.

"Asher." His cousin gave him a broad smile as she opened the door wider and held it for him. "*Wilkom.* Come on in."

He entered the steamy kitchen filled with the aromas of several different dishes, and grinned. "You've certainly been busy. One would think something special was in the works."

Then he looked past Joan at the woman still at the stove and his teasing expression faded.

Martha Eicher.

He knew she and Joan were *gut* friends, of course, but he hadn't heard that she'd returned from her trip to Shipshewana. If he'd known she would be here, he might have waited to make the delivery on his return trip.

A moment later he'd mustered up what he hoped was a polite smile. "*Gutentag*, Martha. I see you made it back from your trip."

She returned his smile, though hers seemed to require very little effort. "*Gutentag.* And *jah*, it's *gut* to be back in Hope's Haven. And I for sure and for certain couldn't let Joan get married without me here to see it."

He nodded, then turned back to Joan. "I hope I'm not interrupting but I promise I don't plan to stay long." As he spoke he carried the box to the table and set his burden down. "*Oma* asked me to deliver this for the wedding. It contains bowls, platters and other serving pieces."

Asher hid a grin as he watched Joan eagerly peek into the boxes. His cousin had always had a weakness for pretty things.

Joan lifted a delicate rose-patterned china platter with a delighted smile. "*Danke.* And please thank *Aenti* Dorcas as well."

Then she turned serious. "How are Lottie and the boys? Are they getting on well with Debra Lynn?"

Asher nodded, still aware of Martha's quiet scrutiny. "*Jah.* They do miss you, for sure and for certain. As for Debra Lynn, she hasn't been with us a full week yet but I think she'll be a *gut* fit for what the *kinner* need."

"*Gut.* It makes it easier for me to move on knowing they'll be well cared for."

Asher gave her arm a pat. Joan really did have a *gut* heart. "Set your mind at ease and focus on your wedding plans. You did well by them this past year and now they are someone else's charges." He moved toward the door. "With that I'll leave you to your preparations."

He met Martha's gaze briefly and gave her a goodbye nod, then made his exit. The fewer words he had to exchange with her, the better.

As Asher made his way back to his buggy, he grimaced at the awkwardness of the encounter. He hoped his struggle to be polite to Martha hadn't been obvious. And of course it hadn't helped that Martha had responded so graciously. He'd done his best to avoid her these past twelve years. Not that it had been difficult.

After her *mamm* died she'd stepped down from her role as assistant teacher. She'd also stopped attending any of the singings or other activities the youth and unmarried members of the community participated in. He'd always suspected at least part of her reason for doing so had been due to guilt over her ill-advised plans for that summer when so much had changed. At any rate, by the time he'd been old enough to join the youth activities himself she'd no longer been in attendance.

He'd seen her here and there over the years, of course, most notably at Sunday services and other community-wide gatherings. But there had been no need for them to interact in any but the most distantly polite of ways.

Which was how he'd attempted to handle things this time. Once he'd gotten over his surprise.

But something about the encounter this time had felt different.

Was there finally enough distance from the past to put it behind them?

Not that he expected them to ever be close friends, but perhaps they could be at ease in each other's company again.

* * *

Once the door closed behind Asher, Joan rounded on Martha. "Are you ever going to tell me just what happened between the two of you?"

Martha kept her back turned as she worked at the stove. She was here helping Joan and her *shveshtra* with all the cooking that needed to be done for the wedding. There were only four days left until the big day, and Martha was spending all her available time helping with the preparations. It had never occurred to her that Asher might drop by.

At one time she and Asher's older *bruder* Ephron

had been best of friends. When the two of them were sixteen Ephron had decided he wanted to spend the summer with his cousin who lived in Columbus as part of the *Englisch* community. He invited her to come along, pitching it as a great adventure to round out their *rumspringa*. She'd allowed herself to be convinced, only learning later that Ephron had let his family believe the whole thing had been her idea and that he was just going along to keep an eye on her.

Asher, who was twelve at the time and adored his *bruder*, had begged her to reconsider, to not take Ephron away for the summer. Unwilling to unmask Ephron's true role to his little *bruder* she'd given him a noncommittal response, which of course had only angered him.

And when Ephron had decided not to return at the end of summer, Asher had held her responsible.

But nothing she could say to Joan would heal the breach between her and Asher, so she avoided meeting her friend's gaze and held her peace.

However, Joan wasn't ready to let it drop. "I know he's four years younger than you, but back in his adolescent days it was as clear as the sun in the sky that he had a schoolboy crush on you. And then almost overnight he was glowering at you as if you'd drowned his puppy."

"Let's just say it was a misunderstanding between us and leave it at that, please." Martha hoped her friend would finally drop the subject. Then she looked up with a more genuine smile. "Besides, today is for talk of your wedding, not what's between me and your cousin, ain't so? And there's definitely plenty remaining to be done."

Joan grimaced. "Don't remind me."

"Is everything ready for the arrival of James's *familye* and friends tomorrow and Wednesday?"

That was enough to keep Joan distracted, for now at least.

But not enough to distract Martha herself.

While Joan chattered on about where everyone would be staying and what last-minute changes had been made to the arrangements, Martha's thoughts centered on her history with Asher. She'd been an assistant teacher for a couple of years after she'd graduated. Asher, who was closer to her younger *shveshtah* in age, had still been a scholar at that time. Back then he'd looked at her with admiration and perhaps had even, as Joan suggested, had a bit of a schoolboy crush on her. But that was before that awful summer twelve years ago when he felt she'd betrayed him deeply.

The fact that she couldn't do anything to redeem herself in his eyes had left her with a melancholy ache that had never quite gone away.

When she and Joan finally took a break for a quick lunch of church spread sandwiches, Martha found herself being closely scrutinized by her friend. Was she going to ask about Asher again?

But to her relief, when Joan spoke it was on a completely different subject. "I've been thinking about what you told me the other day."

"I said a lot of things." What had Joan gotten into her head now?

"I mean what you said about not knowing where you belong anymore," Joan explained.

"Oh." Martha felt her cheeks warm. The last thing she wanted was her friend's pity.

Before she could come up with a more articulate response, however, Joan spoke up again. "I've been wondering if it's not so much that you're feeling out of place at home, as that it's more that you want to have a home and *familye* of your own?"

"Of course that's what I want." Martha tried to keep the edge out of her voice—she knew her friend wasn't trying to be hurtful. At any rate, that was the safe answer. She actually wanted more than that.

She wanted to feel needed and as if she had a purpose again.

To feel that she really mattered to someone in an until-death-us-do-part kind of way.

But she couldn't say that out loud, not even to her best friend. It sounded too needy, too pitiful.

Joan nodded. "And have you found someone that you've formed an attachment for? Someone who you would want to have court you?"

Martha picked at her sandwich. "*Nee*, I mean, not anyone in particular. But that's not to say I wouldn't be willing to consider a man who showed an interest..." But no one had, not since Ephron Lantz left the community twelve years ago.

"Have you taken any steps at all to find someone? Attended the singings, made it clear you're available and interested?"

Why was Joan pressing so hard? Didn't her friend know how difficult this conversation was for her? "*Nee*. I'm twenty-eight years old, too old for the singings. And I'd hardly know how to let the available bachelors in our community know I'm interested." Though the available part was obvious.

"You're not too old. Don't forget, I'm twenty-eight

as well and before I met James six months ago I didn't have prospects either."

Martha didn't have a response for that.

But she needn't have worried, Joan wasn't finished. "But age is not an excuse. Even in your younger years you didn't attend the singings or smile at the young men."

Martha was beginning to feel attacked. "You know why."

Joan sighed. "*Jah.* You were brave and industrious and very, very responsible after your *mamm* passed away. You tried to take her place and keep your *daed*'s home running smoothly and take care of your younger *shveshtra.* But you didn't have to sacrifice your own life to do that." Her expression softened. "That's not what your *mamm* would have wanted."

No longer hungry, Martha pushed her saucer away and moved to the counter, carrying some of the dirty dishes to the sink. "As the oldest *dochder* it was my duty," she said simply. Then before Joan could protest again she added, "But that's all in the past and can't be changed now."

Joan followed Martha to the counter with another stack of dishes. "True." She set her load down and folded her arms. "Tell me, what are you looking for in a suitor?"

Martha cut her a sideways glance. "I didn't say I was looking."

Joan rolled her eyes. "Humor me. If you *were* looking, what qualities would you be looking for?"

Martha thought about that a moment. She was past the age where she should think in terms of romance.

Much better to focus on the practical aspects of such a relationship. "Someone responsible, honorable, *Gotte*-fearing." Then she added, "And someone who would respect me and not take me for granted." That last took care of the mattering-to-someone part without falling into the fairy-tale aspect.

Joan gave her a thoughtful look. "A lot more practical than the romantic description I thought you might come up with."

That took Martha aback. Did Joan think she was merely settling? "There's nothing wrong with being practical. And you told me when you and James began courting that holding out for a love match was a *gut* way to end up a spinster."

Joan shrugged. "I did. But I also remember you arguing with me that love was an important part of a fulfilling marriage."

It was what she had seen between her own parents, and what she saw with each of her *shveshtra* and their *mann*s. But Martha had come to accept that it was not for her. She lifted her chin. "I still believe that. But I've also come to believe that not everyone is able to achieve that happy state. And I may just have come around to your way of thinking—that a practical approach, as long as both partners agree, can make for a solid, amicable marriage."

Her friend gave her a speculative look. "If you really mean that, then I have a suggestion." She tugged on her sleeve. "James mentioned to me that he has a cousin, an upstanding young man only a year older than us. Laban is single, owns his own business and is very responsible. In fact, he has all the qualities you just listed. *And* he's looking for a *fraa*. He'll be attending the wedding as one of James's *newehocker*s. I would be happy to have James introduce the two of you."

Martha placed a hand on her hip. "Joan Lantz, are you trying to play matchmaker?" How long had her friend been planning this?

Joan took Martha's hands. "I just want my best friend to find the same kind of happiness I have."

She studied Joan's sincere expression and found she couldn't be upset with her. "Have you met this fine upstanding cousin of James's yet?"

"*Nee*. But James assures me he's a *gut* person." Then she grinned. "Just think, if things work out between you, you could move to Fredericksburg and we could be neighbors again. We could watch our *familye*s grow up together just like we talked about when we were younger."

That did sound attractive—at least the part about her and Joan being neighbors again. But to do that she'd have to move away from her *shveshtra* and their *familye*s and her *daed*. Could she do that and be happy? When she'd been away at Brenda's, other than an occasional pang of homesickness at night, she'd been too busy to really miss her *familye*. But she'd known her stay would be temporary. If she ended up married to James's cousin, it would be a permanent move.

"At least let me introduce you to him." Joan's voice had taken on a cajoling tone, as if she sensed Martha's hesitation. "You don't have to make any sort of commitment beyond that. If the two of you find you're interested in pursuing something more, you can begin a correspondence the way James and I did."

Joan was right. She didn't have to make any big decisions right now—there was no point worrying over a decision she might never have to make. And it would be *gut* to have something to focus on besides her own unhappiness. This could be just the thing she needed.

Whether this worked out as she wished or not, at least it felt like she was moving forward. Despite her reservations, Martha felt a little tingle of excitement at the possibilities.

As for the romantic aspect, while that could be nice, actually more than nice, mutual friendship and respect were enough to base a solid marriage on.

Weren't they?

Chapter 4

Wednesday morning Asher was no closer to having an answer for Daniel about buying the house than he'd been on Monday when the tenant first approached him. He'd prayed about it and thought about it, but he still wasn't sure what to do. Even though he couldn't come up with a solid reason to hold on to the place, whenever he thought of letting it go something inside him balked.

Had it been selfish of him to put off answering Daniel, making him wait several weeks for a response? Would waiting make him any more certain of the right answer?

Hope Haven's Amish Marketplace loomed up ahead and he turned Axel into the parking lot. Guiding the horse and buggy around to the far side of the building, Asher parked the vehicle next to Stoll Woodworking Shop's freight entrance. Setting the brake, he hopped down and knocked on the door. A minute later Noah Stoll, the owner, opened the door himself.

Noah was an impressive person. At thirty-one he was a skilled woodworker whose creations were well sought after, the developer and owner of this marketplace, the father of three *kinner* and the husband of Martha Eicher's younger *shveshtah* Greta.

"*Gut matin*," Noah greeted with a smile. "I hope you're here with a delivery for me."

"I am. I have the eight panels you ordered, as well as a few other pieces I thought you might be interested in."

Noah nodded. "Let me help you bring them inside and we'll take a look."

A few moments later the panels had been placed on a worktable near the door. Asher spread out the eight tin sheets he'd made to fill Noah's order. The others he set aside in one stack.

Noah picked up the top piece, studying it with a critical eye. "Professional work, as always." Then he looked at the full set. "And all of them identical. Mrs. Milligan is going to be pleased with the precision of these."

"*Danke*." It was always *gut* to have one's work appreciated.

Then Noah turned to his left. "Andrew, the tin panels for the Milligan job are here."

There was the sound of a stool scraping the floor, and a moment later one of the other craftsmen in the shop came over. "Great." Andrew gathered up the eight panels. "I'll get right on this."

Then Noah turned back to Asher. "Now let's see what else you've brought."

Asher spread three other panels on the table. "These two panels with the pineapple pattern on them would go well in a pie safe or large cupboard. And this smaller one with the rooster pattern would work for a spice cabinet." Then he shrugged. "But don't feel obligated if you don't think you can use them. I can always build a frame for them and put them in Charity's gift shop on consignment."

Noah stroked his beard thoughtfully. "Actually, I think I'll buy these from you. I can use them in pieces for the showroom and to display as examples for customers to look at. It might result in additional sales for both of us."

"I'm all for that," Asher said with a grin. "And speaking of that," he picked up a folder that had been under the panels, "I brought these for you to use for that very purpose." He pulled a sheaf of papers from the folder. "These are copies of some of the patterns I use in my work."

"*Wunderbaar.*" As Noah paged through the papers his brow rose. "Some of these are new to me."

Asher leaned a hip against the worktable. "I periodically come up with new designs to try out. Some of these are fairly recent." As recent as last night.

"You designed these?"

"*Jah.*" Asher didn't know whether to be pleased or insulted by the incredulous surprise on Noah's face.

"Well, *danke* for bringing these. My customers will appreciate having them to look at." Then he straightened. "*Kum,* I'll put these away and then you can join me for a cup of coffee."

Asher thought about declining, then changed his mind. It would be *gut* to have a discussion, no matter how casual, with another adult, one that didn't involve the *kinner* or the farm.

A few moments later they were both inside the showroom, sipping on cups of the hot brew.

Noah gave him a searching look. "How are things going with Shem and Lydia's *kinner*? With Joan getting married tomorrow there must be some adjustments happening, ain't so?"

Not only had the woodworker been a *gut* friend of Shem's, he and his wife Greta had also been a source of help and support in the early days after Shem and Lydia's death last year. "The *kinner* really miss Joan for sure and for certain. But Debra Lynn Fisher is stepping in to take her place and I'm sure in time the *kinner* will take to her like they did Joan."

Noah took a sip from his cup. "Debra Lynn is young but that could be *gut*—she'll have the energy to keep up with them. Naomi isn't much older."

Naomi Petersheim was the sitter who watched over Noah and Greta's *kinner* while both were at work.

Noah gave him a searching look. "And how are you doing?"

Asher shrugged. "I miss having Joan around as well but we're doing okay."

"*Nee.* I meant how are *you* doing. Having charge of the farm on your own as well as responsibility for your *grossmammi* and the *kinner* is a lot for anyone to deal with."

Was Noah like all the others who still looked at him as a sickly youth who was incapable of taking on adult responsibilities? He'd outgrown that childhood infirmity by the time he was seven years old, but the reputation lingered.

A closer look, however, showed only genuine concern in Noah's expression, no judgment or doubt. So Asher gave him a straight answer. "It's a lot to handle, for sure and for certain, but I think I'm managing."

Noah nodded. "After your *daed* passed away and you took over the place and the care of your *grossmammi*, Shem said you were more than capable of handling the responsibility. He also said people rarely gave you the credit you deserve, himself included."

Shem had said that? Asher hadn't had any idea his oldest brother had felt that way.

"Still," Noah continued, "even the best of us can only handle so much on our own before we break. I don't know where I'd be if I didn't have Greta and my *brieder* and *shveshtra* in my life to provide support when I need it."

"You are indeed blessed." Asher had no *fraa* or prospects for one and no longer had any siblings in his life.

Noah nodded. "I apologize if I've overstepped by saying all of that, but I just wanted to let you know that if you need a break or need some help with anything, Greta and I are available to step in." He held out his hand.

Asher accepted Noah's gesture, shaking his hand firmly. "I appreciate that." And he did, even if he couldn't see himself taking advantage of the offer any time soon.

But as Asher left he carried himself a bit straighter. This past year had been difficult. The fact that Noah had recognized some of what he was going through and had offered to help if needed had made him feel less alone than before. And even more than that, knowing

Shem had thought him capable had applied balm to a wound he hadn't even been aware he carried.

Even if some others still thought of him as a boy, he now knew his oldest *bruder* had grown to respect him and what he was capable of.

He was actually whistling as he climbed back into his buggy.

Chapter 5

Asher stood near the paddock with a small group of men, enjoying the unseasonably temperate weather. The wedding reception luncheon was over and he, along with a number of the guests, had stepped outside for some fresh air.

He was also keeping an eye on his niece and nephews. He could tell Debra Lynn was still a bit overwhelmed by the rambunctious triplets when they were out in public. Then again, having charge of a five-year-old along with three-year-old triplets would be a bit overwhelming for any one person, no matter their experience.

He should know.

Asher had grown to really love those little ones this past year—all four of them—and he'd protect them with every fiber of his being if need be. But this was definitely not how he'd imagined his life going. To have four preschoolers so utterly dependent on him when he didn't even have a wife was utterly unnerving.

His thoughts were interrupted by the squeal of the boys' laughter, recognizable to him even mixed in with that of the other *kinner*. A quick glance showed them playing tag with one another and having a grand old time. Debra Lynn was nearby, watching but not interfering. He had to look a little closer to find Lottie but he finally spotted her sitting on one of the benches that had been placed strategically around the yard, keeping an eye on her *brieder*. She was such a protective older *shveshtah*.

He turned back to the discussion among the men he was standing with. They were talking about the relative merits of Percherons and Belgians as draft horses.

It was a debate Asher had heard many times before and it wasn't long until his attention drifted once more. Spotting Noah Stoll near the barn, Asher slipped away from his companions and headed in that direction. Noah had placed another order, this one for a half dozen large punched tin panels to use as insets in some cabinets he was building. Asher had had a new idea for the pattern border and wanted to get Noah's okay for it.

He'd only covered half the distance, however, when he saw the triplets headed for the other side of the house. Debra Lynn was focused on helping Lottie retie her boots and hadn't noticed.

Deciding he'd take care of herding them back himself, Asher set off at a near run. Those little monkeys could move surprisingly fast.

Turning the corner, he was just in time to see them barrel right into none other than Martha Eicher.

He mentally groaned. Of all people...

As expected, she handled the situation graciously. "*Ach*, what have we here?" She reached out and steadied one of the boys as another grabbed her skirt to keep from falling. The third abruptly landed in a sitting position, his eyes going wide with surprise.

"Are you boys all right?" she asked.

Asher arrived on the scene before his nephews could respond. "I'm sorry." He was slightly out of breath and he took a moment to get control before continuing. "The boys can be a force to be reckoned with when they run off together like this. I hope they didn't hurt you."

Martha smiled. "I'm fine. And there's no need to apologize. The little ones have a lot of energy and they need an outlet for it."

Asher nodded, trying to ease some of the stiffness from his demeanor. "*Jah*, that they do."

She looked around as if she expected to see someone else. "I hear Debra Lynn Fisher took Joan's place as nanny."

Asher helped the fallen boy to stand and brushed at the seat of his pants. It was Zach, he thought. "*Jah.* She's doing a *gut* job but the *kinner* still miss Joan."

Martha nodded. "It'll take a little time for them to get used to the change but I'm sure it'll all work out."

Debra Lynn bustled up just then, with Lottie in tow. "I'm so sorry, Asher, I just turned my back on them for a minute to help Lottie with her shoes."

The girl looked frazzled and Asher gave her what he hoped was a reassuring smile. "Don't worry, it'll get easier when you've all had more time to get used to each other."

Martha spoke up. "If I can offer a suggestion? If you want to be able to keep a closer eye on them, try finding a place where they can run free but still be contained. I think the buggy shed might do the trick."

Debra Lynn gave her a dubious smile but Asher nodded. Martha did know something about taking care of restless *kinner* and he wasn't too proud to accept her help. "That's an excellent idea." He took two of the boys by the hand and nodded to the third. "Zeb, let Debra Lynn hold your hand." He obviously got the name right as the boy obeyed. He grinned down at all of them encouragingly. "Maybe we can collect a few more *kinner* and their keepers on the way."

He gave Martha a nod and then headed off with his little troop.

It seemed he and Martha could get along after all, if only in a general sense. And as long as the encounters were brief and focused on something other than each other.

* * *

Martha watched the little group walk away. When Asher had first approached her, there had been that politeness to his demeanor, the emotionless tone that added more distance than closeness to their interaction.

But the final smile he'd given just before he'd walked away had seemed more genuine. It had transformed his face. He wasn't married so he didn't have a beard, which made his boyish face seem all the more youthful. Sometimes she had trouble remembering he was a grown man of twenty-four.

She had to give it to Asher, though. He might have

some glaring blind spots, especially when it came to his middle *bruder* Ephron, but when Shem and Lydia had passed away a year ago, he hadn't hesitated to take responsibility for their four *kinner*.

Of course, according to some of the things Joan had let slip, Asher had left all the discipline and structure up to her and his *grossmammi* Dorcas. He apparently still dealt with the *kinner* as if he were a favorite *onkel* rather than someone in charge of their well-being.

Then she shook her head. It wasn't her place to judge. Nor was it her problem to solve.

Martha inhaled deeply. She'd stepped outside looking to escape the crowded rooms for just a few minutes and get a bit of fresh air.

Despite Joan's worry about the weather it had been a glorious day, cloudless with moderate temperatures. The wedding ceremony itself had been both solemn and joyous. Joan had looked radiant. James had beamed throughout the ceremony, obviously happy, and his three-year-old *dochder* was charmingly giggly. The luncheon that followed had been loud and celebratory and all that a bride could want for her special day. In fact, from all appearances, today had been proof that a marriage didn't have to be based on a love match to make one happy.

As promised, Joan had introduced her to James's cousin Laban. He'd seemed a nice enough man and he owned and operated a leatherwork business, which meant he was industrious. The dark-rimmed glasses he wore gave him a scholarly appearance and his speech was measured, something she definitely appreciated. But there hadn't been any opportunity yet for them to spend time getting to know each other beyond that.

"May I join you for a walk?"

Martha turned at the question to face the subject of her thoughts. She smiled, pleased Laban had sought her out. "Of course."

She set a sedate pace as they slowly made their way across the yard.

"I like to be direct," Laban said, "so I'll say at the outset that I know your friend and my cousin have conspired to play matchmaker for us."

Martha wasn't sure from Laban's tone whether he approved or not. "*Jah*, Joan told me that as well."

"*Gut.* I think we should talk about whether we think we at least have a chance of suiting each other before we agree to a courtship."

A practical approach. "That sounds reasonable."

"Joan told me you have a lot of experience being in charge of a household."

She was surprised that was his first topic, but she nodded. "*Jah.* My *mamm* died when I was sixteen. I took over the care of our household and practically raised my two younger *shveshtra*. They're grown and married now, though, and I'm ready to move on to the next stage of my life. I want to establish a home and *familye* of my own."

"And what of your *daed*?"

A thoughtful question that showed he understood the importance of *familye*. "He has a new *fraa*, so he won't be left to fend for himself. In fact, I think they will like having the place to themselves." Without her to intrude on their privacy or routine.

Laban nodded. "That is *gut*, because my home and business are in Fredericksburg."

The implication was that he would expect her to

move. Not that that came as a surprise. She would miss her *familye* if she had to move away from Hope's Haven, but she'd expected as much. Besides, she could always make return visits. That's what hired cars were for.

She returned her focus to Laban, who'd continued speaking without waiting for her response. "It's taken a few years but I've finally established my business well enough to show a nice profit. And I've recently purchased a home with some land, enough for a garden, barn and small pasture. I'm looking for a *fraa* who would be a partner for me, who's not afraid to work, to keep my house and to help with the garden and livestock."

She had no problem with any of that. But a small part of her wished he'd said *our house*, not *my house*. "Of course."

Then he met her gaze with a direct look. "Since it's important that we be frank let me ask what expectations you might have."

Pleased he'd asked, Martha answered quickly. "I expect to be respected and appreciated for what I'll bring to the life and home of the person I marry."

He dipped his head in acknowledgment. "I wouldn't want a *fraa* who expected anything less."

Martha was momentarily distracted by the sight of Asher near the buggy shed. He had stooped down so he was level with his niece, and whatever he was saying to her had brought a shy smile to her face. It was *gut* to see that he'd earned the love of the *kinner*. She'd known him to be a *gut* person from his days as a scholar when she was assistant teacher. Nice to know that, despite how he obviously felt about her now, he hadn't outgrown that quality.

There was something about that little scene between Asher and his niece that tugged at Martha in a way she couldn't quite pin down. When he looked up and caught her staring she felt her cheeks warm and she hastily turned away.

There'd been speculation and directness in the way he'd looked at her, something she was sure had a lot to do with the unhappy history they shared.

Laban cleared his throat, bringing her thoughts back around to his question. "Since we seem to be compatible, I see no reason we shouldn't pursue a formal courtship."

A totally practical way to approach this relationship. "I agree."

His chest seemed to expand slightly. "Then I suggest we correspond over the next several weeks to learn more about each other as James and Joan did before we make a final decision."

She smiled. "That seems the prudent next step."

He paused and turned back toward the house. "Now it's probably time for us to rejoin the wedding party inside. Shall we?"

She fell into step beside him, not sure how she felt about how quickly things were moving. If things went as well between her and Laban she might very well be planning a wedding of her own soon.

But this was what she wanted.

Wasn't it?

Chapter 6

The next morning, Martha was a little later getting out of bed than usual and so had to rush through her morning routine. Thoughts of all that had occurred at the wedding yesterday had kept her awake late into the night.

As she hurried down the stairs her thoughts turned back to the wedding. So much had happened yesterday, things beyond those that went along with being a *newehocker*.

Talking to Laban had given her hope that she might finally have an answer to her prayers for a *mann* and home of her own. If he hadn't exactly been the man of her dreams, that was to be expected. She was too old for such romantic schoolgirl notions anyway. A fine, upstanding man with financial stability and a clear vision of what he wanted from life was worth much more than a romantic daydream. As for relocating all the way over to Fredericksburg, having to move away from her family and community might be difficult, but surely such a prize was worth it.

And Laban might not be the most romantic of men, but she'd take responsible and sincere over romantic any day.

After that one conversation where they'd agreed to write to each other, there hadn't been another opportunity for them to speak privately. Laban was heading back to Fredericksburg this morning so there wouldn't be any other such opportunities in the near future. It was disappointing that he hadn't been able to stay at least one day longer so they could get to know each other better. But she understood his dedication to his work.

Should she start the correspondence immediately or wait for him to initiate it? Perhaps she could just pen a short note to let him know she had enjoyed their conversation and looked forward to hearing from him. Of course she could also include a note about some of her skills that would make her a good helpmeet for him. Or was that too much like boasting?

She pondered that as she helped Leah in the kitchen. Although by this time the only thing left for her to do was set the table.

Martha turned at the sound of the kitchen door opening. Her youngest *shveshtah* bustled inside, carrying her daughter Grace. Martha set the stack of plates down and quickly crossed the room as she realized Hannah was breathless and obviously agitated.

"*Ach du lieva*, Hannah. What's wrong? Has something happened? Is Micah okay?"

Hannah nodded as she got her breathing under control and set Grace down. "He's fine. It's Debra Lynn. She fell off a stepladder this morning."

"Oh, help! Is she all right?" Martha drew her *shveshtah* farther into the room and closed the door behind her. Leah quietly greeted the new arrivals and then picked Grace up and offered her a biscuit and some jam.

Taking a seat at the table, Hannah recounted more of the morning's excitement. "They sent for Micah and he did what he could. Turns out she has a broken arm and a lump on her forehead that needs attention. He's gone with them to the clinic."

Hannah's *mann* was a paramedic, and ever since he'd rejoined the community last year he'd been called on many times by his neighbors when there were injuries that needed quick attention.

"*Ach,* poor thing." But why had Hannah rushed here with the news? Then she realized the implication. "What are Asher and Dorcas going to do for a nanny?"

Hannah gave her an apologetic smile. "They don't know yet. Their place is in the opposite direction as the clinic. I was hoping you could deliver the news. I'd do it, but I've got a large order of cookies to finish decorating by noon today."

Her youngest *shveshtah* was a very talented and in-demand baker in the community. "Of course." In fact Martha was actually glad to have a purposeful task to handle today. "Actually I'll spend the day there to give Asher time to figure out what they'll do until Debra Lynn is ready to return."

Hannah gave her a brilliant smile as she took her hand. "I knew I could count on you to help out."

Martha remembered the last time she'd seen Asher and how fleeting his smile had been. But even if he'd never completely forgiven her, surely Asher wouldn't refuse her help at a time like this.

* * *

Asher rolled over in bed and cracked open one eye to glance at his bedside clock. It was about forty minutes earlier than he normally got up. But he could tell going back to sleep was out of the question.

Interacting with Martha Eicher again yesterday had dredged up a lot of memories, both pleasant and unpleasant. And it hadn't helped that she'd seemed as easy to speak to then as she had when he was a boy.

As a kid he'd thought his older *bruder* Ephron had been the lucky one because he and Martha were such *gut* friends and he himself had been nothing to her but Ephron's little *bruder*. It had turned out, however, that being friends with Martha was what had ultimately led to his *bruder* walking away from his *familye*, from Hope's Haven, and even from the Plain life. Not an altogether lucky circumstance after all.

But dwelling on such thoughts wasn't productive. Nor was it an uplifting start to his day. He pushed his covers aside, along with all thoughts of the past, and got dressed as quietly as he could.

There was no point in waking the others yet. Slipping his suspenders over his shoulder, he padded down the stairs. The aroma of coffee drifting from the kitchen let him know *Oma* was up even before he stepped into the room.

She stood at the counter, kneading the dough for biscuits. He shouldn't have been surprised. He couldn't remember the last time he'd been up before her, no matter how early he rose. "*Gut matin*," he greeted as he headed for the cabinet where the coffee cups were stored. He noticed her cane stood at the ready next to her. Over the last year, *Oma* had begun to rely ever more heavily on her cane when she had to walk any distance. As far as he could tell, it wasn't so much a pain issue as a balance issue. What did this bode for the future? He knew better than to ask her about it, though. She'd just wave away his concerns and tell him she was fine.

Despite the presence of her cane, *Oma*'s smile was as sunny as ever when she returned his greeting. "*Gut matin.* You're up early."

He grabbed the coffeepot from the stove. "But not as early as you. I don't know how you do it."

"It's all part of being a *gut grossmammi*. Let me put these biscuits in the oven and then I'll start on the rest of your breakfast."

He lifted his coffee cup and blew on the steaming beverage. "I'm about to head to the barn to milk Daisy, so take your time." He met her gaze. "Debra Lynn should be here before I return but if not, hopefully the boys will still be asleep until I'm back."

She made a shooing motion. "Go on with you. I'm perfectly capable of looking after those little ones while you're out."

He grinned, then with a nod headed out the door with his cup still in hand. The *kinner* weren't the only ones who missed having Joan around. His cousin had lived here with them almost as long as the four of them had been orphaned, not only caring for the *kinner* but also helping *Oma* with the housework and giving her the adult female company she so obviously wanted.

At the time Asher had still been attempting to adjust to the loss of his older brother and sister-in-law. And to just how much his life and future had been affected by those losses. Of course he'd moved from the house he'd recently purchased so that he could be here. And at first he and *Oma* had tried to handle the *kinner* on their own, but they'd quickly learned they needed help. Then he'd hired a sitter who could only be there part of the day and that too had met with mixed success. When Joan had offered to move in with them, he'd wanted to shout with relief.

Asher set his now-empty coffee cup on a crate and added a little sorghum and corn to Daisy's feedbox. Then he sat on the milking stool and quickly but thoroughly cleaned the animal's teats before reaching for the milk pail.

As he settled into the familiar squeeze-and-release rhythm, his thoughts returned to the subject of the *kinner*'s care.

With Debra Lynn, they'd swapped over from having someone with them full-time to only having a nanny for about nine hours a day. But much had changed in the past year. The *kinner* were older now and had settled into their new routine. And to a certain extent the overwhelming grief they'd felt for the loss of their parents had been tempered by the passing of time. That being the case, he hoped there would be less need for a live-in nanny. Only time would tell.

When he'd finished milking, Asher let Daisy's calf Ferdinand have his portion of the milk then exited the barn with the nearly full pail of milk in hand.

He frowned when he realized Debra Lynn's buggy wasn't in the drive yet. She was only a few minutes late, but he'd hoped she'd get here before the triplets and Lottie woke up. The boys could be a handful when they first got up in the morning. That was the other good thing about Joan, since she'd lived with them she was on hand when the *kinner* went to bed at night and when they got up in the morning. She'd also been able to help *Oma* when she'd had one of her bad mornings.

But Debra Lynn had three younger siblings and her *mamm* needed at least a few hours of her time to help at home.

When Debra Lynn still hadn't arrived by the time he'd cleaned up and strained the milk, Asher's mild irritation turned to worry. Had something happened to her on the way here?

Before he could decide what to do he heard the unmistakable sounds of the boys stirring.

Oma turned and moved toward the hall but he stopped her with a hand held palm-up. "Let me. You have enough to do getting everyone's breakfasts ready."

Asher hurried down the hall knowing what he'd find when he got there. Sure enough, two of the boys were having a pillow fight and the third was cheering them on while he jumped on the bed.

He paused on the threshold as he suddenly remembered the horseplay he and his two older *brieder* had engaged in when they were *kinner*. Of course, with the difference in their ages it had been different than it was with the triplets. But it still left a hole in his heart to know he, Ephron and Shem would never laugh together like that again.

Then he straightened. Why was he in such a

reflective mood today? Was it because of Daniel's offer to purchase his house? Or because of his encounters with Martha this week? Or something else altogether?

Shaking off those questions, he entered the room with a smile. "Is anybody hungry? *Oma* has breakfast ready."

"*Jah!*" The toddler on the bed launched himself into Asher's arms with all the trust of a three-year-old who had no doubts he'd be caught. Luckily, Asher managed to catch the daring toddler despite having so little warning.

Unaware of his close call, the little boy giggled and hollered, "Again."

Asher set him down, realizing by the bruise on his forehead it was Zeb. "Not right now." He turned to include the other two boys in his next statement. "Put the pillows back on the beds and let's get the bedding off the floor."

Five minutes later they were trooping down the hall. Before the trio reached the kitchen, Asher spotted Lottie coming down the stairs. Unlike the triplets, she'd dressed herself, except for her *kapp*, which she carried. The little girl hadn't learned to put her hair up yet.

"*Gut matin*, Lottie," he greeted.

She smiled shyly in response and joined her *brieder* as they trooped into the kitchen.

They entered the room to find *Oma* finishing up at the stove. Her expression softened when she saw them.

"*Gut matin, schlofkopps.*" Then she frowned when she noted the boys' state of dress. "Is that any way to come to the table?"

Asher hid a grin at how quickly they'd gone from sleepyheads to rascals. "It's my fault. I thought it would be okay for them to eat breakfast in their night-clothes just this once." He hoped that by the time breakfast was over Debra Lynn would be here and she could handle getting the three squirmy boys dressed for the day.

Oma's frown held for another heartbeat, then she nodded. She looked over at Lottie, however, and the frown returned. "Asher, the food is cooked. Dish it up please." Then she grabbed her cane, turned and held out her free hand to her granddaughter. "Come with me, Lottie. At least I can help you with your hair."

Once they'd exited, Asher had the boys put the silverware on the table while he spooned the scrambled eggs and baked oatmeal onto the plates. The platter of biscuits and jar of plum jelly were placed on the center of the table. *Oma* and Lottie returned just as he was securely belting the last of the boys in the ladderback stools he'd constructed just for them.

Later, when they'd finished breakfast, Lottie began clearing the dishes. It was one of her assigned chores and she did it without being told and without complaint. Would Zeb, Zach and Zeke eventually grow into equally sweet, biddable *kinner*?

Asher moved to the threshold and glanced out through the screen door. Debra Lynn was now more than an hour late and he was becoming more and more worried by her tardiness.

"No sign yet?" There was a touch of worry in *Oma*'s voice.

"I'm sure it's only something trivial like she overslept." Still, he wondered if he should head out and check the route Debra Lynn normally took to see if she'd had any kind of accident or buggy problem. Or at the very least go to the neighboring farm and use their phone shed to call and check on her.

He was torn between his worry that something had happened to the girl and his reluctance to leave *Oma* alone with the *kinner*. But concern for Debra Lynn won out. "*Oma*, if you think you'll be okay for a little while, I think I'll take the buggy out for a short ride."

He saw understanding in her gaze as she nodded. "Go on with you. We'll be fine."

He headed straight for the horse shed, but to his relief, before he took more than a few steps he heard the sound of a buggy coming up the drive.

At last.

"Debra Lynn's here," he called loudly over his shoulder as he changed direction. Rowdy was already greeting the new arrival with enthusiastic barking. Luckily Debra Lynn's horse had gotten used to Rowdy by now.

But there was no point in taking a chance. "*Kum*, Rowdy," he said firmly, and the dog reluctantly bounded to his side. Asher frowned as the buggy drew closer. That was a different horse than the one Debra Lynn had used the past few days. Had something happened to JonJon? Was that why she was late?

A second later he realized the buggy wasn't the same either. What was going on?

Before he reached the buggy, the occupant had parked it and climbed out. He abruptly stopped in his tracks.

Martha Eicher?

What was she doing here?

Chapter 7

Martha turned to face Asher, hoping to forestall any overly polite greeting he might feel compelled to offer. "I know you were expecting Debra Lynn and must have been concerned when she didn't show up at her regular time." She patted the head of the dog as she spoke. "I got here as quick as I could." She straightened and moved to the front of the buggy, where she hitched Cinders to the nearby fence post.

Asher had followed her. "I don't understand. Where's Debra Lynn? And why are you here? Is she all right?"

His confusion was understandable. And it was an emotion she appreciated much more than the stiff politeness he'd shown in the past. "I'm afraid she had an accident this morning and Micah was called to check on her injuries."

Asher ran his hand over his jaw. "I was worried something had happened. How's she doing?"

At least he seemed to have forgotten to be stand-offish. "Micah thinks she'll be okay but I'm afraid she has a broken arm. She's at the clinic getting it tended to. Hannah came over to ask if I'd let you know."

"*Danke.* I appreciate you making the trip out here."

Well, the seeming truce hadn't lasted long—he was back to using that overly polite tone. "Of course." Their homes were on opposite ends of the community so it wasn't a quick trip. "I know this leaves you unexpectedly without a nanny so I came prepared to take Debra Lynn's place today. And for another day or two if you like, to give you some time to make other arrangements." There, she'd managed to get it all out before he could interrupt her. Now she waited to see how he'd respond.

Asher's expression reflected his hesitancy. But finally he nodded. "*Danke.* I gladly accept your offer and I'll try not to take advantage of your generosity." He waved a hand to the house. "*Kum*, I'll let *Oma* know what's happened and formally introduce you to the *kinner*."

Relieved he wasn't being stubborn, Martha walked beside him to the house. All the while, however, she was aware that he was uncomfortable and likely trying to reconcile his feelings for her with accepting her help. Wanting to break the silence stretching between them, she cast about for something to say. "Joan told me the *kinner* were a joy to care for and leaving them was her biggest regret about leaving Hope's Haven."

He raised a brow. "Joan is very kind. They're a blessing to us, of course, but they can be a handful—especially the boys." His expression thawed a bit as he smiled. "As you experienced for yourself yesterday." Then he opened the door and allowed her to precede him.

Once Martha entered the kitchen, she turned first to Asher's *grossmammi*. "*Gut matin*, Dorcas."

Dorcas blinked, obviously startled to see her. But she nodded in response to the greeting. "*Gut matin*."

Although Dorcas's tone was polite and her smile sincere, there was that touch of reserve in her demeanor that echoed her grandson's.

"Debra Lynn broke her arm this morning," Asher quickly explained. "And Martha has generously volunteered to take her place for a couple of days."

While they spoke, Martha took a quick look around. Lottie, the five-year-old, was already dressed and busy with morning chores. The triplets, on the other hand, were still in their nightclothes and were watching her with open curiosity.

"*Danke*, Martha, that is generous indeed," Dorcas replied, bringing Martha's focus back around. The older woman rose with the aid of a cane and moved toward the stove. "Have you had breakfast yet? It'll only take a few minutes to fix you a plate."

Martha waved a hand to stop her. "*Danke* but that's not necessary, I ate before I left home. And please don't feel as if you need to take care of me. I'm here to help where I can, not add to your workload." She looked around. "Just let me know where to get started."

Dorcas nodded. "Lottie and I were just about to go out and collect the eggs. While we do that it would be helpful if you could get the boys dressed."

Before Martha could do more than nod, Asher spoke

up. "I'll show you where their room is." He turned to the triplets. "Let's go, boys, time to get dressed."

The trio reluctantly stopped their play and moved toward Asher.

Martha studied the near-identical faces. How did one tell them apart?

"Just a minute," she said, stopping Asher before he left the room.

"Did you need something?"

"I should probably tend to Cinders."

Asher waved a hand. "If that's your horse, I'll tend to her and your buggy after we're done getting the boys dressed."

We? But she nodded. "*Danke.*"

With a dip of his head he turned and led the way while Martha brought up the rear. They headed down the hall, stopping only when they reached the second door on the right. "Here we are." Asher opened the door and stepped aside for the others to precede him.

Martha studied her surroundings as she entered. Three twin beds were arranged in a U shape on the wall to her right and took up most of the space in the room.

A tall dresser stood to the left of the door and a long, low bench was centered on the wall across from the beds, near the windows. Under the bench were three pairs of boy's shoes neatly lined up, awaiting their owners.

Martha brought her attention back to the task at hand. "Are their clothes in the dresser?" she asked as she moved farther into the room.

"They are. The top drawer has their shirts, the second has the pants and suspenders. And the bottom two have nightclothes and assorted other items."

As Martha pulled the clothes out of the drawers, she talked to him without turning around. "I assume they share the clothes."

"They do."

She turned, holding three identical sets of boy's clothes. "And is there a trick to telling the boys apart?"

That question earned her a grin. "For today you can tell which one is Zeb because he has a bruise on his forehead. He took a little tumble yesterday."

Martha checked the boys and sure enough one of them had a purplish mark just above his left brow. Zeb.

"As for Zach and Zeke," he placed a hand on the boy closest to him, "this is Zach. Which I know doesn't help you since there's no easy marker like Zeb's bruise. However, if you can get them to smile, Zeke's dimple is more pronounced."

Now if she could just remember that.

Asher took one set of clothing from her. "Don't feel bad, though, if you get them confused, it happens to the best of us. You can just do what I do." His grin grew more pronounced. "Ask Lottie. She can always tell them apart."

Good to know. "I'll need information about their regular routine and anything else you feel it's important for me to know while I'm here." She'd prefer not to have this conversation in front of the boys but she didn't have much choice.

Asher's response, however, was an offhand shrug. "*Oma* could tell you that better than I could."

Martha refrained from comment but she couldn't help wonder just how involved Asher was in their

day-to-day lives. Part of the reason for his seeming
ignorance of the *kinner*'s routine was probably due to
his being out of the house during most of the day. But
she suspected it was also partly due to his abdication
of responsibility in the *kinner*'s daily care.

For the next several moments the only conversation
was with the boys as she and Asher got them dressed.
Asher was jovial, teasing the boys and making them
giggle. Still, by the time the three boys were suitably
attired, Martha felt as if she'd just wrangled a roomful
of frisky cats. How had Joan managed to handle these
tiny whirlwinds day in and day out?

She straightened and met Asher's gaze. "What
now?" She looked at the unmade beds and little-boy
clutter. "Should we get the room in order?"

Asher looked around as if he wasn't quite sure how
to answer her. Then his head turned toward the doorway. "I hear *Oma* and Lottie in the kitchen. Why don't
we join them? Tidying the room can wait."

                         * * *

Asher was relieved to see that *Oma* and Lottie were
indeed in the kitchen, each holding a small basket
of eggs. The two had been smiling over something
but as soon as his grandmother spotted Martha she
sobered.

Martha either didn't notice anything amiss or chose
to ignore it. She stepped forward with a smile. "Can I
take that from you?" she offered.

But *Oma* shook her head as she continued across
the room. "*Danke*, but I've got it." Then she turned to
him. "The pump by the back porch is dripping again.

And there's a loose post on the chicken yard fence. It looks like something's been pushing on it."

Asher swallowed a sigh. It seemed there was always one thing or another that needed attention. But he merely nodded. "I'll get them tended to in the next day or so."

Then he turned to Martha. "If you'll excuse me, I'll go take care of your horse and buggy." And with that he made his exit and gladly left the ladies to care for the *kinner*. His thoughts, though, were still on the buggy's owner.

When Martha had been the assistant teacher he'd been in sixth and seventh grades. He'd watched her as she worked with the younger students, admired her patience and empathy as she helped them with their work. And somewhere along the way he'd developed a crush on her. The fact that she was older than him by nearly four years hadn't mattered to his adolescent self.

Of course, it hadn't helped that for a while his middle *bruder* Ephron seemed poised to court her himself. She must have looked on him as nothing more than a kid, one of her pupils.

And then the summer between seventh and eighth grades everything changed. Not only between him and Martha, but for his entire family. Whether intentional on her part or not, it was her fault Ephron had taken that first step toward leaving them—his family, his community, even the Amish faith.

Before this week it had been a long time since their paths had crossed in any but the most superficial of ways. In fact he couldn't remember the last time they'd had any direct conversation. Now he'd had reason to interact with her multiple times in one week. And it appeared she'd be spending most of the next day or two here.

Despite what had passed between them twelve years ago, in addition to his more recent barely masked rudeness, Martha had come here to help without being asked.

He reached the buggy and led Cinders closer to the paddock before loosening the traces. He looked down at Rowdy, who was right on his heels. "What do you think, boy? Is she doing it because she's trying to make reparations for past wrongs or is she merely offering a simple gesture of neighborliness?"

Rowdy barked and ran off, heading for the far side of the barn. "You're no help at all," Asher grumbled good-naturedly.

Regardless of Martha's motives, though, he should be grateful. And *Gotte* instructed that one should forgive those who harm them. Asher was no longer that twelve-year-old boy who'd just seen one of his heroes topple. He should be man enough—and Christian enough—to forgive her past actions and put it behind him. To leave it in *Gotte*'s hands.

Perhaps her coming here was a test he'd been given, a chance for him to come to terms with his own feelings.

His own failings.

Still, it was difficult to see her and not remember how deeply her betrayal had cut him back then. His family had never been the same after that fateful summer.

That summer when she'd played on Ephron's sympathies to get him to leave Hope's Haven. After which he'd never truly returned except for a few brief visits he'd made out of obligation.

Better to focus on the present rather than the past.

How would Martha handle the *kinner*? It had been a long time—twelve years—since she'd helped at the school, and none of her students had been toddlers.

Time would tell, he supposed. But she had shown a trace of that humor and patience from her teaching years when helping the boys get dressed earlier, which was a *gut* sign. Of course she'd also seemed to focus on routines and plans. It would be interesting to see if the fun or the discipline won out.

Then he considered a problem closer to home. Martha had said she'd help with the *kinner* for "a day or two." Debra Lynn's broken arm was likely to put her out of commission for at least five or six weeks. Who could he call on to fill in for her? One of Joan's *shveshtra* perhaps? Though the ones still at home were much younger than Joan or even Debra Lynn.

The most expedient thing would be for him to put the call out for help with a few neighbors. Hopefully someone would step up or would know someone who could. Even if it meant getting someone different from week to week. Not ideal but they could manage that way for a few weeks if necessary.

Leading the now-buggy-free Cinders to the stable, he gave the mare's coat a good brushing before turning her loose in the paddock.

Chapter 8

Martha kept her expression carefully neutral. It seemed Dorcas still hadn't quite decided how she wanted to handle having the person who'd driven her middle grandson away spending time in her home. Ah well, she could bear up under Dorcas and Asher's stiff hospitality for the few days she'd be here. And maybe she could show them she wasn't such a villain while she was at it.

"Dorcas, if you don't mind, can you tell me a little about what the routine is for the *kinner*? I didn't have a chance to speak to Debra Lynn or Joan."

Dorcas nodded and moved to the table. "Of course. But since you're only going to be here a couple of days, I don't think you need to try to learn everything. We should keep it very simple, ain't so? In fact we can split the responsibility. I'll keep a watch on Lottie. She can help me take care of the cooking and normal housework. You can focus your attention on keeping the boys occupied with both play and simple chores, and take care of any messes they make."

Martha wasn't certain that would keep her busy enough. After all, how much of her time would keeping up with a trio of three-year-olds take? But there seemed no point in arguing. As Dorcas said, it was just for a couple of days. "Is there anything in particular Joan or Debra Lynn kept the boys occupied with?"

Dorcas's look said she shouldn't have had to ask such a basic question, but the woman's tone was polite enough. "For one thing, before she left, Joan was working with the boys in the mornings to teach them to help straighten their rooms, including making their beds. Of course they're still too little to do much more than help. But I think they were making progress with that. Debra Lynn was supposed to continue working with them but she hasn't been with us for quite two weeks yet and she's been a bit overwhelmed."

Martha nodded decisively, glad to hear the boys had been given some responsibility. "That's definitely something I can work with them on." And she might look around for a few other easy tasks they could help with as well.

Dorcas stood and moved back to the stove. "After I have lunch under way, I plan to start getting the garden prepared for spring planting. You and the little ones can join me there—*kinner* need to have some outside time."

It seemed a little early to be thinking about spring planting but Martha merely nodded. "We should have their beds straightened by then." Then she had another thought. "What about Lottie? Will she need any help with her room?"

Dorcas paused, an uncertain expression on her face. "I'm not sure how much help Joan or Debra Lynn gave her. Why don't you check in with her and see if she needs help."

With a nod Martha left the kitchen and headed for the living room where the four *kinner* were playing with a set of plastic farm animals.

She smiled down at the little girl. "Lottie, I've already seen your *brieder*'s room. Would you like to show me yours?"

Lottie looked as if she'd just been asked to walk on broken glass, but she obediently nodded, stood and headed for the stairs. As the two of them climbed to the second floor, Martha tried to draw her into conversation but found herself receiving only monosyllabic answers to her questions. When they finally reached the preschooler's room, Lottie opened the door and led the way inside without saying a word.

Martha looked around and discovered that, unlike the triplets' room, Lottie's was neat and tidy. So much so that there was no sign of clutter of any sort. Her clothing, toys and books were put away or neatly organized on her dresser top. Her bedding might be somewhat askew but it was neatly smoothed over.

"Lottie, this is such a nice room. I can tell you take wonderful *gut* care of it."

"*Danke.*"

Martha considered showing the little girl how to fix her bed properly then immediately discarded the idea. It was done well enough and there was nothing to be gained by making her feel like she'd failed.

"I appreciate you showing me your room. Now I need to get back downstairs and see if I can get your *brieder* to do as *gut* a job on their room as you have on yours." Then she gave Lottie a smile. "Would you like to help me with that? You don't have to if you'd rather not," she added quickly. "But you've done such a wonderful *gut* job on yours I thought you might like to help me teach them how to do the same."

Lottie hesitated a moment longer, then nodded. Martha noticed when she'd praised the girl's skill that there'd been a flash of surprise in her expression and she'd stood a little straighter. Was being on the receiving end of praise so unusual for her?

Martha made a mental note to do more of it while she was here.

When the two of them returned to the living room, Martha got the triplets' attention. "Boys, this morning we're going to learn how to straighten up your room, just like big kids do." She smiled. "And once we're done we can go outside and help your *grossmammi* Dorcas work in her garden."

When they arrived at the door to the triplets' room, the *kinner* entered first while Martha paused on the threshold and took a good look around. Making the bed was the biggest and most obvious chore. But there were a few other things that needed attention as well. A few stray socks on the floor that hadn't quite made it to the hamper. Hats that were perched on the bench rather than hung on pegs. Some wooden blocks that had ended up under the bench.

With a decisive nod she decided to start with the biggest task first. Without knowing how Joan had gone about it, she decided her best approach was to draw on her memories of how her *mamm* had taught her and her *shveshtra*. She could also draw on her experience with the scholars she'd dealt with in her time as an assistant teacher. Little ones learned best by example.

She smiled down at the boys. "Let's get started, shall we?" She moved to the nearest bed. "Who sleeps in this one?"

Zeb, he-of-the-bruised-forehead, responded with a vigorous nod and a loudly uttered "Me."

With a grin she handed him the pillow from the bed. Then she handed the other two boys the quilt—it was bulky enough to require both of them to hold it. "You boys hold on to these until Lottie and I are ready for them."

Once the boys nodded, she turned to their *shveshtah*. "Lottie is going to help me straighten the sheet on this one and then you boys can help with the other two."

Martha and Lottie went to work, smoothing the bottom sheet, tucking in the top sheet at the foot of the bed and then smoothing it all the way up to the top.

Once that was accomplished, Martha congratulated Lottie on a job well done and thanked her for her help. Then she turned back to the boys. "Zach and Zeke, it's time to put the quilt on top. Do you think you're big enough to help me and Lottie do that?"

Both boys nodded an emphatic yes.

"*Gut.* Now Lottie and I will each take a corner and you boys can take the other two corners." Martha made sure she and Lottie had the top corners and the two boys had the bottom. While the boys stood at the foot of the bed, she and Lottie drew their corners up to the head and then smoothed out the wrinkles. All the while she was aware that Zeb was not happy with being left out.

When they were done she heaped praise and thanks

on her helpers. Then she turned to Zeb. "Would you place the pillow on the bed now?"

The little boy obliged, with an energetic lift from Martha that made him giggle. After giving Zeb his own praises, she stepped back, admiring the work they'd done with a broad smile. "*Gut* job, everyone. It looks wonderful nice."

Then she turned to the next bed. "Let's do this one now." They repeated the process on the other beds, rotating the roles based on whose bed they were working on. And as they worked, Martha took every opportunity to let them know what a good job they were doing.

Once they had straightened all three beds Martha turned their attention to the rest of the room. She did her best to make a game of it, asking them to see how many things were out of place and to put them where they needed to be.

She also made certain there were lots of opportunities to giggle as they worked. And she considered it progress when she even got a smile out of Lottie.

She could see why Joan had grown to love these little ones so dearly.

Chapter 9

Twenty minutes later Martha stood in the garden, trying to divide her attention between her charges and Dorcas. Dorcas was wielding a hoe with authority, but Martha remembered how she had leaned heavily on her cane as they walked from the house to the garden and was worried the older woman would lose her balance.

On the other hand, she watched the boys with a mix of dismay and resignation. The ground was still a bit soggy, which meant the dirt was more like mud in spots. Each of the boys had been given a short-handled garden fork, and they were having a grand old time digging holes. It was Martha's job to make sure the only things the boys stabbed with their forks was the dirt.

So far that hadn't been an issue. But their enthusiasm for the digging had resulted in some very dirty clothes and arms. And it was not just the digging in the dirt that claimed their interest. They had discovered several earthworms and some beetles that demanded closer examination.

She saw baths in their near future. Not to mention, with all the picking up of fallen boys and finding herself in the way of a few tossed clods, she now wore an uncomfortable layer of dirt herself. It was a good thing the Lantz home had an indoor bathroom.

Lottie was in better shape. She was quietly helping Dorcas set stakes in the section of the garden where the climbing plants would be located, and other than her shoes had managed to remain relatively dirt-free. Martha had tried to draw her into conversation, to build on some of the trust she'd earned earlier when they'd been setting the boys' room in order, but the girl had returned to monosyllabic answers and shy smiles.

"See!" One of the boys held his hand out to her. Martha stooped down to study the rock he was proudly holding up for her to look at. It was an irregularly shaped piece of quartz about the size of a chicken egg. Though dirty, she could see it was an opalescent white, stained with small flecks of gray and brown.

"*Ach*, it's beautiful."

The other two boys rushed forward to see what their *bruder* had found. Unfortunately, in her stooped position, their jostling overset her balance and she found herself flat on her back with one of the boys on her chest.

She wasn't certain whether she or the toddler was more surprised by their situation. A moment later the boy's lip started trembling. Which one of the triplets was this?

"Are you okay?"

He nodded but still seemed uncertain about whether to cry or not.

She gave him a big smile hoping to reassure him. "*Gut.* I'm okay too." She sat up, careful to keep him secure in her lap. "I imagine I looked mighty silly down on the ground like this."

"*Ach du lieva*, what happened?"

Martha looked over to the other end of the garden where Dorcas was studying them in some concern. And she'd been worried about Dorcas losing her balance. It seemed their roles were reversed.

Martha waved a hand reassuringly. "I just lost my balance. We're fine."

The older woman moved in their direction. "Do you need some help?"

But Martha shook her head. "*Danke*, but we're fine." She helped the child in her lap to stand.

Before she could get up herself, however, she froze at the sound of a voice from somewhere behind her.

"What have we here?"

She smothered a groan, recognizing that voice.

Turning her head, she saw Asher standing at the edge of the garden, staring down at her. And while he wore a deadpan expression on his face, there was a glint in his eyes that seemed suspiciously like amusement.

* * *

Asher had been heading back to the house for lunch when he spotted the group working in the garden. He'd altered his course, deciding to join them. But he'd barely taken a step or two in their direction when he witnessed one of the boys overset the very proper Martha.

Concerned, he had immediately picked up his pace but by the time he reached the garden fence it was obvious everyone was okay.

Now the overset nanny was staring at him with what he could only describe as a mix of embarrassment and annoyance.

Before he could step forward and offer her his assistance, however, she had straightened and turned away. The sight of the normally dignified woman scrambling to get up from her seat in the dirt tickled his sense of humor, and it was all he could do not to grin.

A moment later she had managed to stand and was trying to unobtrusively brush the dirt from the back of her skirt. Unfortunately for her, her efforts were woefully inadequate.

Giving her a chance to regain her composure, Asher studied the rest of the group in the garden. The appearance of the individuals ranged from the dirt-covered triplets to *Oma* who only had a few smudges. Lottie had also managed to stay mostly dirt-free.

But it was Martha whose appearance surprised him the most. Her hands were almost as dirty as those of the boys, and her clothing looked very much more disheveled than it had when he last saw her. Most of it could be put down to her fall, of course, but not all of it. Were the triplets responsible? Or had she let down her guard and gotten down in the dirt to play with them? If so, he would give quite a lot to have seen that.

But now was not the time to ask such questions. So instead he turned to *Oma*. "Do you need any help?"

She shook her head. "*Nee*. I'm sure you need to rest after your busy morning."

He hid a grimace. *Oma* meant well, but in her eyes

he was still that invalid toddler he'd been when she moved in here to help his newly widowed *daed*.

One of the triplets, Zach he thought, rushed up and showed him a wriggling earthworm he'd captured. Asher admired the boy's find, but cautioned him to handle it gently. "Earthworms are for sure and for certain *gut* for our garden. They help the soil stay loose and absorbent and add back nutrients as well."

He stooped down, looking the toddler straight in the eyes. "Why don't we let him go now?"

The little boy looked doubtful, but finally nodded and set the worm on a freshly turned bit of soil.

A second toddler—Zeb?—clamored for his attention and showed him a white rock he'd found. Asher dutifully admired it, all the while aware of Martha standing nearby helping Zeke retrieve and dust off his hat.

Martha busied herself with collecting the boys' digging tools. Was she deliberately avoiding meeting his gaze?

Oma walked up, wiping her brow with the back of a hand while she used the hoe as a cane. "I hadn't realized it was lunchtime already. You must be hungry. Go on in and clean up—we'll be right behind you as soon as we put the tools away."

Asher smiled while he retrieved her cane from where it leaned against the fence and took the hoe from her. "Let me handle that." Then his smile took on a teasing note. "It looks like some of you will need more time to clean up than I do anyway."

From the corner of his eye he saw Martha's cheeks redden.

Not looking his way, she spread her arms in a gesture meant to include all four *kinner*. "*Kum*, boys, Lottie. Time to clean up for lunch."

Asher motioned toward the house. "The hand pump is right over there by the back porch. And you can find some rags in that wooden crate under the porch window."

She gave him a nod that would have been dignified if not for the spot of dirt on her nose. He grinned after her as she began to herd the *kinner* toward the back porch.

Then he caught *Oma* studying him thoughtfully and he quickly schooled his features and busied himself gathering up the rest of the tools.

"Martha seems to have a way with the little ones." *Oma*'s tone was almost offhand. "I heard them all laughing earlier when they were straightening up the boys' room."

So Martha had put them to work. Asher shrugged. "She did work as teacher's assistant for two years."

"That's right. You were still a scholar then, weren't you?"

At his nod, she brushed at her skirt. "It's a shame she won't be here for more than a couple of days. I have a feeling she would be *gut* for my *kins-kinnah*."

A shame? That brought him up short. Had *Oma* overcome her reservations about Martha? More important, had he?

He gave his head a mental shake. "We shouldn't impose on her generosity by asking for more of her time than she's already offered us."

"Of course." *Oma* began to move toward the house. "And speaking of imposing, I should help her clean up the little ones." She patted his arm as she passed. "Lunch will be on the table shortly."

Asher slowly moved to the small shed where the garden tools were kept. For a few moments he really had forgotten his long-held feelings regarding Martha.

Oma was right, she was *gut* with—and for—the *kinner*. And that's what he needed to focus on right now.

As for what had happened in the past, that couldn't be changed. And maybe she had learned from it.

And, if he was being entirely honest with himself, in his heart he knew that Ephron wouldn't have needed much of a push to follow her on her little adventure that summer.

* * *

It was nearly half an hour later before Martha felt the little ones had been made clean and presentable enough to sit at the table. As for herself, she'd done her best to clean her dress since she had no change of clothing with her, but she was afraid it was a poor job at best. She realized Dorcas and Asher would understand why she came to the table in such a state but it still felt uncomfortable.

As they settled into their places, Martha was pleased to see all of the *kinner* had been taught to observe the time of quiet prayer before beginning their meal.

Afterward, as Asher passed her the platter of rolls he met her gaze. "So how has your morning been?"

Surely he didn't expect her to discuss the little ones in front of them?

But she was rescued from answering when one of the boys proudly piped up. "We made our beds."

Asher turned to his nephew in mock-surprise. "You did?"

"They are all very *gut* workers," Martha responded. "Lottie helped as well."

"Now, that's a wonderful *gut* thing, for sure and for certain."

Martha looked across the table, ready to change the focus of the conversation. "Dorcas, this potato salad is delicious. Do I taste something smoky in here?"

The woman nodded, seeming pleased by Martha's interest. "I usually add a dash of smoked paprika."

Martha smiled. "It adds such a lovely touch. I'll have to try it at home." Or in her future home, wherever that might be.

Which reminded her. She needed to write to Laban when she arrived home this evening.

At least now she had something interesting to write about.

Later, after the *kinner* had been put down for an afternoon nap, Martha joined Dorcas in the living room.

The older woman glanced up from her knitting but her hands continued to work. "Have my *kins-kinnah* settled down?"

"*Jah.* Is there something I can help you with while they're sleeping?"

Dorcas smiled but shook her head. "*Nee.*" She gave Martha a surprisingly warm look. "Why don't you rest while you can? I know the boys can be a bit of a handful. The room Joan used while she was here is upstairs, second door on the right."

"*Danke*, but if you don't mind I'd rather go outside

for some fresh air. I should be back before the *kinner* wake up."

Dorcas merely nodded and went back to her knitting. "As you wish."

Martha hesitated a moment as she studied the woman's bent head, feeling something had shifted between them. Then she moved back to the kitchen and made her exit through the side door.

Was it her imagination or had some of Dorcas's reserve eased a bit? Not that she'd been exactly warm, but her smile had seemed friendlier.

A moment later she pushed that thought aside as she heard what sounded like hammering coming from one of the large outbuildings. Impulsively deciding to investigate, Martha altered her course and headed toward the sound.

The large double doors were open and when she looked inside, she realized it was an equipment shed. From her perspective she could see a plow, a harrow, and a flatbed wagon. There were other things farther back, but she ignored them as she saw the source of the hammering noise—Asher was seated on a low stool working on the plow.

Not wanting to interrupt him, she started to back away. But it was too late—Rowdy spotted her and came racing up, barking a greeting.

Asher turned and when he saw her set his tools down and stood. He grabbed a rag to wipe his hands. "Is there something I can help you with?"

She held up her hands. "*Nee.* I was just out for a walk. I didn't mean to interrupt your work."

He shrugged. "I was ready for a little break anyway. I take it the *kinner* are napping."

She nodded.

"I know you're just stepping in to help us as a favor. I hope they haven't made you regret your offer."

"Not at all. The little ones have a lot of energy for sure and for certain, but they're actually quite sweet and respectful when you approach them properly."

He smiled wryly. "You obviously haven't lost your touch with *kinner*."

Unsure how to respond to that, she searched for a way to change the subject and waved to the machines behind him. "Are you having problems with the equipment?"

"*Nee*. I'm just doing some much-needed maintenance so it'll all be ready for the spring planting."

Not quite ready to leave the shed, she tried another topic. "Hannah told me Micah figures it will be about six weeks until Debra Lynn's arm mends enough for her to come back to work here. Do you know yet what you're going to do?"

Asher rubbed the back of his neck. "I'll put the word out that we're looking for a person to help for a few weeks. Hopefully someone will step forward." Then he gave her an apologetic look. "But this isn't your worry. You've been more than generous with your time."

She waved off his concern. "It's no problem. I enjoy spending time with your *kinner* and besides, that's what neighbors do for each other." Would he see this as an olive branch to put their past behind them?

"Still, I'm grateful."

She couldn't read anything in his tone or expression.

Then he bent down to scratch Rowdy's head and she took that as her cue to leave.

She straightened. "I'll let you get back to your work. Do you mind if I walk around your place for a bit?"

"Not at all. Feel free to wander wherever you like." And with a nod he went back to work on his plow.

As Martha walked away she felt her steps were a bit lighter. Maybe Asher really was ready to forgive her for her perceived wrongs.

* * *

As Asher sat on his stool he realized Rowdy had abandoned him to accompany Martha. Not that he blamed the animal—he'd prefer to be outside on a nice day like today too.

He'd been well aware of Martha's discomfort when they sat down to lunch, no doubt due to the stains that still adorned her dress and *kapp*. Just now, however, he hadn't sensed any of that discomfort. Either she'd forgotten or it no longer bothered her.

He had to admit, the sight of the normally proper and neat-as-a-pin Martha wearing a stained garment was amusing. But oddly, not in a serves-her-right kind of way. Rather, it was more in a friendly, teasing way, as if it had been Joan standing there.

There had also been the slightest tug of that old attraction he'd once felt for her.

Maybe it was just as well she'd only be here for another day or so.

Chapter 10

As Martha brushed Cinders in the horse shed at home that evening she found herself reviewing the events of the day. Hard to believe Joan's wedding had taken place only yesterday.

The four Lantz *kinner* were great youngsters. The triplets were as full of energy, curiosity and mischief as any other three-year-old boys. The fact that there were three of them, of course, only multiplied their impact. That was a challenge but not a burdensome one. And speaking of challenges, she hadn't quite figured out how to tell them apart yet but she was confident that she would. She'd had experience with several sets of identical twins when she'd served as assistant teacher and she'd learned that no matter how much they resembled each other in physical appearance, once you got to know them there were subtle differences you could pick up on if you paid attention. She figured it would be the same with triplets.

Lottie, on the other hand, was not only less rambunctious, she was outright shy. That made it easy to overlook her, especially in such a busy household. Martha would have to make a point to see that she didn't let that happen. But she was concerned about the extent of Lottie's shyness. Shyness in and of itself was not a bad thing, of course. However, in some cases it could be crippling. And Martha was afraid that was the case with the five-year-old. Even with her *familye* Lottie seemed to be separate, a loner who stood on the edges, observing more than participating. Martha had worked with *kinner* like her before and there were things that could be done to help bring her out of her shell, at least enough to be comfortable joining in occasionally.

Then Martha grimaced. What was she thinking? She wouldn't be around the Lantz household long enough to either learn to tell the triplets apart or to work with Lottie on overcoming her shyness.

Maybe there was something she could do for Lottie from the outside? How would Asher react if she went to him with her concerns for his niece?

She gave Cinders a final pat and headed for the house, still mulling over those questions. She was surprised to see it was nearly dusk—she hoped Leah and her *daed* hadn't waited supper on her.

When she stepped in the kitchen, Leah was cleaning the last of the supper dishes. Her *shteef-mamm* glanced over her shoulder and gave Martha a smile. "*Wilkom* home." Then her expression shifted to a frown of concern. "*Ach*, Martha, what happened to your clothes? Are you all right?"

Martha glanced down at her skirts. She'd almost

forgotten about the mud. "I'm okay. I just took a little tumble with one of the boys when we were out helping Dorcas get her garden ready."

Leah smiled. "*Kinner* can find ways to startle you, that's for sure and for certain." Then she waved toward the stove. "I've been keeping your supper warm for you. It'll just take a minute to serve it up."

Martha shook her head. "*Danke*, but I can take care of it after I clean up. Is *Daed* in the living room?"

"*Jah*. A new copy of *The Budget* came in today."

"I think I'll freshen up before I go in and speak to him." And with a smile, Martha turned and headed up to her room. She was glad to finally be able to change out of her dirty dress and into a clean one. A few minutes later she returned to the first floor where she found Leah had joined *Daed* in the living room and was doing some mending on one of his shirts.

"You stayed late," *Daed* said after they exchanged greetings. "How was your day with the *kinner*? Four little ones must have been a handful."

"No more so than a classroom full of scholars."

Leah smiled. "That's right, I forgot you were a teacher at one time."

"Assistant teacher, but *jah*, having that experience to draw on was a big help today as well as the three months I spent with cousin Brenda."

Daed lowered his periodical to meet her gaze. "What do Asher and Dorcas plan to do until Debra Lynn can return to help them?"

"Asher intends to look for someone to take her place temporarily. In the meantime, I told him I'd go back tomorrow and lend a hand." She quickly looked from one to the other of them. "That's assuming you don't need me here. I know I just got back after three months away, so if you need me—"

Leah interrupted with a wave of her hand. "Don't worry about me and your *daed*. Having you here to share my day is a joy, for sure and for certain. But remember, I kept house on my own for over thirty years and I can continue to do so as long as needed." Then she smiled. "And it's wonderful *gut* of you to volunteer to help the Lantz family."

It was just as Martha had suspected—her presence wouldn't be missed. Tamping down that momentary flare of self-pity, she dug up a smile. "I don't mind. The *kinner* are little *lamm*s. And it may take an extra day or two for them to find someone."

Then she stood and changed the subject, injecting a touch of cheerfulness in her tone. "Now, I've been smelling that soup since I came in and I think it's high time I taste it." She held a hand up as Leah started to stand. "Please don't get up. I can serve myself and clean up after."

Leah gave her a probing look as if trying to puzzle something out. Then she returned Martha's smile with a nod and went back to her mending.

Later, as Martha sat at the table and absently stirred her soup, she felt a stab of guilt. It wasn't Leah's fault that she felt so comfortable running the household these days. Martha had always considered herself a fairly even-tempered person who would be able to accept whatever role in life *Gotte* had in store for her. It was lowering to discover that wasn't exactly true.

Perhaps, if things went well with Laban, she'd have a chance to make a clean start elsewhere soon. Until then, she would just have to make a more deliberate effort to be, if not happy with, at least accepting of her lot.

Trying to push those less-than-uplifting concerns away, she thought again of Asher's niece. Had the child always been so painfully shy or had her parents' death pushed her over the line? There was just a little over six months before Lottie would start school, time enough to help her learn to cope with it so it wasn't so isolating. Perhaps she could speak to Debra Lynn about ways to do that.

Naturally she'd speak to Asher first—she certainly didn't want to overstep. But she didn't see how he could possibly object to something that was only intended to be helpful. Of course, it meant she'd have to explain her observations about Lottie's behavior to him. But that was something that needed to happen, whether he welcomed her help and advice or not.

A day ago she would have said he wouldn't welcome any such intrusion from her. But they'd seemed to make progress today. In fact, by the end of the day he'd even seemed willing to relax in her presence and carry on a conversation as if they were friends. Was that just a temporary truce or could they really get past his objections to her?

If only she had more time interacting with him, perhaps they could have become actual friends again. But this time as equals rather than teacher and student.

Then she paused with her spoon halfway to her mouth. What if she offered to take Debra Lynn's place not just for a few days but for the entire time the girl would need to be off? It would solve a number of problems. She would have time to get used to the idea that her role in her *daed*'s house had changed significantly. She'd be able to rebuild her relationship with the Lantz family. And she'd have time to work with Lottie. Not to mention she would have the opportunity to exchange several letters with Laban and have a better sense of whether that relationship would lead to something more.

Of course, this was assuming Asher hadn't already found someone else.

Or more important, that he would be willing to welcome her into his home for the full six weeks.

She dug into her soup with more gusto, looking forward to what the future could bring with a much happier outlook than just a few minutes ago.

* * *

Martha arrived at the Lantz place extra early the next morning. She intended to speak to Asher about her offer to stay on as soon as she arrived but things didn't quite work out that way. When she stepped inside the kitchen Dorcas gave her a quick over-the-shoulder greeting from her position at the stove. "*Gut matin.* The boys are awake early this morning. Asher is trying to round them up for breakfast."

Martha nodded as she set her tote down on a chair. "I'll lend him a hand." She hurried down the hall and found Asher in the midst of a pillow fight with the boys.

"Looks like everyone woke up with plenty of energy this morning."

Martha swallowed a grin as all four of the room's occupants froze and turned to her with identical guilty expressions, as if they'd been caught with their hands in the cookie jar.

Asher fluffed the pillow he'd been swinging vigorously moments earlier. "*Gut matin*," he said as he casually tossed it on the bed.

Was that just a hint of embarrassment she heard in his voice? Instead of commenting she headed for the dresser. "Your *grossmammi* Dorcas is getting breakfast ready," she said as she opened the top drawer. "But I believe we have time to get you all dressed for the day before we head for the kitchen."

The toddlers hesitated, but Asher nodded. "You heard Martha. Put your pillows down—time to get ready for breakfast."

Almost as one, the boys dropped their pillows and moved toward Martha, but she crossed her arms. "Is that where the pillows go?" she asked, keeping her voice merely inquisitive.

The boys looked at one another then turned and retrieved the pillows. When the trio had placed them on the beds, she gave them her brightest smile. "*Gut* job." She held up a clean shirt. "Now, who's willing to go first?"

With Asher's help the boys were quickly dressed and headed down the hall. When they arrived in the kitchen, they found that Lottie had arrived ahead of them and was helping Dorcas set the table. Martha noticed a place had been set for her as well.

Since the girl and Dorcas seemed to have preparations in hand, Martha helped Asher seat the boys on the three stools that had obviously been made with them in mind. Each was tall enough for a toddler to be able to comfortably eat at the table. They also had armrests, a high back and a footrest to provide added support.

By the time that was done the table was set and ready for the rest of them to take their places.

"Up we go, sweet pea." Asher lifted his niece onto the shallow wooden box that rested on her chair and acted as a booster seat. Once she was in place, he pushed the chair under the table.

Martha sat with Zach and Zeb on either side of her. Across the table, Dorcas was similarly situated between Lottie and Zeke. Asher, of course, sat at the head of the table with Zach on his left and Zeke on his right.

They could have been any Amish family sitting down for a meal. Maybe one day she would have a family like this, surrounded by her own *kinner*, a *mann* of her own...

For a moment she felt an almost physical ache for that image to become reality.

She stared down at her food, trying to imagine Laban in that picture. But it didn't feel right. She supposed it was because she didn't know him well enough yet. Hopefully, in time...

With a mental start she realized she hadn't written to Laban yet. Speaking to her *daed* and Leah about her idea to spend the next five to six weeks here and then planning how she'd make the best of that time with the *kinner* had driven all other thoughts from her mind last night.

She'd write to him tonight, though, for sure and for certain.

* * *

It wasn't until the *kinner* were down for their afternoon naps that Martha had a chance to speak to Asher alone.

She found him down by the chicken coop making repairs to the fence. At the moment he was setting a new pole, manually pounding it into the ground with a post driver.

With his back to her, Martha couldn't see those boyish features that made him look so young. Instead she saw his broad shoulders, the smooth power of his movements and the way the muscles in his upper arms strained against the fabric of his sleeves every time he slammed the driver on top of the post.

She suddenly saw him in a whole new light. She knew he was no longer a teenager, of course, that he was twenty-four years old and a full-grown man. But on some level, it was hard to let go of that youthful image of him as Ephron's little *bruder*.

At this moment, however, she actually saw the adult he had become. Asher really wasn't a boy any longer. He was a man, with a man's responsibilities—he had a *grossmammi* and four *kinner* who depended on him and a farm to run. He was the man of the house here, in every sense of that title.

Why wasn't he married yet? Or at least courting someone? He'd make some deserving girl a wonderful *gut mann*. And having a *fraa* would not only give him a helpmeet to love and be loved by, but it would be *gut* for the *kinner* as well.

Asher paused and took off his hat, wiping his brow with a rag. A moment later he must have sensed her presence because he turned and met her gaze.

"Is there something you need?" There was nothing more than inquiry in his tone and expression as he put his hat back on. "Or are you just off on another walk?"

For some reason Martha suddenly felt rattled. She quickly tried to collect her thoughts. "When you have a minute, there was something I wanted to speak to you about." She waved a hand. "But it can wait until you aren't quite so busy."

"No need to wait." He waved toward the back porch. "Do you mind if I get a drink of water while we talk?"

She nodded and fell into step beside him as he headed toward the water pump. Her newfound image of him was still with her, making her feel slightly off balance.

He cut her a sideways look. "What did you want to talk about?"

She gave her head a mental shake, regaining some of her composure. "I was wondering if you'd found anyone yet to take Debra Lynn's place."

He grimaced. "Not yet. But I just put the word out late yesterday. I'm sure *Gotte* will provide."

She found it was more difficult to state her offer than she'd expected. What if he made it clear he didn't want her around long-term? Then she took herself to task. Surely she wouldn't be so stubborn. No point in drawing this out. "What if I told you I'd be willing to take it on?"

He stopped in his tracks for just a moment and stared at her in disbelief. She couldn't tell what he was thinking.

Then he moved forward again. "I'd say *Gotte* has most definitely provided."

His obvious relief eased her worries.

They'd reached the pump by then and he grabbed the cup that hung by a nail on the side. He met her gaze as he filled it, his expression probing, as if he was trying to figure out a puzzle. "But are you sure you want to commit a full six weeks to this? Didn't you just return home after being away for three months?"

Was he trying to talk her out of her offer? Did he not want her here after all? "*Jah*. But this will be different. I'll still be in the community, still be around should *Daed* or Leah need me for anything." Not that they were likely to. "But I doubt that will happen, the two of them are pretty self-sufficient."

Asher's expression shifted momentarily, as if he'd noted something in her tone. But he drank deeply from his cup of water then moved on without commenting on it. "If this is something you're truly willing to do, *Oma* and I will be relieved and happy to accept your offer. And it'll be easier on the *kinner* not having to get accustomed to yet a third nanny in a matter of just a few weeks."

"*Gut*, then it's settled." She hesitated a moment, not sure whether she should bring up the other issue she wanted to talk to him about. Then, with a mental shrug, she cast a quick look at the porch door to make sure they were truly alone, and forged ahead. "I know it's primarily the *kinner* you need my help with, but I got the impression from Joan that she also helped with other things around here. I'd be happy to do the same but I don't want to step on any toes. Your *grossmammi* doesn't seem to want my help. I'm not sure if it's something to do with me or if she just prefers to do things herself."

Asher rubbed the back of his neck. "The first month or so that Joan was with us, she had her hands full just watching the *kinner*. It was only after the five of them were better acquainted and had developed a routine of sorts that she was able to take on other things. *Oma* may just feel that, like Joan, your focus needs to be on the little ones until you are all comfortable with each other."

Which would take more than just a few days. "Are you sure that's all it is? I don't want to trespass on what she feels is her domain." She knew all too well what that felt like.

Asher refilled the cup and Martha got the feeling he was giving himself time to form his answer.

"*Oma* doesn't like to be reminded that she can't do as much as she used to," he said carefully. "I think she worries about no longer being useful."

Martha could relate to that as well. "I understand. I promise to keep that in mind should I try to take on some of her chores." She changed the subject. "I know Joan moved in here when she served as the little ones' nanny. And that Debra Lynn traveled back and forth from her home each day. Was that her preference or did Joan stay here because she was your cousin?"

"*Nee.* Debra Lynn could only take the job if she could return home each evening to help her *mamm* with some of the household chores."

That's what she'd figured. "Do you have a preference for what I do in that regard?"

He met her gaze, obviously surprised. "I can't ask you to move in."

Did that mean he didn't want her here? Or that he didn't want to impose? "That's wasn't my question. As you mentioned earlier, I just returned from a three-month stay at my cousin's home, so it wouldn't be any more of a problem if I moved in here for six weeks.

In fact, moving in would save me a thirty-minute buggy ride to and from home every day." She met and held his gaze. "But I wouldn't want to intrude if you'd prefer otherwise, especially since I'm not family like Joan."

Asher smiled. "Practical, as always. In that case, it would be very helpful if you were here to put the *kinner* to bed in the evenings. And even more so in the mornings so I don't have to wait for your arrival to start my day. And if you can start tomorrow it's a church Sunday so I'm certain *Oma* will be happy to have some help caring for them during the service."

Martha nodded, relieved. This was going to work out very well for her too. "Then when I return tomorrow, I'll be prepared to stay until Debra Lynn returns." And perhaps by that time, she and Laban should have reached an understanding.

Asher hung the cup back on the hook. "*Gut.* And *danke.*" He straightened. "Now, unless you have more to discuss, I should get back to work on the fence."

Martha nodded and watched him walk away. Then she turned and slowly walked back inside. She almost felt guilty accepting Asher's thanks when this was going to work out equally well for her.

Hopefully Dorcas would be pleased with the new arrangement as well.

Life was so much better when one had a purpose.

Chapter 11

Asher slowly turned back to his work on the chicken yard fence. To say Martha's offer to take over as nanny until Debra Lynn could return had surprised him was a decided understatement. Welcome, of course, but entirely unexpected. And then she'd surprised him a second time by offering to live here while she took on the role.

He couldn't have wished for a better solution to his problem, or a more timely one. Because whatever else Martha was, she was *gut* with *kinner*, at least she had been when she worked as assistant teacher. And it would also keep him from having to introduce yet another new caretaker to his niece and nephews.

She was being surprisingly generous, especially considering how standoffish, and at times downright antagonistic, he'd been. It was humbling to realize that although he hadn't made the effort to move past their dispute, she not only had but was also seemingly able to act as if it had never happened.

Of course that was easier to do when one was the guilty party.

He grimaced. If he was to truly move on he had to quit thinking that way, had to quit trying to assign blame.

There'd been one point in their conversation where he'd gotten the impression that she had her own reasons for wanting to help him. He had to admit he was curious as to what that was about. But he wouldn't begrudge her her secrets as long as the *kinner* were well cared for. He certainly wasn't one to look a gift horse in the mouth.

All that aside, it would be interesting to have Martha in the house for six weeks. Not necessarily comfortable, but interesting.

He tacked the wire to the newly set post, still mulling over the current situation. He'd wanted a chance to prove he could let go of his resentment, to forgive as *Gotte* commanded.

It seemed he was going to get his chance.

Whether he wanted it or not.

* * *

Martha stopped in the living room when she returned to the house. "I'm back. I assume the *kinner* are still asleep."

Dorcas nodded. "I haven't heard a peep out of them."

"*Gut.*" Martha came more fully into the room. "I spoke to Asher while I was outside. I offered to take Debra Lynn's place until she's able to return and he accepted. But I wanted to make certain you were okay with it as well."

Did she imagine Dorcas's momentary pause before she continued stitching?

"That is wonderful generous of you. And *jah*, I accept as well."

Martha waved off the praise, knowing she was doing it as much for herself as for the Lantzes. "I'm happy to help. And I hope you don't mind, but we also agreed to my moving in here for the duration of my time with you rather than my spending the time traveling back and forth." She waved a hand. "But please don't think I'll cause you more work. I'm perfectly capable of taking care of myself."

Dorcas, however, would have none of that. "Nonsense, it's you who are helping us so of course we'll make your stay as easy on you as we can." She set her knitting down and reached in her basket for another skein of yarn.

Martha stood there a moment, unsure of what she should do next. The *kinner* were still napping, she didn't have a room yet to go to and she hadn't brought any reading material with her. All her offers to help Dorcas had been politely rebuffed and she wasn't ready to make another attempt just yet. Should she just go back outside and take a walk or check on Cinders?

Before she could decide she heard someone padding down the stairs. To her relief it appeared Lottie was finished with her nap. Which meant the boys couldn't be far behind.

When the little girl made it to the bottom of the stairs, Martha gave her a smile. "Did you have a *gut* nap?"

Lottie nodded.

Asher's niece seemed as subdued as her *brieder* were boisterous.

Martha looked forward to helping her come out of her shell a bit and better prepare her for school in the fall while she was here. After all, she had experience with helping first graders get used to being in the classroom. And equipping Lottie with a touch of extra confidence when she walked into the classroom for the first time would be rewarding.

But first she needed to make a deeper connection with the child, had to win her trust. She smiled down, meeting Lottie's gaze. "I'm about to go outside and check on Cinders, my buggy horse. I have an apple I plan to cut up and share with her. I could use a helper if you'd like to come with me."

The little girl looked startled at the invitation, but quickly smiled as she nodded.

Martha turned to Dorcas. "We're just going out to feed Cinders. Hopefully we'll be back before the boys wake up from their nap."

Dorcas waved them on. "Don't hurry on my account. The boys and I will be fine."

Lottie followed her to the kitchen and Martha made quick work of slicing the apple while she kept up a steady stream of conversation about Cinders that didn't require any kind of response from her companion. Once the apple was sliced, Martha placed it in a plastic bag and held it out. "Would you carry this for me, please?"

With a nod, Lottie accepted the bag.

As they stepped outside, Martha tried to draw the little girl into a conversation. "Have you ever fed a treat to a horse before?"

"*Jah. Onkel* Asher lets me give Axel and Web carrots sometimes."

Web? Asher still had Ephron's old buggy horse?

"And I used to bring Acorn treats every day too."

There was a sadness in Lottie's voice as she said that last bit. "Who's Acorn?"

"She was *Mamm*'s horse."

Was that sadness in her tone brought on by thoughts of her *mamm*? Or had something happened to the horse itself?

But she didn't want to press the girl to tell her more than she was comfortable revealing. So instead Martha returned to the original topic. "Cinders is very gentle and she really likes apples so she'll be wonderful glad to see you and the treat you've brought her."

"I like her color."

At last, she'd initiated some actual conversation on her own. "I do too. The gray flecks sprinkled on her black coat make a wonderful pretty picture, ain't so? I haven't seen another quite like her."

Lottie swung the bag she carried. "Have you always had her?"

They'd reached the paddock and Martha leaned against the fence rail while Lottie climbed up on the bottom board.

Martha smiled fondly in response to the little girl's question. "Cinders was born right on our place when I was fourteen years old. My *daed* planned to sell her but I fell in love with her and I begged him to let me raise her. He finally gave in."

Lottie folded her arms on the top rail and laid her chin on them. "I loved Acorn like that. After *Daed* and *Mamm* died, though, *Onkel* Asher sold Acorn."

So that's what had happened. Martha could tell from Lottie's tone that this was something that had really hit her hard. Did Asher know how much his niece had cared for the animal? "I'm sorry. I know how difficult it is to be separated from an animal you love."

The little girl merely nodded.

"I tell you what," Martha said impulsively. "While I'm here for the next several weeks, you can help me take care of Cinders. Would you like that?"

Lottie's eyes widened. "I thought you were only going to be here a couple of days."

"I talked to your *onkel* a little while ago about staying until Debra Lynn is able to return. Is that okay with you?"

Lottie nodded. "*Jah.* And I *would* like to help you take care of Cinders. Do you think you could teach me how to brush her too?"

Pleased by the lightening of the girl's mood, Martha smiled. "I think that's a *wunderbaar* idea."

As Cinders trotted over to check them out, Lottie happily held out a slice of apple on the palm of her hand.

It wasn't long before the other horses in the paddock came over to investigate. Martha watched as Lottie carefully tried to divide the apple slices among them all.

The girl had a *gut* heart, and a tender one. Martha was more determined than ever to do all in her power to help her overcome the shyness that held her back.

* * *

That evening back at her *daed*'s house Martha retired to her room earlier than usual. It hadn't taken her long to pack her things for her stay with the Lantz *familye*. After all, she'd barely unpacked from her last trip away from home. She'd made quick stops at the homes of both of her *shveshtra* after she left Asher's, borrowing a few things she thought might come in handy during her time with the Lantzes.

Six weeks. Would anything about her circumstances have changed in that time? She'd like to think she and Laban would have at least reached an understanding by then. But what if they hadn't? Just because things had worked out for Joan and James didn't mean they would work for her and Laban.

Then she gave herself a mental shake. Joan had been fond of telling her she was the world's foremost expert on borrowing trouble.

She'd prefer to think of it as taking a realistic approach but perhaps there was a bit of truth in Joan's assessment. There was no point in thinking things would go wrong until they were further along in their relationship.

She had to remember that *Gotte* was in control and things would work out as they should.

Besides, she and Laban hadn't even exchanged their first letters yet. But there was no time like the present.

She pulled a pen and writing tablet from her bedside table and then paused, feeling suddenly uncertain.

Then she forcefully shook off her insecurity and put pen to paper.

Laban,

I trust you had a safe trip home and are now rested from your travels.

It was gut *to meet you at James and Joan's wedding. Before introducing us, your cousin told Joan what an upstanding person you were and what a* gut *provider you would be. After speaking with you I have confidence he was correct.*

I've made a few changes in my life in the short time since you've left. I've taken on an assignment as nanny for a household with four kinner, *all of them preschoolers. They are the same* kinner *Joan took care of before she married James so you may have heard her speak of them. It's temporary, for only about six weeks while the regular nanny heals from a broken arm. But I am looking forward to it. That is probably something you should know about me. I enjoy working with* kinner, *especially the very young ones. The two years I served as assistant teacher are among some of my fondest memories.*

Another thing you should know about me is that my skills are of the household type. My youngest shveshtah *Hannah is an amazing baker and cake and cookie decorator. My middle* shveshtah *Greta designs and creates breathtaking quilts. Both of their products are in demand among our own people as well as the* Englisch *and they both have shops in a local Amish Marketplace. I don't have any creativity of that sort.*

But what I can *do is manage a house, plant and tend a garden, I can make my own cheese and do those things required to make a home and family comfortable and well cared for.*

My dreams for the future are quite simple—a mann *and* kinner *of my own and a household to*

manage. I would also like to be a gut helpmeet
for my mann, helping him in whatever way I
can. Along those lines, if it's not too premature
to discuss this, I'd like to learn more about your
business, both the skills side and the business
side, so that if we do decide to pursue a match,
I'll be prepared to provide you with whatever
support you might need.

I'll admit I've never visited Fredericksburg
before, but Joan visited James and his family
there about two months ago and she reassures
me that it's a lovely place, much like Hope's
Haven, in friendliness if not in geography. As
another person who's spent time in both places
I'd like to get your impressions of how they are
the same as well as different to help me picture
it better.

I will leave it at that for now. The return address
on the envelope is where your correspondence
can reach me over the next several weeks. I look
forward to receiving your letters and learning
more about you and your own plans.

Sincerely
Martha Eicher

Martha reread the letter, chewing her lip as she did
so. She'd tried to be straightforward and businesslike
but she wasn't certain how well she'd succeeded. Had
she been too forward, too presumptuous?

Deciding she was overthinking it, she quickly folded
the paper and placed it in an envelope. Second-guessing
herself wouldn't serve any productive purpose and

she'd wasted enough time. Getting the letter out in the mail and on its way to Laban was what was most important.

Then she remembered tomorrow was Sunday so it would have to wait one more day.

And maybe Laban had done the same thing and their letters would cross in the mail.

As she turned out her light and slipped under the covers her thoughts turned to the Lantzes. She found that she was looking forward to the time she'd be spending with them. And not just because it would get her away from home.

As she drifted off to sleep her final thought was about how nice it would be if she actually succeeded in mending her relationship with Asher while she was there.

* * *

Almost as soon as Martha stepped down from the buggy the next morning, Asher was right there to help with her bags. "Let me show you to the room you'll have." She let him take the plastic tub with the craft and play items she'd brought for the *kinner* while she took the wheeled suitcase.

He fell into step beside her as they moved to the house. "*Oma* thought you might be more comfortable downstairs than in the room Joan had upstairs. You'll be closer to the triplets that way and they're likely to need more of your attention than Lottie."

Martha frowned. "I'm not so sure about that. But Lottie will require a different kind of attention, for sure and for certain."

He gave her a puzzled look, but let her comment pass.

"I converted my office into a bedroom for you. I'm afraid it's not very big but we furnished it with a comfortable bed and a few other pieces, namely a chest, a bedside table and a chair."

"*Danke.* I'm sure I'll be quite comfortable there."

He shifted his burden. "How did your *daed* and Leah feel about your moving in here?"

"They understood that you have a need I could help with, and that it's only temporary."

They'd reached the house by this time and pausing only a moment for her to greet his *grossmammi*, Asher led the way past Dorcas's room and the triplets' room to a door at the end of the hall. He set her bin inside then straightened. "I'll let you get settled in before the boys wake up. I have a feeling that won't be much longer."

Martha entered the room and took a quick look around. As Asher had warned, it was on the small side, but it would do—she didn't need much space. She opened her suitcase and carefully removed the three everyday dresses she'd packed—she was already wearing her Sunday best. She also unpacked and put away the associated undergarments and such items as were required to complete her simple wardrobe.

She placed her Bible on the bedside table and then moved to the bin. First she pulled out the storybooks and simple jigsaw puzzles she'd borrowed from her *shveshtra*. She'd always enjoyed working puzzles and hoped it was something the Lantz *kinner*, especially Lottie, would enjoy as well.

The rest of the bin's contents were mostly things left

over from her days working as assistant teacher. There were some notebooks with extra-wide line spacing, appropriate for teaching a first grader to print. It also included art supplies like child's scissors, construction paper, colorful magazines, crayons and markers. All of that could remain in the bin until she was ready to use them.

In a matter of a few minutes Martha had her things organized and put away. As soon as she stepped out of her room she heard sounds of activity from the boys' room.

Deciding there was no need to wait on Asher to assist, Martha went to their room and announced it was time to get ready for the day.

After three mornings of working with them, getting the triplets dressed was becoming easier to do. For one thing, the boys were getting used to having her around. And they were starting to take an interest in helping to make their beds beyond just holding the pillows and watching.

But getting them dressed in their Sunday *mutza* suits, fed, and working on straightening their rooms in time to leave the house for the church service almost got the better of her.

Finally, slightly breathless and frazzled, Martha ushered the four little ones out of the house and toward the waiting buggy.

Lottie sat up front with Asher and Dorcas, while Martha sat in the back with the boys. It was the best way to divide them up since the boys weren't happy with being separated.

When they arrived at the Bixler place, where the current Sunday service was to be held, Asher joined the other men gathered near the barn. Martha and Dorcas took the children and joined the women and children in the house.

Martha spotted Debra Lynn right away. The girl was sporting a cast and sling but otherwise seemed in good spirits. As soon as Debra Lynn caught sight of her, she came over.

"I understand you've taken my place with the Lantzes until my arm's healed."

"*Jah.* But don't worry, the job will be all yours again as soon as you're ready."

Debra Lynn waved off Martha's words. "*Ach*, I'm not worried. I'm just relieved they were able to find someone as qualified as you are who was willing to step in so quickly."

Martha wasn't quite sure how to respond to that so she changed the topic and inquired after Debra Lynn's family.

When the girl moved on to speak to someone else, Martha looked around for Joan. Unfortunately she wasn't able to get to her friend before everyone lined up to head down to the basement where the service would be held. And since Joan now entered with the married ladies, they didn't even walk in together as they usually did. It was almost worse than if Joan had already moved to Fredericksburg. Her friend was still here but somehow separate.

The boys were well behaved during the service, playing with the little toys Martha had brought in her tote and nibbling on the snack crackers that she'd packed.

After the service, Martha rounded up a couple of the adolescent girls to keep an eye on the four Lantz *kinner*, then she turned to join the other ladies who were preparing to serve lunch.

When she entered the kitchen she immediately spotted Joan, surrounded by friends congratulating her on her marriage. Joan, James and little Hilda would be leaving for Fredericksburg soon to start their new life together as a *familye*, and this was the last time many of them would see her for a while. Martha was definitely going to miss having her best friend to talk to, especially on occasions like this.

Finally, after everyone had been served and the kitchen cleaned, Martha took the opportunity to pull Joan outside with her for a break and a breath of fresh air. And to finally have a chance to talk, just the two of them.

"Marriage seems to agree with you," Martha observed. And it was true. Joan had an extra glow about her, a soft air of happiness.

Joan's cheeks pinkened. "*Jah*. James is a *gut mann*. And I already love Hilda, she's such a sweet child."

Across the way they could see a group of children playing. Despite Joan's new *dochder* Hilda being a relative stranger, she seemed to fit in with the group, playing tag with the unfiltered exuberance of a confident three-year-old. By contrast Lottie stood on the sidelines, watching.

"I understand you've temporarily stepped in as the nanny for Shem's *kinner*."

The statement pulled Martha's attention back to her friend. She shrugged. "Asher and Dorcas needed someone to help out and I was available."

Joan gave her a pointed look. "If I'm not mistaken you were more than just available, you were also eager, ain't so?"

Martha sighed. "*Jah*, it did work out well for me too. But Leah has things well in hand at home. My presence is not needed, nor will it be missed."

"Still, I think you're overreacting. Leah would never try to push you out, and deep down you know that."

"I know." Uncomfortable with the direction of the conversation, Martha quickly changed the subject. "So, do you have any tips or suggestions for me on how best to deal with the *kinner*?"

Joan smiled. "You've always been *gut* with *kinner*. I'd say you just need to trust your instincts."

While flattering, that certainly hadn't been very helpful. Martha waved back toward the children. "Speaking of *kinner*, has Lottie always been so withdrawn?"

Joan paused and followed Martha's gaze with a frown. "I can't speak to how she was before her *eldre* died. But Lottie had a more difficult time adjusting to her new situation than the boys did. For one thing she was four when it happened so she could hold on to the memories longer than her *brieder*. Zeb, Zach and Zeke were only two-year-olds at the time and they also had that special bond of being triplets to provide a level of support for one another that Lottie lacked."

She resumed their walk and Martha followed suit.

But Martha wasn't ready to let the subject drop. "I've noticed she seems to avoid joining the other *kinner* during playtime."

"You know how some little ones are just naturally shy, I'm sure that's all it is. And who wouldn't look reserved when compared with those *brieder* of hers, ain't so?"

There was no denying that. But still Martha felt there was something more at work here.

"Now, enough about that," Joan said, giving her arm a squeeze. "Tell me, what did you think of Laban? He certainly seemed taken with you."

Martha was pleasantly surprised at that. "Did he?"

"*Jah*. He told James he thought you seemed to be a fine woman who would make a great helpmeet."

Not a very romantic reaction. But she reminded herself that romance was only a secondary consideration.

"You didn't answer my question—what did you think of him?"

"He seems to be a very sensible and industrious man. I think we would get along well." She could be just as businesslike as Laban. "We'll be corresponding for the next several weeks to get to know each other better. In fact, I wrote to him last night."

Joan gave her a delighted smile. "*Wunderbaar!* I'm sure you'll hear back from him soon."

Their discussion moved on to other topics and before long they were joined by others who wanted to speak to Joan before she embarked on her new life in Fredericksburg.

As Martha gave way to the others she felt a lump rise in her throat. She knew it was silly to get so sentimental about this—she and Joan would always be friends no matter how many miles separated them. But not in the same way. Their relationship had already changed and Martha was feeling as if she'd been left behind.

Again.

Chapter 12

Asher listened to the soft clip-clop of Axel's hooves on the hard packed dirt road as they drove home from the Bixler place. A drowsy Lottie leaned her head against his side. It was a warmly welcome pressure. There was a comfortable silence in the buggy, giving him the opportunity to let his mind wander.

He'd spotted Martha and Joan earlier as they'd tried to get some time alone to chat. He knew how close the two women were—they'd been friends since they were in first grade together. He'd noticed how frequently they'd exchanged letters while Martha was out of town. Would they continue to do so now that it would be Joan who was away? Or would Joan's new status and responsibilities interfere?

Whatever their discussion had been, it had left Martha in a reflective mood. He could sense a somber sort of preoccupied air about her even now. Was it sadness over her friend moving away? Or was something else troubling her?

Hopefully she wasn't already having second thoughts about her offer to stay on with them as nanny. It had surprised him how excited his nephews and niece were when he told them last night that Martha would be staying until Debra Lynn returned. Lottie, who apparently already knew, hadn't smiled so broadly in quite some time. Even *Oma* appeared pleased. It seemed that in the two short days she'd spent with them Martha had made a very positive impression.

Not that he should be surprised. If one overlooked the one glaring issue between them, Martha was a very kind, patient and generous sort of person, especially when it came to *kinner*.

When they arrived home, Asher had to help Martha rouse the boys who'd fallen asleep during the ride. Then he left her and *Oma* to escort the little ones inside while he took care of the horse and buggy.

By the time he returned to the house he found the kitchen empty. But he could hear sounds of giggling coming from the front of the house. He followed the sound to the living room and what he saw brought a smile to his own face.

Martha sat on the sofa with all four *kinner* gathered around. Two of the boys—he wasn't sure which two— were sharing her lap while Lottie and the other triplet sat on either side, so close they were almost on top of her. Martha held an oversized picture book and was reading from it in what he thought of as her storyteller voice.

Back in her days as assistant teacher she'd read to the younger scholars on rainy or heavy snow days when they couldn't go outside to play. Back then she kept the scholars hanging on her every word, much as the four youngsters on the sofa were doing now. It was something about the emotion she imbued her words with, about the way she managed to frequently look each of them in the eye when she was telling the story, and how involved she herself seemed to be that kept her listeners both engaged and entertained. Even Joan hadn't captured their interest so fully.

He'd seen Martha's middle *shveshtah* Greta do the same thing at community gatherings when she'd watched over the *kinner*. Had the younger Eicher girl learned it from her older *shveshtah*? Or had they both learned it from their *mamm*?

Whatever the case he considered Martha the master of this particular skill.

As he watched the five of them on the sofa he felt a sudden longing to be a part of that group rather than the outsider, to scoop Lottie up and seat her on his lap while he sat beside Martha on the sofa.

Was it time for him to think about finding a *fraa*? He studied Martha wondering why she'd never married. Surely she didn't still carry a torch for Ephron?

As if feeling his stare, Martha looked up and spotted him standing there. She gave him a welcoming smile. "Look, there's your *onkel* Asher," she said to the *kinner*. "Should we invite him to join us?"

He was pleased to see the nods and hear the chorus of assents. And he was sorely tempted to actually join them as he'd longed to earlier. But he decided it would be best to maintain a bit of distance with Martha.

So with a regretful smile he shook his head. "*Danke*, I'm sure it's a wonderful *gut* story. But I need to change clothes and then I thought I'd take care of the evening milking a little early."

"Of course."

Did he imagine that touch of disappointment in her expression?

But then she smiled and turned back to the book. "Now where were we?"

As Asher made his way to the stairs he felt a little niggle of regret that he hadn't taken her up on her invitation. After all, Joan had hinted once or twice that he ought to spend more time with his nephews and niece outside of meals.

* * *

That evening, Martha had her first experience with putting the four Lantz *kinner* to bed. She'd given some thought to how she would tuck them in at night and had come up with a plan. It was always *gut* to be prepared. Once they had cleaned up and had their nightclothes on, she asked Lottie to join the boys in their room while she told them a story.

Martha remembered a bedtime story her own *mamm* had told her and her *shveshtra* many times, one Martha suspected Mamm had made up herself. It featured a frog and a dragonfly and included a lesson on the virtue of kindness.

When she was done she gave each boy a kiss on the forehead as she adjusted their covers then led Lottie from the room.

Once in the hall, she smiled down at the boys' older *shveshtah*. "Your turn." She took the little girl's hand and together they climbed the stairs to her room. As she combed Lottie's hair she softly sang a lullaby. By the time she tucked Lottie in bed with her cloth doll the girl's eyes were definitely droopy.

Just before Martha left the room, however, a softly uttered *gut nacht* reached her. The words were soft and trusting. And they infused Martha's heart with a surprising warmth.

She was still feeling that warm glow when she made it back downstairs. While she was upstairs Dorcas and Asher had settled in the living room. Asher sat in the recliner reading a farming magazine and Dorcas had pulled out her knitting.

Martha hesitated on the threshold, unsure whether to join them or not. Before she could decide, however, Dorcas looked up and met her gaze. "Are the *kinner* settled in their beds?"

Martha nodded and moved fully into the room. "*Jah.* They had a long day so they were ready to snuggle down."

Dorcas began putting away her knitting. "Well, I feel like I've had a long day as well. I think it's time for me to turn in." She nodded to a side table. "There's the latest copy of *The Connection* if you'd like to have something to read." Then she looked from Martha to Asher. "I expect the two of you will be turning in soon as well."

Feeling as if that was more a declaration, no matter how gentle, than a suggestion, Martha nodded meekly.

Not that Dorcas had anything but appearance of propriety to worry about. After all, Asher was four years younger than her. And she was focused on Laban.

But she did want to speak to Asher privately. And

the sooner the better. Unfortunately she was having trouble figuring out how to get started.

Asher cleared his throat, feeling the need to break the silence. "You did a *gut* job getting the *kinner* to settle down for the night. I didn't hear any horseplay coming from the boys' room."

"*Danke.*" She waved a hand. "But it wasn't difficult. They're *gut kinner* and Joan taught them well."

He smiled. "It helps that Lottie is so much calmer than the triplets."

To his surprise, she didn't return his smile. If anything she grew more serious. "I'm glad you said that. I want to speak to you about Lottie."

That didn't sound *gut*. "Is something wrong?"

"*Jah*, but not in the way you think."

How did she know what he was thinking? "Then what?"

"She's too calm, too well behaved."

There was no indication that she was being anything but sincere. Now he was really confused. "Isn't well behaved a *gut* thing?"

"Not necessarily. She's a five-year-old who doesn't seem to know how to play with others her age and just have fun."

That got his back up. "If you're trying to say that Lottie is unhappy—"

She interrupted him with a wave of her hand. "*Nee.* Not unhappy exactly, just painfully shy." Her expression was earnest, her tone patient but firm. "I saw this a few times when I was an assistant teacher."

He crossed his arms. "But shyness is not *gut* or bad, it just is, ain't so?"

"In most cases. But I said *painfully* shy. If we don't help her overcome this now, she'll have trouble when she starts school next fall."

Her genuine concern made it hard to dismiss her words. Still… "Don't you think you might be over-reacting? After all, Joan never worried about this and she spent a lot more time with Lottie than you have."

She leaned forward slightly, as if trying to show him how earnest she was. "Joan got those sweet *lamms* through a very difficult time in their young lives. I'm sure it took a lot of patience and time to help them deal with their grief and adjust to their new situation."

Asher remembered those early days when the *kinner* had cried all the time, when Lottie had refused to sleep unless they put her bed in the room with her *brieder*, when they'd all seemed inconsolable. It had most defi-nitely been Joan who'd held them, rocked them, tried to soothe them. She found ways to distract them during those early weeks and months when he and *Oma* had been struggling with their own sense of loss.

And truth be told, he'd been glad to leave it to her while he dealt with not only his own grief but also all the other issues brought on by the death of his oldest *bruder*. Like moving in here again and handling the farm all on his own. It had taken him some time to accept and adjust to the changes to his own circumstances.

Martha was still speaking and he quickly turned his focus back to her.

"I'm not blaming anyone, for sure and for certain. It's just that I can see it because I'm walking into this house with fresh eyes. And because of my experience in the classroom."

"Experience that's about twelve years old." He regretted his sharp tone as soon as the words left his lips.

But she merely raised a brow. "That doesn't mean it's not still valid, ain't so?"

He gave a short nod. "Very well. Assuming there really is an issue here that needs attention, is there something you have in mind to help Lottie with this?"

"What *we* should do," she said pointedly, "is to find ways to get her involved, to not allow her to always fade into the background. But we should do it in a way that doesn't feel threatening and doesn't set her up to fail."

He hadn't missed her emphasis on the word "we." "How can it be nonthreatening if we make her do something she doesn't want to do?"

"We don't *make* her do anything. We ease her into things slowly. For instance, for the next Sunday service we find one *kinner* about her age and set things up so they can interact one-on-one. It'll be much easier than expecting her to join in with a crowd of *kinner*."

Asher had no idea how to identify a child who would be a *gut* fit for such an interaction. "Do you have someone in mind?"

She clasped her hands, her expressive eyes alight with her enthusiasm for helping his niece. "*Jah*. My *shveshtah* Greta's *suh* David is the same age as Lottie and is a very friendly little boy." She nodded thoughtfully. "I might even invite Greta to come by for a visit with her *kinner* so Lottie and David can get to know each other in a familiar place before the next Sunday service."

"It sounds like you've given this a lot of thought."

Martha certainly liked to plan things out. But he had to admit, she'd been here just a few days and already she was on her way to making a major impact on their household.

Martha's expression was self-deprecating. "I have."

He was beginning to believe she might be right. "If you think this is the best way, then perhaps you can invite Greta and her *familye* to join us for lunch this coming Sunday."

She tilted her head to one side. "Do you think your *grossmammi* will mind?"

He didn't hesitate. "Not at all. She enjoys having company." Now that he thought about it, she really hadn't done much socializing lately except with Joan. Was that at least partly his fault? Had he failed to make sure she found time to invite her friends over or to visit them in their homes? At a minimum he should at least have realized how isolated she'd become before now.

"*Gut.* And between now and then we should find things for Lottie to do that she is *gut* at to help build her confidence. Do you have any idea what that might be?"

"I'm sure there are any number of things Lottie enjoys doing." Though he couldn't think of any right off the bat.

She gave him a look that made it seem she'd read his thoughts. But she merely nodded. "*Jah,* I'm sure there are." She met his gaze with a challenging one of her own. "Lottie has lived under your roof for a year now. Have you noticed her take an interest in anything that might be appropriate for this?"

Asher tried not to squirm. To be honest, because his

niece had been so quiet and agreeable, he hadn't really paid much attention to her. That wasn't a truth he felt comfortable admitting, even to himself.

"We can start with something simple," she continued after a short pause. "I brought some jigsaw puzzles with me to see if it might be something she'd like to do. And I've noticed she's really quite *gut* with a box of crayons and a coloring book."

Relieved she'd come up with some activities rather than waiting on him to take the lead, he nodded. "Those are both *gut* things." Then he frowned as he thought about it. "But they seem more like activities to do alone than with others. Aren't we trying to get her to interact with others more?"

"We're also trying to build her confidence. It's true, though, that it would be *gut* to find something more active to add to our list of things to try."

Time to give in and go along with her approach. "Like what?"

"Do you have horseshoes or perhaps a croquet set?"

He slowly nodded. "Assuming they weren't thrown out years ago, we have both. They should be down in the basement somewhere."

She smiled as if he'd performed some wonderful feat. "*Gut*. If you'll help me dig them out, I can start teaching Lottie how to play. In fact it would probably be *gut* to teach all the *kinner* how to play so she doesn't feel too much of the spotlight is on her."

"I can take care of finding the equipment and toting it upstairs for you. But what if you try to teach the puzzles and games to Lottie and it turns out she doesn't take to them?"

Her brows rose as she considered his words. "If you

mean she doesn't do well, we both know she doesn't have to be a champion player for us to succeed, she just has to be confident that she knows how to play and won't embarrass herself." Martha waved a hand. "But if you mean what if she doesn't enjoy those particular activities, then we'll just keep searching until we find something she *does* enjoy."

Martha seemed so confident it was hard to disagree with her. "That makes sense. I'll head to the basement first thing in the morning and get that game equipment brought out to the back porch. It'll be there for you whenever you get ready."

"*Gut.* Now that that's settled, there is one more thing I'd like to talk to you about."

Gauging from her tone of voice he wasn't going to come off in a *gut* light, whatever the "one more thing" was. "What is it?"

"It concerns the buggy horse that belonged to Lottie's *mamm.*"

The unexpectedness of the topic threw him for a moment. "Acorn? I sold her to Obed Miller along with the buggy. He was looking for a horse and buggy for his *dochder* and made us an offer shortly after the funerals."

"Did you know that Lottie was particularly fond of Acorn? And that she still misses the animal?"

The questions, spoken matter-of-factly, hit him like a physical blow. "She never said anything to me about it."

"I imagine she didn't know you were going to sell the animal until it was already gone, ain't so?"

He thought back and slowly nodded. "Still, she could have said something even then." He knew he sounded defensive, but how was he supposed to have known his niece's feelings if she didn't speak up. He obviously didn't have any parental instincts others seemed born with.

"She would have been four then, wouldn't she? And she'd just lost her parents. I imagine her place in the world seemed very strange and uncertain to her at the time."

Of course it would have. Lottie and her *brieder* had been shaken and grieving over their loss. "How do you know about her feelings for Acorn?"

"She told me." Martha's tone was blunt but without accusation. "We were discussing Cinders and she just blurted out how much she loved and missed Acorn. I could hear the longing in her voice."

How had he missed that? He'd noticed she liked animals, and that they in turn took to her. She'd managed to pet Hissy, the skittish barn cat that never let anyone get close. And she also had a way with Daisy's calf Ferdinand. It reminded him of the way Ephron had been when it came to animals.

That thought brought him up short. Was that why he'd failed to notice what was going on with his niece, why he'd never gotten as close to her as he had to the boys? That was a sobering thought.

When he met Martha's gaze, he saw the speculation in her eyes. It was as if she was waiting to gauge his reaction to what she'd told him. But there was no judgment there.

He owed it to her not to be evasive or dismissive. "I'm not sure how to fix this."

Her expression softened into one of sympathy and she spread her hands. "You can't go back and change the past, Asher. I didn't tell you about this to make you feel guilty. I told you because I thought it was important that you know about Lottie's feelings going forward, that it might help you understand her better."

Though her intentions were *gut*, her words didn't do much to make him feel better. But none of this was her fault and she was right about the need to move forward from here. He tried a self-deprecating grin. "And all this time I was thinking the triplets were going to be the ones who would keep you on your toes."

She smiled. "*Ach*, they will do that, for sure and for certain. But that's actually a *gut* thing. It means they are normal, well-adjusted toddlers." Then she sobered. "But just because they're rambunctious and Lottie is quieter doesn't mean we can or should ignore her."

"So I'm learning."

"The *gut* news is that Lottie is a sweet, intelligent little girl. All that's required is to give her some encouragement and confidence."

He still couldn't figure out how she'd homed in on all this in the short time she'd been with the *kinner* when he hadn't seen any of it in the year he'd been under the same roof with them. "Any other observations about the *kinner* you feel led to share?"

He immediately regretted his tone when he saw the way she stiffened.

"That's enough for one sitting, ain't so?" Then she stood. "And now I think I'll follow your *grossmammi*'s lead and head to my room. *Gut nacht.*"

"*Gut nacht.*" He watched her go, feeling a wretch, not only for his tone but also because he'd missed all those signs with Lottie.

Gotte, *please help me to learn the lesson You have*

provided for me in this, teach me to be humble in dealing with others, help me to see and be sympathetic to the pain of others, and above all help me to do gut *by those You have placed in my care.*

Then he added, *And also help me to appreciate the blessings Martha is bringing to our* familye.

He pushed himself up from his chair and turned out the lights before heading up to his room for bed.

* * *

As Martha sat on her bed and brushed out her hair she thought about her conversation with Asher. She tried not to take offense at the way their conversation had ended. The information she'd given him about his niece couldn't have been easy to hear, especially since it appeared he felt guilty about not having seen it for himself. It was no wonder he'd felt defensive.

She'd seen the contrition and self-reproach play out on his face, had heard the remorse and regret in his voice, and it had tugged at her, made her want to offer comfort. Of course acting on those feelings would have been not only inappropriate but also unwelcome.

Martha had no regrets over having told Asher what she'd learned. And she took heart in his obvious intention to do better going forward.

Hopefully she could nudge him toward actually taking a more active, more fatherly role with the *kinner* in the future.

He was a *gut* person, he just needed to be reminded of that from time to time. Actually, she'd add that to her list of things to take care of while she was here.

He might not like any of the prompting or nudges

she gave him in that direction, but she had hope after the way he reacted tonight that he would at least listen to her.

In fact, once he saw the results, he might actually come to look forward to it.

As she slid under the covers she had a smile on her face.

Chapter 13

When Martha woke Monday morning it took her a few moments to remember where she was. As soon as she did, however, she popped out of bed and hurried through her morning routine. She wanted to be up and about well before the *kinner* woke up.

One of the things she'd discussed with Joan yesterday was how to best help Dorcas without making her feel that she was being elbowed aside, something Martha was definitely sensitive to. Joan had suggested that whatever she did, she couch it in such a way that Dorcas felt she would be helping Martha or other members of the household rather than the other way around. That had given Martha an idea of how to approach Dorcas with what she saw as the number one place she could help her—taking care of the laundry. It was a chore made especially difficult for the older woman since the washing equipment was in the basement and required she utilize the stairs, something that was becoming increasingly difficult for her. Along those same lines, Martha figured she would also work on finding ways to cut down on Dorcas's trips upstairs. She would just have to take care to be respectful of Dorcas's feelings.

But first, the laundry. If Dorcas was like most of the women in the community, Monday was laundry day, so she needed to set her plan in motion quickly.

Saying a silent prayer that she'd find the right words, Martha stepped into the kitchen to find both Dorcas and Asher already there. But apparently Asher hadn't beaten her there by much because he was just now pouring himself a cup of coffee. When he glanced her way she saw a flash of something very much like a welcome in his gaze. But he turned back to his cup so quickly she wasn't sure.

"*Gut matin*, Asher, Dorcas. The coffee smells *wunderbaar*."

Dorcas, who was peeling apples to go in the baked oatmeal, smiled over her shoulder. "That mug on the counter is for you, help yourself."

"*Danke*."

As she poured the hot brew, she broached the subject of the laundry. "Today is washday, ain't so?" She posed the question as casually as she could.

Dorcas gave her a curious glance. "It is." Then she turned back to her work. "If you have things you'd like to add to the washing—"

"*Nee*," Martha protested quickly. "I was actually wondering if you'd mind if I took care of it? I've been trying to come up with new ideas on how to teach the *kinner* responsibility and I think getting their help with the laundry would be just the thing."

Dorcas frowned. "I can understand trying to teach Lottie to help with laundry, but it's surely not appropriate for the boys."

Martha kept her tone reasonable. "If it's because they're so young, I promise I won't push them too hard, I'll just get them familiar with how it all works and let them help with things like stripping their beds, getting it all down to the basement and handing me things."

She added a teaspoon of sugar to her coffee. "If it's because they're boys, learning how to take care of themselves is always *gut*, ain't so? And even if they are blessed enough to always have a woman in their lives who'll take care of such things for them, then I believe it's still *gut* to understand the effort that goes into that care."

Then Martha gave Dorcas an apologetic smile. "But I never had any *brieder*, so I'm not sure what my own *mamm* would have done or if this is appropriate, so I'll defer to you on this." Even if she got Dorcas to agree to let her teach only Lottie, she'd still have succeeded in getting Asher's *grossmammi* to turn the chore over to her.

Asher sipped on his coffee as he listened to the conversation between *Oma* and Martha unfold. It had been a masterful bit of diplomacy on Martha's part, for sure and for certain. She'd managed to wrestle the undesirable laundry chore away from *Oma* while leaving the older woman's dignity intact.

And she'd made it seem like *Oma* was doing her a favor in allowing her to take it on.

Deciding to lend her his support, Asher cleared his

throat. "Actually, *Oma*, Martha's right about it being *gut* for menfolk to know how to do such tasks. When I lived alone for those five weeks last year, I had to ask Joan to come over and teach me how to do laundry and cook some basic meals."

Oma looked at him with a frown. "Why didn't you ask me to teach you? Or better yet, you could have come here and I would have taken care of it for you."

He heard the hurt in her voice and rushed to reassure her. "I know you would have but I didn't want to add to your workload." He set his cup down. "Shem and his family had just moved in and were keeping you plenty busy."

"Not too busy to help my grandson."

Asher tried not to grind his teeth. Would *Oma* always see him as a little boy who needed to be coddled?

To his relief Martha spoke up again. "So that's settled then. After breakfast this morning I'll get the *kinner* to help me gather up all the things to be washed and give them their first laundry lesson."

Then she caught his gaze. "If you'll strip your bed and put the bedding and your other laundry outside your door, Lottie and I can carry it down when I help her fetch her things."

Before he could respond, *Oma* spoke up. "I can take care of that. Asher has other work he needs to get to."

He saw the very pointed look Martha shot his way and quickly spoke up. Not that he wouldn't have otherwise. "That's okay. I have to go back upstairs and fetch my work gloves anyway. I can even carry it to the foot of the stairs when I head down."

Martha's expression had relaxed considerably when she realized he was willing to go along with what she was trying to do. Apparently she hadn't been sure of him.

Then Asher straightened. "I think I hear the triplets stirring. Want some help getting them up and dressed?"

But she shook her head. "You go ahead with the milking. The boys and I have reached an understanding on how to get ready for the day." And with that she set her coffee mug down and moved toward the hallway.

As Asher walked out to the milking barn a few minutes later, he mulled over what had just happened. How much of her so-called request this morning was truly about teaching the *kinner* new skills and how much was a sensitive way to take some burden from *Oma*? After last night's discussion he'd guess it was more the latter than the former. Martha might be too much of a plotter and planner, but she had *gut* intentions.

It was for sure and for certain going to be an interesting six weeks.

* * *

Martha entered the triplets' room to find all three boys in Zach's bed, giggling and whispering to one another. But there was no guilt in their faces when they turned to her so she merely gave them a big smile. "*Gut matin*, boys. Time to get up and get dressed."

They scrambled out of bed, pulling off their nightshirts as if racing to see who could finish first.

She was already starting to be able to tell the trio

apart. Of course it helped that Zeb had that identifying but fading bruise. Beyond that Zeb was also a fearless child, which was probably how he'd acquired the bruise in the first place. There was no feat that he feared.

Zach, on the other hand, was the ringleader of the group, seeming to initiate most of their activity. The other two obviously took their cues from him.

And Zeke was a little sweetheart, always eager to please or curl up in your lap for a quick hug before rejoining his *brieder*.

As she helped the boys get dressed for the day, she thought about Asher's reaction to her plan to take over the laundry. She'd avoided meeting his gaze as she discussed her idea with Dorcas because she wasn't sure if she'd see suspicion and censure there. When she'd finally risked a glance his way, she'd seen the knowing gleam in his eye but still couldn't tell if he approved or not.

When he agreed to carry his laundry downstairs, however, the look he gave her was almost a wink. Which for some reason lifted her spirits significantly. His approval meant a lot to her.

Only because it signified he might actually be ready to forgive her, of course.

When she'd tied the last shoelace she ushered the boys to the kitchen. As expected, Lottie was already there and helping to set the table. Asher returned with a pail of milk, and in short order everyone was seated at the table.

She waited until everyone had been served and started eating before she told the *kinner* about her plans.

"I have something new for us to do today," she said

cheerfully. "It's Monday, which means it's laundry day. The five of us are going to take over that task so *Grossmammi* Dorcas can work on some other projects. Won't it be fun to learn something new?"

All four faces looked at her with varying levels of uncertainty, but Martha went on as if she hadn't noticed. "The first thing we need to do is strip our beds and gather up all the dirty clothes from our rooms."

Asher smiled at Lottie. "Since both of our rooms are upstairs why don't I give you a hand while Martha helps your *brieder*?"

Martha noted the way Lottie's face brightened at that. Apparently she didn't hold her *onkel*'s sale of Acorn against him.

Martha gave him an approving smile then turned back to the *kinner*. "All right then, as soon as we're finished with breakfast we'll get to it."

Later, when Martha and the three boys entered their room, Martha headed for the nearest bed. "While I strip the sheets, you boys can take the pillowcases off the pillows." Then she gave them a grin. "Let's see if you can get that done before I get the sheets taken care of."

With gleeful grins, the triplets began removing the pillowcases with a great deal of gusto and much giggling. She'd barely gotten started on the second bed when they were done. She paused and placed her hands on her hips. "*Ach*, but you three are wonderful fast, that's for sure and certain." She waved toward the clothes hamper in the corner of the room. "Why don't you put your things from the hamper into the pillowcases while I finish stripping the beds?"

In no time at all they had everything gathered up and stepped back in the hall. Each boy held a stuffed pillowcase that he dragged behind him, and Martha held the sheets.

"Just a minute," she instructed. "I need to get my laundry too." Since she'd already taken care of gathering everything up, it was just a matter of grabbing it and stepping back into the hall.

"All right, I think that's everything. Let's see how Lottie and your *onkel* Asher are doing."

When they reached the end of the hall they found Lottie and Asher waiting at the foot of the stairs with their laundry in a pile at their feet.

"All right, everyone, it looks like it might take us a couple of trips to get this all down to the basement."

Asher looked at the *kinner*. "It seems Martha doesn't know about our secret moving device."

"What's this?" Martha was not only surprised by his bit of teasing but intrigued as well. "I like secrets."

"Let's show her, shall we?" Asher was obviously enjoying her curiosity.

He picked up an armload of the laundry and led the way to the basement stairs, stopping just short of the entrance. In fact he paused in front of what appeared to be a large cabinet door just to the left of the staircase.

Martha hadn't paid it much attention before now, but since this obviously had something to do with whatever the big secret was she studied it more closely. It was mounted low on the wall, the bottom edge falling even with her knees. And there were no hinges so she'd guess it was a sliding door.

She didn't have time to notice much else before Asher slid it open with a flourish. At first she wasn't sure what she was looking at. The cupboard was deep but totally empty. Then she noticed a pair of ropes, one going down along each side of the cupboard. She turned to Asher, who was grinning at her.

"Is this a dumbwaiter?"

Asher nodded. "Shem and I installed it before he and his *familye* moved in here. It was a surprise for Lydia, he wanted to spare her from having to carry loads up and down the stairs."

Asher's expression had sobered momentarily at the mention of his *bruder* and sister-in-law. But then he smiled again. "So yes, it may take more than one 'trip' down to the basement to get this all down there, but the good news is that the trips won't be via the stairs."

Martha nodded her approval. "A wonderful useful device, for sure and for certain." Then she straightened. "If you don't mind, why don't you and the *kinner* get these clothes down to the basement while I talk to your *grossmammi* about her laundry and the towels?"

With a nod, Asher turned to the *kinner* and had them load their burdens into the dumbwaiter.

When approached, Dorcas indicated she would get her laundry to the dumbwaiter herself. Not wanting to press the matter, Martha nodded and headed for the basement. Once there, she was greeted by the sight of Asher and the four *kinner* unloading the laundry items.

When they'd finished he sent the cabinet back upstairs so it would be ready for *Oma*'s load. Asher didn't return upstairs immediately, though. While Martha demonstrated the art of sorting the laundry items to the *kinner*, she peripherally watched him cross the basement and start rummaging around in a pile of things that were stacked along one wall.

Several minutes later he turned back to her with a pleased smile. "I've unearthed quite a bit of game equipment." He waved a hand over his finds. "Do you want me to take all of this out to the back porch?"

Naturally this attracted the little ones' attention and Martha followed them across the basement.

She studied his finds with an approving smile. There was a croquet set, horseshoes, a cornhole board and a lawn bowling game. "This is all in wonderful *gut* shape. *Jah*, if you don't mind, please do move all of it where we can get to it more easily."

"Can we play now?" Zeb asked.

She shook her head. "We must get our chores done first. Your *onkel* is going to bring those games upstairs and then he also has other things to do. But we can play this afternoon and we might even be able to convince him to play with us."

Asher's only response was a noncommittal grin as he started loading things into the dumbwaiter.

Trying not to be disappointed, she ushered her charges back toward the laundry.

Martha spent the next several hours teaching her young companions how to do the household laundry. She charged the boys with sorting the clothes, a task that they tackled with mixed success. Lottie helped her with the actual washing, though Martha was careful to keep her well away from the wringer machine.

Later, when the washing was done, she again had them help with hanging the clean clothes on the line outside. Since none of them were tall enough to reach the line, she assigned them tasks they *could* do. Lottie handed her the items to be hung and the boys took turns handing her the pins, taking time out occasionally for spontaneous games of tag.

When they were finally finished Martha praised

them for a job well done. Then she grabbed up the hampers and they trooped back to the house.

Dorcas had apparently been watching for them. There was a platter of freshly baked sugar cookies on the table and she was just setting a pitcher of milk beside it. "After all that hard work I thought you all might be ready for a little snack."

With eager nods the little laundry helpers crowded around the table. Martha set the hampers down and quickly had the boys seated in their stools. To her surprise Lottie managed to climb up on her booster seat on her own.

"So how did the laundry lesson go this morning?" Dorcas asked.

"I helped," Zeb said as he reached for a cookie.

Not to be outdone, Zach chimed in with a "Me too."

Martha quickly intervened. "Everyone helped and they did a very *gut* job."

"I'm sure they did," Dorcas agreed with a smile.

* * *

Asher moved back to the horse barn where he'd been working on repairing some tack. He'd stepped out earlier when he'd heard the sound of childish laughter and squeals. It hadn't been difficult to spot the source—Martha and his niece and nephews were hanging the laundry on the line. Rather Martha was hanging the wet items on the line with Lottie's help. The boys, on the other hand, appeared to be getting in one another's way more than helping. Their exuberant play was what had been generating all the gleeful sounds that had pulled Asher from his work.

Not that Martha and Lottie were somber onlookers. As he watched, Martha had whispered to Lottie and then the two of them had grabbed up a sheet from the basket, and each taking an end they had swooped at the squealing boys, corralling them in its folds.

The laughter had been contagious and Asher had taken a step toward joining them when he caught himself. Would he be a welcome addition to their horseplay or would his presence put a damper on their fun?

As he turned away he thought about what an ironic twist that Martha should be the one being so playful and he should be the one left on the sidelines.

About thirty minutes later he looked up to see Martha leading her horse in from the paddock, Lottie at her side. Martha paused a moment when she spotted him at the workbench, then gave a tentative smile. "I hope we're not intruding. Lottie and I thought we'd treat Cinders to a *gut* brushing before lunch."

Asher returned her smile. "Come on in—you won't be bothering me a bit." So Martha had found a way to give Lottie a replacement for Acorn, at least for the time being. Why hadn't he thought of that?

While he continued examining and mending the tack, Asher listened to the gentle way Martha instructed Lottie and the way she drew her out. She even managed to elicit a few giggles from his niece.

He couldn't remember the last time he'd heard the little girl sound so carefree.

Martha was most definitely *gut* with children. And children seemed to love her, despite her sometimes severe demeanor.

They did say children were a *gut* judge of character.

Chapter 14

After lunch Martha had a little bit of trouble getting the *kinner* to settle down for their naps. But after two stories and a softly sung hymn their eyes started to droop and she was able to leave them to their sleep.

As she'd gotten in the habit of, Martha decided to go out for a walk while her charges slept. She enjoyed the chance to stroll around the Lantz place and do a bit of exploring. Each day she'd discovered something different. Asher's homeplace was more spread out than hers, and the outbuildings were different as well.

Asher was nowhere to be seen today, not that she'd been looking for him. And just to prove it to herself she deliberately stayed away from the equipment shed and horse barn. Instead she moved toward another outbuilding, the one next to the equipment shed.

However, when she realized the metallic tapping sound she'd been hearing for several seconds came not from inside the equipment shed but from the outbuilding she'd been headed for, she paused. It had to be Asher making that noise. Perhaps she should change direction and explore elsewhere.

But what was he doing? Was he building something? Curious, she went around to the side of the building and peered inside one of the large windows. Sure enough, Asher stood at a worktable situated near the center of the room wielding a hammer. But she couldn't really see what he was working on.

Before she could see more, Rowdy came around the corner and barked an enthusiastic greeting. Asher looked up at the disturbance and to her embarrassment caught sight of her standing there watching him.

His brows rose in surprise, then he grinned and motioned for her to come inside.

Feeling as if she'd been caught spying, which she supposed she had, Martha had no choice but to nod and walk around to the door.

He was still at the worktable when she stepped inside, but he'd put his tools down and sat on a stool with his arms crossed.

Before he could speak, she attempted to explain herself. "I'm sorry for spying on you but I heard you in here hammering away and my curiosity got the better of me. But I for sure and certain didn't want to disturb you."

He waved a hand. "No need to apologize. And as for what I'm working on, come closer and take a look."

As he spoke she'd taken in something of her surroundings and was surprised by what she saw. The walls were covered with punched tin panels. Sculptural pieces like lanterns, sconces, fixtures and ornaments hung from the rafters. There were simple patterns and breathtakingly elaborate ones. Most were done on tinlike metal but there were some on copper as well. It was almost too much to take in.

As her focus returned to Asher and she approached the worktable she saw the hammer and metal punch that lay close to hand. Then she caught sight of the piece he'd been working on. It was unfinished but the pattern on the paper overlay was a beautifully intricate design that included geometric and floral shapes.

"Asher, your work is *wunderbaar*. You're a true artist, for sure and for certain. How come I never knew you created such lovely pieces?"

Asher shrugged. "I don't make a secret of it but neither do I boast of it."

She moved around his workshop, admiring the completed pieces. "Do you already have a market for your work?"

He picked up his tools again. "Noah Stoll is my biggest customer—he orders panels to inlay in furniture pieces when his customers want that extra touch. And Charity Umble lets me place some of my items in her gift shop on consignment."

She nodded. "Actually, I shouldn't be so surprised that you produced such beautiful pieces. I remember some of the sketches you did when I was assistant teacher. They were very *gut*. And Teacher Helen always called on you when she needed a poster or sign made."

Asher mentally winced. Much as he appreciated her compliment, he couldn't help but wonder if she still saw him as that scrawny schoolboy.

"How did you come to learn to punch tin?"

Her question pulled his thoughts back to the present. "I found a book on various crafts on one of our school trips to the library and there was a section on tin punching. I asked *Daed* for a piece of scrap tin to try my hand at it and found it was something I enjoyed."

"So you're self-taught?"

"*Jah*." He looked away. "It's not very difficult. It only requires patience and a steady hand."

"You're just being modest. There's bound to be a lot more to it. Like having an artistic eye."

"Actually, the artistic part comes in creating these patterns." He waved a hand around the room. "Once you have the pattern in hand, just about anyone can follow it."

"What are you working on here?"

"It's going to be an inset for a cabinet door. Noah's ordered eight of these for a customer he's working with."

She waved a hand to the tabletop stand where he kept his various punches and hammers. "It looks like you have quite an assortment of tools."

He nodded. "There are different punches depending on the shape and size of the hole I'm trying to create."

"I had no idea." She gave a tentative smile. "Would it bother you if I watched you work for a little while?"

Did she realize what a distraction she created for him? But he couldn't very well say so. So instead he temporized. "I'm not used to working with an audience."

Her expression fell. "Oh. Of course. Well, I'll just—"

Feeling like an oaf at her obvious embarrassment, he relented. "Of course you're welcome to stay. I just need to focus on what I'm doing so I don't make mistakes."

This time her smile was beaming. "I'll be quiet as a mouse."

And just who'd decided that mice were particularly quiet? Shaking off that whimsical thought, Asher indicated a nearby stool. "Have a seat if you like."

As he turned back to his work he could feel her gaze on him like a feather touch on the back of his neck. How was he supposed to focus?

Martha watched him work, doing her best to be as still and quiet as possible so as not to be a distraction.

He was amazingly precise with the spacing and the size of his punches. There was a soothing sort of rhythm to his work.

Occasionally he'd stop to change the punch he was using and he'd give her a quick explanation about why and what the new tool would do that the previous one wouldn't.

When he finally paused and leaned back, she reluctantly stood. "Thanks for letting me observe. And for explaining what you were doing. That was quite interesting and I'm even more impressed than before. But I need to get back to the house. The *kinner* will be up from their naps soon, if they aren't already."

He nodded. "Of course."

Still she lingered. "Will you be working on these much longer?"

"I'll finish this one up and then stop for today."

"Do you work on these every day?"

"*Jah*, this time of year anyway. Once I start with the spring planting I'll have to just fit it in when I can— mostly on rainy days."

"It sounds as if you regret having to cut back on the time you devote to it."

He shrugged. "I enjoy working with metal and it does bring in a little extra money. But the farm has to come first."

His tone was matter-of-fact, with not even the slightest hint of resentment. "Do you mind if I watch you work again sometime?"

His raised brow indicated his surprise but he merely shrugged. "Not at all. You're welcome to stop by anytime I'm in here."

"I'd like that, for sure and for certain."

With a nod, he turned back to work, effectively ending their discussion.

As she walked back to the house Martha realized there was a lot about Asher she didn't know.

Chapter 15

When the *kinner* woke from their naps, Martha was ready. She settled the boys on the living room floor to play with their building blocks, then she turned to Lottie. "Do you like jigsaw puzzles?"

Lottie's lips twisted as she considered the question. "I never worked with one before."

"You haven't? *Ach*, I think we should remedy that right away, don't you?"

She pulled two boxes out of her large tote bag. One had the picture of a field of flowers. The other had a group of playful kittens. She'd gotten both of them from Greta. They were simple puzzles for younger children, each comprised of about a hundred large sturdy pieces. "You figure out which one you'd like to work on while I go get the table." She'd informed Dorcas of her plans earlier and Dorcas had told her where to find a folding table she could use.

As Martha walked away she noticed Lottie sitting on the sofa and studying the two boxes closely. At least the little girl seemed to be willing to give the activity a try.

When Martha returned, she set up the table near the sofa. "Have you made up your mind?"

Lottie nodded and held out the box with the kittens.

"Excellent choice. Why don't you just dump the pieces on the table and I'll show you how to make it."

While Lottie did as instructed, Martha cast a quick glance at where the boys were playing. Satisfied they were fine for the time being, she turned her attention back to Lottie.

"First we turn all the pieces faceup so we can see the pictures on them." Martha put words to action, turning up the pieces closest to her.

With a nod Lottie went to work. Once all the pieces were faceup, Lottie looked to her, awaiting further instructions.

"Now we try to match up all the pieces so they form the picture on the box." Martha studied the pieces, looking for two that went together. "Here we go. See where this piece has a part of the ball of blue yarn and this other piece has another part of the ball? If we put them together like so," she connected the two pieces, "then we have the whole ball. See?"

Lottie nodded but still looked doubtful. Martha tapped the ball of yarn on the box and then the edge of one of the connected pieces. "See right here, we have a little piece of the gray kitten, like in the picture."

The little girl looked from the box to the puzzle pieces and back again before she nodded. Was she ever going to speak?

"Let's see if we can find another piece that has the gray kitten on it."

Martha spotted it almost immediately, but bided her time until Lottie spied it. The little girl studied the loose pieces until a delighted grin split her face and her hand swooped in to lift a piece triumphantly. "I found one," she announced with a proud grin.

Pleased the girl had responded verbally, Martha gave her a big smile. "You certainly did. Now, why don't you connect it to the yarn pieces."

It took the child a few tries and Martha resisted the urge to do more than just add encouragement, but at last Lottie had them connected properly. They continued working on the puzzle, building on the central pieces, for about fifteen minutes. At one point Martha got up to take care of some roughhousing the triplets were engaged in, and when she returned she saw Lottie had added two additional pieces on her own.

"*Ach*, Lottie, *gut* job!"

The girl flashed her a brilliant smile, then ducked her head, turning her attention back to the image on the puzzle box.

It seemed puzzles were going to be a hit with the little girl.

A moment later, Zeke came over and studied the puzzle. "What's that?"

"It's a jigsaw puzzle."

"Can I play?"

"Of course. I have some right here in my tote bag that are perfect for you and your *brieder*." She pulled out a set of wooden puzzles that had a dozen pieces each. One had farm animals, one had an underwater scene and one had insects.

By the time she'd laid the puzzles out on the sofa Zach and Zeb had joined them.

"I want this one." Zach reached for the one with insects.

Zeb took the underwater one and Zeke took the farm animals.

The boys settled on the floor with their puzzles, and before Martha could show them how to work the puzzles they'd dumped the pieces in a pile, mixing them together.

Martha cast a quick glance Lottie's way. Satisfied the girl was still absorbed in the kitten puzzle, she joined the boys on the floor and went to work helping them sort through the pieces.

"What have we here?"

At the sound of Asher's question, the boys scrambled up to greet him. Lottie looked up but stayed where she was.

Asher's question was answered in a jumble of simultaneous responses from the boys.

"We're playing puzzles."

"Martha's teaching us."

"Do you want to play with us?"

Asher moved forward and grinned down at Martha, who still sat on the floor. "Puzzles, is it? Now, that sounds like fun, for sure and for certain."

"*Jah*, it is." For some reason she didn't feel at all embarrassed to be caught in so undignified a position.

He gave her one last grin then turned to Lottie. "*Gut* job, Lottie. It looks like you have a talent for puzzles."

The girl responded with bright pink cheeks and a smile. "*Danke.*"

Then Asher gave a mock-frown. "But it's a beautiful sunshiny day outside. Inside games like puzzles should be saved for evenings or rainy days, ain't so? Who wants to go outside and play one of those games I brought up from the basement this morning?"

There was an immediate chorus of "Me!" from the boys.

Lottie, on the other hand, seemed less excited by the prospect. But she obediently turned from the puzzle she was working on.

Martha held her hand out to the little girl. "Don't worry. We'll leave everything spread out on the table and we can work on it some more later."

With a nod, Lottie took her hand and together they followed Asher and her little *brieder* from the room.

When they stepped out on the back porch where Asher had placed the equipment earlier, there was an immediate debate as to which game they should try out first.

Finally Asher held up his hand. "I promise we will eventually play all of them. Why don't we take turns picking. Lottie, as the big sister, you can go first."

Lottie's eyes widened and she looked alarmed at having been singled out.

But Martha stepped up to encourage her. "I think that's a wonderful *gut* idea. So Lottie, which one would you like to try first?" She gave the girl an encouraging nod.

With a doubtful glance at each of the adults Lottie took a step forward. When she pointed to the cornhole board Asher got the impression it was a random choice. Did she really not care? Or had she just been in a hurry to get it over with?

But he gave her a big smile. "*Gut* choice. Come on, let's get it set up."

He handed Lottie the mesh bag that held the bean-bags and then had the boys help him carry the board out to a suitable spot in the backyard. Once they had the slanted board set, Asher explained the basic goals of play. "You take one of the beanbags and toss it toward the board. The idea is to get it in the hole or as close to it as you can without letting it slide off the board entirely."

Then he held his hand out to Lottie. "I'll go first to show you how it's done." Lottie handed him two beanbags and after eyeing the hole a moment, he gave one of the bags a toss. He missed the hole by about six inches. His second toss was closer but still a miss.

"Looks like your *onkel* is a little out of practice." Martha's tone held a hint of amusement even though her expression remained impassive.

Asher stroked his chin and looked at the children. "I think we should let Martha give it a try next. What do you think?"

Amid a chorus of "*Jah!*" Martha accepted a couple of beanbags from Lottie.

She gave the first a soft underhanded toss and to Asher's surprise it went straight into the hole.

Asher studied her with a raised brow, and she gave him a satisfied grin. "Did I mention that cornhole toss is a regular activity at Eicher family gatherings?"

He rolled his eyes. "No, I think you forgot to mention that."

She laughed outright at that then turned to the *kinner*. "Who wants to go next?" All three boys had their hands in the air immediately. Even Lottie quietly lifted her hand.

Martha quickly organized them, deciding which order they'd go in by drawing straws. Then Asher stepped up. He had the children toss from much closer to the board. The boys tossed their beanbags willy-nilly, even walking up to the game board and just dropping it in.

At one point he saw Martha slipping away. Following her progress with his gaze he realized she'd spotted *Oma* taking the laundry down from the line. He couldn't hear their discussion but it was obvious Martha offered to help and that *Oma* waved her away. It wasn't done in an irritable or insulted manner, however. *Oma* was smiling warmly and shooing Martha back to their game with the same indulgent attitude she'd show one of her own *kinner*.

To his surprise, after some additional discussion, *Oma* set the half-full laundry basket on the back porch and followed Martha over to where they were playing.

"Your *grossmammi* wants to join us," Martha said in a pleased-with-herself voice. "Let's give her a turn."

Zach retrieved two of the beanbags and handed them to her.

"You can toss from here," Asher said, indicating a point halfway between the distance he and Martha had tossed from and the spot Lottie had stood on.

But *Oma* gave him a don't-baby-me look and stepped back to the spot he had tossed from earlier. Setting her cane aside and pulling her shoulders back, *Oma* tossed her first beanbag and it went wide.

"That's okay, *Grossmammi*, you can do better next time." Lottie's words were accompanied by an encouraging smile.

Asher wasn't sure if he was more surprised by the fact that his grandmother had joined them or that his niece had just spoken up to try to make her feel better.

Oma gave the little girl a soft, appreciative smile then turned back to the game and gave her remaining beanbag another toss. This time it hit the board and slid neatly into the hole.

The *kinner* cheered and the triumphant flush on *Oma*'s face was a joy to see. Asher caught Martha's gaze and mouthed a silent *Danke*.

Then he turned to the others. "It seems Martha, Lottie and *Oma* are *gut* with the cornhole toss. The boys and I will have to do some practicing to keep up."

As Zach took his next turn Asher looked around at the smiling faces surrounding him. Why hadn't he taken the time to play with the *kinner* before? To make sure *Oma* took the time to do so as well?

He had taken on the responsibilities thrust on him when he'd been forced to become man of the house. But he hadn't allowed himself to enjoy the blessings that came with it.

Why?

Chapter 16

Once the kitchen was cleaned after supper, Martha joined Dorcas and Lottie as they headed for the living room. Lottie eagerly resumed her work on the puzzle while Dorcas reached for her knitting, which she kept stored in a basket that was always on the floor beside her rocker.

Asher sat in the recliner reading a periodical of some sort and the boys were on the floor playing with some wooden animals, a plastic tractor and some wooden building blocks of various sizes and shapes.

Martha stooped down beside the boys and admired their efforts to stack and arrange the blocks. At Zeb's invitation she helped them construct pens for the animals.

After a while she left the boys to their play and moved to the sofa where Lottie was still working on the puzzle. The girl was focused entirely on putting the pieces together, seemingly blocking out everything, and everyone, else in the room.

"You're doing a wonderful *gut* job on that puzzle," she said, trying to claim Lottie's attention.

Lottie glanced up with a smile. "*Danke.*" But then she immediately went back to working the puzzle.

Had Asher been right about an activity like this making her more of a loner rather than less of one? Then again, Lottie had fully participated in their cornhole game this afternoon.

Perhaps they needed to strike a balance of some sort.

Later Martha came downstairs after tucking Lottie in and paused at the foot of the stairs. The sound she'd only been peripherally aware of earlier was clearer here. It sounded like a harmonica and it was coming from out on the front porch. Was it Asher playing the instrument? Of course it was. Dorcas had already retired for the night.

The front door stood partially open, though the storm door was closed. She crossed the room then hesitated with her hand on the handle. Would Asher welcome her presence or consider it an intrusion?

Asher came to the end of the tune he'd been playing and didn't immediately start another. He'd been aware of Martha's presence on the other side of the door for several moments now. "The sky is clear enough to see all the stars tonight," he said without turning around.

She stepped out on the porch with an apologetic smile. "I'm sorry. I didn't mean to interrupt you." Then she grimaced. "I seem to be saying that a lot since I arrived here."

He grinned. "For sure and for certain. But you'll get used to our routines soon enough."

"I didn't know you played the harmonica. You do it wonderful *gut*." Then she lifted a hand. "You punch tin, you play the harmonica—you're a man of many talents."

"*Danke*." He quickly changed the subject. "It was a *gut* idea you had, getting the game equipment out for us to play. I can't believe you convinced *Oma* to play with us."

Martha moved to lean against the porch rail. "It only took a little nudging. And tossing beanbags at a cornhole board doesn't require more agility than she can manage."

"It was kind of you to take the time to invite her. I should have thought of it myself."

"Do you mind if I ask what caused the problems with her legs?"

"She doesn't like to talk about it much. All I know is that the doctor diagnosed it as neuropathy and it's causing her balance issues." He rubbed the back of his neck. "She says it doesn't cause her pain, just the mobility issues."

She studied him a moment. "But you don't believe her?"

He waved a hand. "*Oma* wouldn't lie. But she *would* try to brush away any hint of sympathy."

Martha nodded. "She doesn't want to worry you."

Asher grimaced. "It's not working." Then he met her gaze. "And thank you also for taking over the laundry in such a sensitive manner."

She waved off his thanks. "No one likes to feel as if they're no longer needed."

Something about the way she said that made the words seem personal. But before he could dig into that she pushed away from the porch rail. "I'll tell you *gut nacht* now. I'll see you in the morning."

Asher watched her disappear inside then sat down and stared out at the night.

It seemed having Martha around was *gut* not only for the *kinner* but for *Oma* as well.

And maybe for him too?

* * *

Martha sat on the back porch steps the next morning, hugging her knees as she watched the *kinner* at play. Lottie was pushing Zeke on the tree swing and Zach and Zeb were playing tag nearby while they waited for their turn. The sound of their teasing and laughter was wonderful *gut* to hear.

Still, Martha felt that she should be busy doing something. She wasn't used to remaining idle. She'd offered to bring some mending out here to work on while the *kinner* played but Dorcas wouldn't hear of it. "You need to remain focused on the *kinner*," she'd said. "It's frightening how quickly they can get into trouble or mischief if you allow yourself to get distracted."

So here she remained, sitting idly by, watching the little ones at play.

The sunshine and sound of the *kinner* faded to the background as her mind drifted to thoughts of Asher. Was he working on his punched tin artwork right now? And artwork it was, regardless of how he thought of it.

And then there was the harmonica playing she'd heard last night. He was very talented in that regard as

well. Would he play again tonight? She wouldn't mind
stepping out on the porch and—

A sudden scream from Lottie brought her abruptly
to her feet. The little girl had tugged her brother from
the swing and was frantically trying to round up her
brieder.

"Bees!" she screamed. "Run! Run!"

Martha rushed toward them. Why was Lottie so
terrified? Then she remembered how the little ones'
daed had died, an allergic reaction to multiple wasp
stings.

Before Martha could reach the panicked *kinner*
Asher was there and had scooped Lottie up. He held
her tight and stroked her hair, doing his best to
calm her.

Martha turned to the boys, who were crying and
looking for some consolation of their own. She pulled
them all close in a group hug as she leaned back
against the tree and crooned soothing platitudes and
sounds.

At the same time she kept an eye on Asher and
Lottie in case she had to jump in and help him calm
her down.

Asher, on the other hand, was entirely focused
on his niece. "It's okay, Lottie *lamm*. The bees are
gone now."

The aching tenderness in his voice took her by
surprise.

The boys' tears quickly dried but they were still
agitated. She tried distracting them with observations
about a cardinal she spotted in the tree above them.
By the time she was able to turn her attention back to
Asher and Lottie she found them on the tree swing.

Asher had his niece on his lap with his arms around her. The little girl was looking around fearfully.

No doubt she was still afraid the bee might reappear.

Asher gave Lottie a little squeeze, then loosened his hold enough to meet her gaze. "The bee is gone now, Lottie. And even if it wasn't, I give you my word I wouldn't let it hurt you. Do you trust me?"

Lottie gave a tentative nod, but her gaze was locked on his face, her expression intense.

He smiled tenderly. "I know bees and wasps are scary and that it's best to try to avoid them. But remember we talked about what happened to your *daed* and how it was unusual because he was allergic."

Martha was impressed by his patience and empathy and the deft way he spoke to her.

He brushed some stray hairs from her forehead. "I won't let that happen to you or to any of your *brieder*. But even if you or one of your *brieder* ever do get stung and have the same allergic reaction as your *daed*, we have medicine on hand now to make sure you'll still be okay."

Some of the tension visibly eased from the little girl as she relaxed against him.

Asher smiled approvingly. "And it was very brave of you to try to protect your little *brieder*. You're a wonderful *gut* big *shveshtah*."

Martha could have sworn Lottie sat a little straighter.

Asher moved her so he could look her in the eyes. "Are you okay now?"

Lottie nodded.

"*Gut*. Why don't we gather up your *brieder* and go inside and see if *Grossmammi* Dorcas has some of those snickerdoodles ready that she was working on earlier?"

With another nod, Lottie slid from his lap and turned to the boys. "*Onkel* Asher wants to check on the snickerdoodles *Grossmammi* Dorcas was baking."

Their upset forgotten, the boys raced with their *shveshtah* to the house.

Martha walked beside Asher as they followed more slowly. "You were very *gut* with her just now."

He cast a quick glance her way then focused his gaze straight ahead. "You know what happened to Shem and Lydia, don't you?"

She nodded, feeling a deep sense of sympathy not only for the *kinner* but for Asher as well. After all, Shem had been his *bruder*. "An accident involving a swarm of bees and an overturned wagon. It's no wonder the sight of bees frightens Lottie so much."

"It was horrific—and she was there for all of it. As was I."

They'd stopped walking, but Asher no longer seemed aware of his surroundings—he was back in that day a year ago. "After I moved, I still helped out here during the busy times. I was working in the field with Shem the day it happened. We were working hard, trying to finish the planting before a predicted storm hit. Lydia and Lottie rode over in a pony cart to bring us lunch."

His jaw worked a moment and Martha wanted to tell him to stop, she didn't need to hear more. But something told her he needed to speak of this so she held her tongue.

"We stopped work when we spotted them, and as they got closer we could hear Lydia singing. She had such a sweet voice. I can still see the smile on my *bruder*'s face as he watched them—a mix of pride, love, contentment. And then from one breath to the next everything changed."

He bent down and plucked a stem of grass, rolling it between his fingers as he straightened. "It was as if a puff of smoke lifted off the ground. I didn't realize what happened until the pony bucked and bolted. Shem and I raced toward them and he yelled at me to check on Lottie while he went for Lydia—both had been thrown from the cart." He tossed the stem away. "When I got to Lottie she was screaming. She'd been stung a few times and still had some wasps on her. I brushed them off as best I could and then picked her up and ran as fast and as far as I could."

"*Ach*, the poor *lamm*."

Asher nodded. "It was only when I finally stopped and turned around that I saw Shem on the ground, convulsing." His hands clenched at his sides. "For a moment I was paralyzed, not knowing what to do. Lottie was still crying and clinging to me for all she was worth. I couldn't leave her and I couldn't bring her back to that horror."

Ach du lieva, how had he borne having to make such a decision?

She must have made some small sound of dismay or sympathy because he met her gaze with an apologetic twist to his lips. "I'm sorry. I shouldn't—"

Before she could stop herself, Martha reached out and gave his arm a comforting touch. "*Ach*, Asher, please don't apologize. I can't imagine how difficult that must have been for you."

He cut her a quick look of gratitude, then he looked

straight ahead again. "My brain finally engaged and I got the two of us into the work wagon and drove it to where Shem and Lydia lay. Luckily the wasps had pretty much dispersed by then. But it was too late for Shem and Lydia."

Martha had already known how the story would end—Shem had died of an adverse reaction to the wasp stings and Lydia had suffered a broken neck when she was thrown from the cart. But hearing all the terrible details as he'd lived them was so much worse. She gave his arm another sympathetic squeeze then withdrew her hand. Hopefully he hadn't thought her too familiar.

But he merely scrubbed a hand over his jaw as if he hadn't noticed. "Lottie had nightmares for weeks afterward. And she still gets them occasionally. It's why we no longer have a pony cart—she gets hysterical when she gets near one. And it's why her room is next to mine and the boys are still down on the first floor."

Which meant he'd been the one to comfort his niece whenever she had those nightmares, the same way he'd comforted Lottie just now. Had she been too quick to judge his parenting skills?

* * *

After lunch Asher headed for his workshop. He had one more panel to finish before he made his delivery to Noah tomorrow.

As he went to work, he thought about how resilient the *kinner* were. They hadn't seemed to suffer any lasting effects from the morning scare. They'd eaten the snickerdoodles *Oma* had prepared and Martha had even coaxed smiles out of them before they left the table. And once they were done with their treats she announced that she'd brought some paper and crayons with her if anyone wanted to join her in a bit of artwork. Without her saying so he knew she was looking for activities they could do indoors.

By the time he'd headed back outside she had them all eagerly chatting about what they would be drawing.

And when he returned for lunch they all had finished drawings to proudly show him.

Still, Lottie's earlier panicked reaction to seeing a bee was concerning. He had hoped she had finally outgrown such an extreme hysteria. Would she ever?

Thanks be to *Gotte* that he'd been nearby.

And that Martha had been there to calm the boys while he tended to Lottie.

He had to admit, even though it showed a regrettable touch of pride on his part, it had felt *gut* to see the appreciation and admiration in Martha's eyes. And the unexpected feel of her hand on his arm, soft as a butterfly and just as fleeting, had been comforting. And perhaps something more if he were to be honest.

But he refused to go down that road again. It hadn't served him well when he was in school. And there was no reason to believe it would end any differently if he let himself feel that way again.

Rowdy's tail-wagging bark brought him out of his reverie a heartbeat before he realized someone stood in the doorway.

"Do you mind if I join you?" Martha asked.

It was a bit disconcerting to have her appear on the heels of his earlier thoughts. But he nodded. "*Nee,* come on in. But you'll have to excuse me if I keep working. I'm scheduled to deliver these panels to Noah tomorrow."

"Of course." Martha stepped fully inside with a tentative smile. "I'll try not to be a distraction."

In that, he feared, she was destined to fail.

Martha sat on a stool far enough away to avoid being a distraction—she hoped—but close enough to watch what he was doing. She found the deftness of his movements and the intricacy of the results fascinating.

Her gaze shifted from Asher's hands to his face. The unwavering focus of his gaze and sureness of his movements lent him an added air of maturity she didn't usually associate with him.

Trying to distract herself from those thoughts, she turned her gaze to the finished pieces he had displayed around the room. Her gaze landed on a pair of lanterns. One featured a repeating starburst theme. The other had an intricate geometric pattern. She could picture candlelight shining through each of them, enhancing the pattern and shedding a stippled light all about them.

Why were such beautiful pieces still here in his workshop? Surely there was a market for such things? In fact there were quite a few lovely pieces here, and all of them appeared flawless. She was especially taken with a set of three panels that featured images of various trees and hillsides, but when placed side by side created a beautiful, seamless landscape.

Was he holding his best pieces back for some reason?

After a while Asher straightened and drew his

shoulders back and twisted his neck as if trying to work the kinks out of his muscles. Then he swiveled around as if just remembering her presence.

He offered a crooked smile. "You must be getting bored with watching me at work by now."

"Not at all. I've been studying your other pieces here. Those lamps are absolutely beautiful. As are those three panels that form a single picture. Did you do them as a special order for someone?"

He shook his head. "I like to occasionally challenge myself with more intricate pieces."

"But these deserve to find a home. Surely there's a market for such special pieces."

He grimaced. "I'm not sure they're so special." Before she could disagree, he continued. "Charity Umble places some of my work in her store on consignment. But she only has limited shelf space for consignment vendors." He shrugged. "And she says her customers prefer the simple pieces, mainly because they're priced less. So I only place one piece like that at a time."

Charity's shop carried a wide variety of gift items— such as candles, honey, jellies, aprons, cloth dolls and small wooden toys—but they tended to be lower-cost items. She could see where his more ambitious work was not a good fit. "Those pieces shouldn't be placed in Charity's shop. They need to be showcased better than that."

He raised a brow at that. "I certainly don't see me opening my own shop."

She grinned. "Perhaps someday. But for now you should look around for someplace that would be a more fitting place to display your beautiful work."

His brow drew down as he seemed to consider her

words. Then he met her gaze with a half smile. "It's something to think about, for sure and for certain."

Pleased that he wasn't dismissing her idea out of hand, she stood. "I'll be thinking of possible places as well. But for now, I'd better get back to the house. The *kinner* will be up soon." She smiled. "And I'm afraid I've broken my promise not to distract you from your work." With that she made her exit.

* * *

Asher went back to work, but he turned her words over in his thoughts. Martha certainly wasn't shy about offering her opinion on things. It sometimes made her come across as a know-it-all, but he was beginning to see that she was just trying to help. And her suggestion this time certainly had merit. Although when he said he'd think about it he'd meant think about the idea, not about possible venues.

Placing his more intricate pieces in a higher-end shop would certainly give him opportunities to sell more of his pieces, though. Not only that, but if he could place those more intricate pieces someplace where they would actually sell, it would justify him spending the time to craft more of them.

But was there an appropriate shop owner out there who would want them, even on consignment?

He supposed he should thank Martha, and not just for her suggestion.

She was making it easier and easier for him to keep his vow to move past what happened in the past and forgive her.

Chapter 17

After the excitement over the incident with the bees, the afternoon was relatively uneventful.

Later, after Martha put the four *kinner* down for the night, she joined Asher out on the porch. He was in the midst of playing the hymn "City of Lights" on his harmonica and she leaned with her elbows on the porch rail, staring out into the night, while he finished.

When the music quieted she heard the sound of his feet scraping the porch floor as he stood. A moment later he joined her at the porch rail, leaving a couple of feet between them.

"I heard you playing outside with the *kinner* this afternoon." His voice was soft and deep.

She nodded. "I thought it best to get Lottie back outside before she built up the incident with the bees as bigger than it was."

"*Gut* thinking."

"I let Zach select the game and he picked croquet."

She grinned. "I think he just liked the idea of the mallets and balls because when I asked none of them had played before."

"And did you teach them?"

"*Nee.* I just set up four wickets and let them practice trying to hit the balls through. To be honest the boys were more concerned with distance than accuracy."

"And Lottie?"

"She focused on trying to get the ball through the wickets, just as I instructed."

"She's very much a rule follower and a people pleaser."

Martha had always considered those *gut* things. But he didn't sound as if he were giving his niece a compliment. Was that how he viewed her as well? "What's wrong with that?"

Asher saw a flash of something in Martha's expression. Surely that wasn't hurt?

He waved a hand. "Nothing, I suppose. But you opened my eyes to how withdrawn she is. I just want to make certain she knows she doesn't have to be serious all the time, that it's okay to have a bit of fun as well."

"Of course." She quickly changed the subject. "How did you learn to play the harmonica?"

"*Daed* played." He smiled as he remembered some of those moments from his childhood, *Daed* playing the harmonica while the rest of them sang along. "And he taught Shem and me."

"Not Ephron?"

The question brought him up short for a moment. Did she still have feelings for his *bruder* after all this time? "Ephron didn't have an interest in learning."

She nodded as if agreeing that it wouldn't be something that appealed to Ephron. "So why do you wait until you're alone to play?"

He frowned. *Gut* question. He'd never considered that before. "I don't know. I guess it just never occurred to me to do otherwise."

"Well, I think you're a bit guilty of hiding your light under a bushel. It would be *gut* for the *kinner* to have some music in their day."

There was that Martha-knows-best tone again. But, as usual, she was probably right. He made a short bow. "I shall consider that."

"*Gut.* Now I will bid you *gut nacht.*"

He stayed at the porch rail as she went inside.

Why had he failed to spend more time with the *kinner* before Martha came along? Failed to play his harmonica for his *familye* the way his *daed* had? And there was one other thing his *daed* had led the *familye* in during their evenings that he'd let fall by the wayside.

Had he truly been too busy? Or was he subconsciously holding himself back for some reason?

* * *

Wednesday morning passed quietly enough for Martha. The boys were getting *gut* at helping to get their beds and room straightened. Besides keeping her own room clean and neat, Lottie had several morning chores she'd been assigned—helping clean the kitchen, gathering the eggs with Dorcas and other little tasks Dorcas assigned her. Martha also made a point to ask the girl to help her groom Cinders every morning after her other chores were done. Martha decided to speak to Asher when she could catch him alone about whether the boys were old enough to start taking on some jobs in addition to keeping their rooms neat, as well. Maybe after the *kinner* were down for their naps this afternoon.

And she had some ideas of what those jobs might be.

But later as they pushed away from the lunch table, Asher turned to her. "Like I mentioned yesterday, I go to town every Wednesday afternoon to deliver whatever punched tin work I've completed for Noah and Charity."

She felt a stab of disappointment, not only that she wouldn't be able to speak to him as she'd hoped, but also that she wouldn't be able to join him in his workshop this afternoon. Strange how, after only two days, she'd come to look forward to spending time there. It was only because the pierced tin work was so intriguing, of course.

"And while I'm at Noah's workshop," he added, "I thought that I'd go ahead and invite him to bring his *familye* here for lunch on Sunday." He turned to Dorcas. "If you're all right with it, that is."

Oma gave him a broad smile. "I think that's a wonderful *gut* idea. We haven't had guests here for a meal in quite some time. Let me just add a few things to my list before you go."

Dorcas moved to the sideboard where she kept a running list of things for Asher to pick up whenever he was in town. As she added some additional items, Martha added a few of her own—some supplies she could use for craft time with the *kinner*.

Once Martha had her charges down for their naps

she felt restless and at loose ends. Deciding she needed a change of scenery, she stopped by the kitchen to speak to Dorcas on her way out. "Cinders hasn't had much exercise since I've been here. If you don't mind I think I'll take the buggy out for a short ride. I shouldn't be gone long."

Dorcas nodded. "We'll be fine. Enjoy your ride."

Fifteen minutes later Martha was turning the buggy left at the foot of the drive. She chose that direction for no reason other than she saw the flash of a cardinal as it flew across the road. She wanted to be back and have time to tend to Cinders before the *kinner* were up from their naps. But it did feel good to ride down the road with no particular destination in mind.

Martha let her thoughts wander. She was disappointed she hadn't heard from Laban yet. While it was still a little soon for her to receive a response to her letter, she'd hoped he would have sent one on his own as she had. But perhaps he'd been too busy catching up on things after being out of town for three days for his cousin's wedding. After all, from all accounts his leatherwork business was quite prosperous.

Speaking of business, she was still trying to come up with an idea for where Asher could place his more elaborate pieces for sale. She just couldn't bear the idea of those beautiful items not finding a home where they'd be appreciated. If nothing else, perhaps Greta could display some of them in the shop window of her quilt shop.

Up ahead she spotted Marylou Mast checking her mailbox and she realized it was time she headed back. When she reached her drive she pulled Cinders to a halt. "*Gutentag*, Marylou."

The young woman offered her a smile. "*Gutentag*, Martha. What brings you out our way?"

"I'm just out for a short drive. Would you mind if I turned my buggy around in your drive?"

"Not at all."

Martha waved to the seat beside her. "Why don't you climb aboard and we can chat while I take you up to the house." The drive wasn't exceptionally long but Martha would feel funny leaving her to walk back while she rode.

Marylou nodded. "*Danke*." She climbed aboard and settled into her seat. "Would you like to come in for a cup of tea and some pie?"

"That's a kind invitation but I'm afraid I can't today. I want to get back before the *kinner* wake up from their naps."

"That's right, you're taking care of the Lantz *kinner*."

Martha nodded. Then she remembered something. "This used to be Shem and Lydia's place, ain't so?"

Marylou nodded as Martha halted the buggy in front of the house. "We've been renting it since we married." She stepped down. "And we hope to be able to purchase it from Asher soon."

Martha smiled as she looked around. "It appears to be a *gut* place to set down roots."

Marylou smiled in return as she stepped away from the buggy. "We think so too. Please tell Asher and Dorcas hello for me."

"I will." And with that Martha turned the buggy around and headed back to the Lantz place.

* * *

That evening after the kitchen had been cleaned up
from supper, Asher decided to act on the conversation
he'd had with Martha yesterday on the porch. He
pulled out his harmonica and held it up. "How about
a bit of music and singing before we turn in this
evening?" he said.

He was pleased to see Martha's surprised grin.

But Lottie claimed his attention. "*Daed* used to
play the harmonica," she said with a wistful smile.

Asher nodded. "Our *daed*, your *grossdaadi*, taught
both of us how to play when we were little boys."

She tilted her head to one side. "I can't picture you
and *Daed* as little boys."

Asher managed to keep a straight face. "Well, we
were, though I admit it was a long time ago. And someday, when you get a little older, I can teach you as well."

"Me too?" Zach asked.

And predictably Zeb and Zeke echoed the request.

"Of course, any of you who are interested."

Oma brought the topic back around to his initial
question. "I think having a singing tonight is a
wonderful *gut* idea. It reminds me of when Elijah was
still alive."

Lottie wrinkled her nose. "Who's Elijah?"

"Elijah was my *daed*," Asher replied.

"What shall we sing?" Martha asked, chiming in.

"Why don't we start with one of my favorites,"
Oma suggested. "'This World Is Not My Home.'"

Asher nodded and played the first few notes. Then
Oma and Martha began to sing. He was pleasantly
surprised by the sweet purity of Martha's singing
voice. She hit the notes with a sureness and clarity that
was a blessing to hear.

The *kinner* didn't know the words but listened with rapt faces. When that song was over, Martha selected the next song, "I Am Free."

When they had finished that one she met his gaze. "I think not only should you choose next, but you should put the harmonica away and sing with us." She turned to the *kinner*. "Don't you want to hear your *onkel* sing?"

When his niece and nephews nodded vigorous agreement, he good-naturedly set the harmonica down. "All right, but remember," he said, waggling his brows, "you asked for this."

The boys giggled and even Lottie grinned. He pulled Zeke, who stood closest to him, up on his lap and began singing "In the Sweet By and By."

"I know a song the *kinner* can sing with us," Martha said when they finished that one. "'*Schloof, Bobbli, Schloof.*'"

Asher recognized it as a lullaby, one he'd heard Joan sing to them on numerous occasions.

Sure enough, when Martha started them off, all four *kinner* chimed in with varying degrees of accuracy.

Afterward Martha stood. "I see some droopy eyes. I think it's time to put some *schlofkopps* to bed."

"Before we do that," Asher said as he reached for the Bible that rested on the small table beside him, "there's one other practice I'd like to reinstate—that of reading aloud from the Bible before we retire for the night."

He saw pleased surprise in both *Oma*'s and Martha's faces, which drove home to him that he had waited much too long to step fully into his role as man of the house. Yes, he'd shouldered the work, but not the responsibility to be the head of this *familye*. He always read from his Bible before he turned in, as he was sure *Oma* did. But it was never too soon for the *kinner* to hear the word of *Gotte* spoken in the home.

Bowing his head for a moment of silent prayer, asking for the will to do better, he then opened the Bible and read the first chapter of Genesis.

When he'd finished his reading, he again bowed his head, leading the group in a moment of silent prayer and reflection.

As he set the Bible aside, Martha looked around at her charges. "Now, I do believe it's time for some nightclothes and bedtime stories."

There were a few token protests but Martha ignored them and ushered them down the hall.

When he and *Oma* were alone, she met his gaze with a smile. "The *kinner* enjoyed this, I think, everyone together, like a *familye* again. I'm wonderful glad you decided to do this."

"I'd like to take credit, but I got the idea because of something Martha said yesterday."

He couldn't interpret the expression that crossed her face before she looked down and brushed at her skirt. "Just like she suggested getting us all together to play cornhole toss the other day. Martha has been *gut* for our *familye*, ain't so?"

"She has."

"And perhaps for you as well?"

What did she mean by that? "Since I am a part of this *familye*, then I agree."

She gave a satisfied nod and then straightened. "I think I'll retire as well. The young and the old require more rest than you young adults."

Asher frowned as he picked up his harmonica. *Oma* certainly seemed to be in an odd mood tonight.

* * *

While Martha put his niece and nephews to bed, Asher stepped out on the porch. Even though he'd taken Martha's suggestion to share his harmonica music with the *familye*, he still felt the need to step out here and play with just *Gotte* in his audience.

He was on the fourth hymn when he heard the door open. He didn't have to look up to know that Martha had joined him. He allowed the music to taper off at the end of the stanza and then set the instrument down.

"I wasn't sure you'd come out here to play this evening since we had music time earlier."

"I like this quiet time out here just before I go to bed. It helps me sleep."

She blinked and suddenly seemed embarrassed. "I'm so sorry. I didn't mean to intrude."

He raised a brow. "Martha, you need to quit apologizing for imagined trespasses. I wasn't implying you were intruding." He could see, though, why she would have taken his words that way. "How about this. I promise to tell you if at any time you are in my way so you don't have to wonder."

She studied him in the light of the moon and stars as if trying to judge his seriousness. Then she nodded and seemed to relax. "I think the *kinner* enjoyed the music time this evening."

He accepted her change of subject. "As did *Oma*. You were right to say something."

She shifted and waved a hand. "I wasn't fishing for compliments."

He smiled. "I know. But you deserve them anyway." Then it was his turn to change the subject. "I hear you took your buggy out for a short ride this afternoon."

Martha nodded. "I thought Cinders would be glad for a chance to get out and about." She rubbed her upper arms. "We ended up at your *bruder*'s old house before we turned around."

He made a noncommittal sound. He still hadn't decided what he would say to Daniel yet.

"I spoke to Marylou for a moment. Sounds like she and Daniel really like living there."

"It's a *gut* place to live." He rubbed his jaw. "Did you know I lived there for a while?"

"Of course." Her expression softened in sympathy. "It was right before Shem and Lydia passed, wasn't it?"

"*Jah.* I lived there for about five weeks, but it was long enough that I think of that place as my house, not Shem's."

"I'm sorry if my reference offended you. I didn't mean—"

He waved away her apology. "Remember our agreement. And *nee*, that's not why I mentioned it." He thought about stopping right there. But there was a part of him that wanted to tell her how things had happened.

"What a lot of folks don't really know," he said, "is that I actually bought the place from him with money I'd saved from my punched tin business."

"Oh." He watched as she seemed to consider his words. "So the two of you didn't simply swap places."

Asher spread his hands, acknowledging her statement.

"Does that mean there was more to it than Shem and Lydia wanting more room for their growing *familye*?"

"That was part of it. But the other half of the arrangement was me wanting a place of my own."

"I see."

Did she? He thought he heard a touch of judgment in her tone. "I don't know how much of my history you know, but I was sickly for the first several years of my life. It's why I started school a year late."

She nodded.

"I love *Oma*," he continued, "but she's never really let go of that image of me as a little boy who needs an extra bit of coddling."

"So you wanted to get out on your own to show everyone you were capable of making it alone."

He grimaced, but nodded. "Something like that. I'd always planned to find a place of my own as soon as I earned enough money to purchase one. And by the time I turned nineteen I had just about met my goal. But then *Daed* passed and I couldn't just up and leave *Oma* on her own."

She smiled in sympathy. "You're a *gut* person."

"I didn't always feel that way." There'd been times when he'd mentally railed against his circumstances. "A few years later, when Shem and Lydia's *boppli* were growing and they were hoping to add to their number, they began talking about needing more room. It occurred to me I could buy his place and he and his *familye* could move here with *Oma* and it would solve everyone's problems."

She raised a brow. "And did it?"

"For the five weeks, until the accident."

She placed her hand on his sleeve. "And once again it was up to you to step up and take charge."

He shrugged. "Ephron made it clear he didn't plan to move back. Not that I expected him to."

They were both quiet for a moment. Then she spoke up. "Was it what you imagined?"

"What?"

"Those five weeks of living on your own. Was it as good as you imagined it would be?"

He took a moment to think that over. "It was and it wasn't."

"What do you mean?"

"It was exhilarating at first, but after the first few weeks it was also a bit lonely. The trouble is, I didn't have long enough to really figure out how it would settle out." He cut her a sideways glance. "And now Daniel wants to buy it from me."

"And will you sell it?"

Good question. "I haven't decided yet."

She turned sideways so she could look at him fully. "Is it because you're not ready to fully commit to this new *familye* you've formed here?"

He frowned at the implied accusation. "The people here have always been my *familye* and always will be."

She waved a hand impatiently. "You know what I mean. Your responsibility and relationship with them changed significantly when Shem and Lydia died."

He stiffened. "In case you haven't noticed, I *have* committed to them. My whole life is focused on making certain they are well cared for." But was that true? Had she been right to question his motives for not giving Daniel an answer yet? Was there a part of him that considered his time as the *kinner*'s guardian temporary?

Was he truly so selfish?

He straightened. "It's been a long day. I think it's time for me to turn in."

* * *

Martha headed down the hall to her room. She'd obviously insulted him but that hadn't been her intention. She'd only wanted to make him think about why he was putting off making a decision. But she had to remember that wasn't her place. She might live here for the time being, but she wasn't really a member of this *familye*. She'd make a point to apologize in the morning.

She felt honored, though, that he'd opened up to her about his past. She could see where Dorcas's overly protective treatment of him might have been a weight to carry, even more so as he'd grown older. Especially given that he'd had to take on man-of-the-house responsibilities at such a young age.

Then she grimaced as she realized she'd forgotten to speak to him about additional chores for the boys. Something else to speak to him about in the morning.

Sitting on her bed she removed her *kapp* and pulled the pins from her hair. She hoped her thoughtless comments hadn't truly insulted him. He'd been so patient when she'd shown an interest in his punched tin, answering her questions, allowing her to watch him at work. It had felt *gut* to be taken seriously that way. She would hate to think she'd repaid him with intrusiveness, no matter how well intentioned.

Strange to think she'd only taken over as nanny here six days ago and moved in only four days ago. In some ways it seemed like so much longer.

Perhaps that was partly because she and Asher had gone so far in repairing their relationship.

At least she hoped that was the case.

Chapter 18

When Asher entered the kitchen Thursday morning, he was surprised to see Martha already there. He wasn't sure how he felt about facing her after the way they'd left things last night.

But she seemed to have no such reservations. "*Gut matin.*" She smiled as she held out a cup of coffee that she'd apparently poured for him.

He nodded as he crossed the room and accepted the brew. "*Danke. Gut matin.*" He noticed the coffee already had cream in it. She was observant, for sure and for certain.

"Do you have a few minutes to talk about something?"

He should have known she had a reason. With a nod, he moved to the table. "Of course."

Martha took a seat as well. "First I want to apologize for overstepping my place last night." Her voice was pitched so it wouldn't carry to *Oma*.

"Sometimes I don't think how my words will come across."

At least she recognized that about herself. He nodded. "Perhaps there was some small element of truth in what you said. But let's agree to drop it, shall we?"

"Very well. But there is something else I'd like to speak to you about."

He took a sip of his coffee. What now? "I'm listening."

"I was thinking that it's time to think about assigning the boys a few more chores to take care of, but I wanted to speak to you first."

He blinked at the unexpected topic and rubbed his jaw to give himself more time to gather his thoughts. "Aren't you teaching them to take care of their rooms?"

"*Jah.* And they pick up their toys when they're through playing." She lifted a hand. "If you think that's enough for now, then I'll leave it be. I just thought, at three and a half, they're old enough for a few more responsibilities."

She was right, of course. "I'll give some thoughts to what might be appropriate."

"Actually, I have an idea."

Of course she did. "And what might that be?"

"I thought they could take responsibility for feeding Rowdy and perhaps some of the other animals."

"Other animals?"

"Like the chickens to start with. I'll be happy to supervise them." She leaned back in her chair. "Of course, if there are other chores you'd like them to do instead of or in addition to these, I'll be happy to work with them on those as well."

"I'll give it some thought but in the meantime feel free to go ahead and work with them on feeding the animals. Anything else?"

"*Nee.*" She glanced over her shoulder. "And I think I hear them now. So if you'll excuse me..." And with that she stood and headed down the hall.

He carried his cup to the counter and caught *Oma* giving him a sideways look from her position at the stove.

"Martha has taken a keen interest in the *kinner*'s well-being, ain't so?"

"She has. But that's why she's here, after all."

"I can see why you liked her so much when she was your teacher."

For some reason her reminder that Martha was once his teacher irritated him. "Time for me to milk Daisy." And with a nod he left the house.

* * *

Once Martha had the boys up and dressed she talked to them about feeding Rowdy. She helped them scoop up the proper amount and place it in the bowl. Then they filled a large cup of water from the pump and poured it in the water bowl. This first time there was as much food and water on the porch around the bowls as in the bowl itself but she figured with practice they'd get better.

After the breakfast dishes had been cleaned, they followed Dorcas and Lottie out to the chicken yard and while their *shveshtah* and Dorcas were gathering eggs, Martha showed the boys how to scatter the chicken feed.

The boys had great fun tossing the feed about and watching the chickens scratch for it. They had less fun carrying the buckets of water to pour in the low trough, but managed nonetheless.

When they returned to the house, Martha rewarded all of their efforts with a story while she helped Dorcas peel potatoes for their lunch. She was gratified to notice that Dorcas seemed as entertained by her story as the *kinner*.

* * *

After lunch, Asher headed for his workshop. When he'd dropped off the panels with Noah yesterday the woodworker had placed two separate orders. One for eight panels to go in a set of cabinets and another order for four smaller but more elaborate panels that were going to go in a pie safe.

He worked on the pattern for the pie safe pieces, scaling it to fit the size called for on this project. As he worked he wondered if Martha would come here once the *kinner* were napping. Or had she already had her fill of watching him at work? After all, it must be getting a bit repetitious from a watcher's perspective.

When he finally had the pattern drafted to his satisfaction, he slid out a blank sheet of metal and cut it to the right size. But before he could make the first punch Rowdy announced that they had a visitor. He turned and sure enough, Martha stood in the doorway.

"May I come in?" she asked.

He nodded and waved to a stool.

She took a seat and studied his current project. "Are you starting something new?"

"I am. Noah placed some new orders and I'm eager to get started."

"Then don't let me stop you."

He hesitated a moment, wondering what she found so fascinating about watching him work. He pulled a three-ring binder from a shelf beneath his worktable. "This is where I keep copies of the patterns I work with and my ideas for new ones. You're welcome to look through it if you like."

Her face lit up in a delighted smile as she accepted the binder. "*Danke.*"

Satisfied he'd given her something besides himself to look at, he turned back to his work. Twenty minutes later he leaned back and glanced her way. To his surprise the binder was closed in her lap and she was watching him.

"That's a beautiful pattern you're working with today. Is it one you designed yourself?"

He nodded.

She sighed. "I know it's wrong but sometimes it's difficult not to be envious of creative people like you and my *shveshtra.*"

She thought of him as creative? "I'm sure you have gifts of your own. Like the way you are with *kinner.*"

She waved a hand dismissively. "That is a matter of loving them. Most people love *kinner.*"

"It's much more than that. But tell me, why are you so interested in my work here?"

"I just enjoy seeing the way a simple piece of metal is transformed into something so lovely under your hands."

He twisted around to face her more fully. "Would you like to try it for yourself?" he asked impulsively.

She held her hands up, palms out. "I haven't the skill. And I wouldn't even know how to get started."

"Don't worry, I'll talk you through it." He grinned. "You can use a piece of scrap tin I was going to throw out so nothing's wasted if it'll make you feel better."

That seemed to ease her concerns and she gave him a delighted grin. "In that case I think I *would* like to give it a try."

"*Gut.*" He pointed to the notebook. "Look through those and pick out a pattern that appeals to you."

While she did that, he examined the pieces in his scrap pile and finally settled on an irregularly shaped piece that seemed to have a large enough surface for her to work with, then placed it on the table in front of her. He straightened and studied Martha's bent head as she thumbed through the design pattern pages.

Asher smiled. She seemed to be studying them very intently, taking the selection as seriously as she took everything else she attempted.

Finally Martha straightened and pointed to the page currently open. "How about the star in the corner of this pattern? It seems simple enough."

He studied it then nodded. "*Gut* choice. And it'll fit wonderful *gut* on this piece of tin." He grabbed a pair of scissors and cut out the appropriate section of the pattern sheet. He then smoothed the paper design over the sheet of tin and taped it carefully in place. "Now you're all set to get started."

"I'm afraid I'll need a little more direction than that," she said drily.

He grinned. "So now I'm the teacher and you're the scholar."

She lifted her chin at a haughty angle. "I'm not too proud to take the role of student when needed."

The glimmer in her eyes let him know she wasn't really offended so he merely smiled. "Okay. First your tools." He pulled one of the punches from his rack along with a hammer and handed both to her. "These should work for your first lesson. Take the punch in your left hand and the hammer in your right." As she complied he picked up the punch and hammer he'd been working with earlier. "Figure out which spot on the pattern you want to start with and position your punch on top of it, like so."

She mimicked his action then looked to him for confirmation.

The trust in Martha's expression, even over so simple a matter, made Asher feel almost like an authority. "Hold the punch firmly so it doesn't slip and keep it as upright as possible."

Martha followed his directions as closely as possible as his patient, concise instruction put her at ease. She shifted slightly to take a firmer hold of the tools, then gave him an I'm-ready look.

"Next you take the hammer and give it a light tap, just enough to make an impression in the metal."

She watched as he performed the action to demonstrate. It seemed straightforward enough. Taking a deep breath, she gave it a try. Then she leaned back with a grin. "How was that?"

"*Gut.*" But his smile was definitely that of a teacher to a scholar who hadn't gotten it quite right yet. "In the future, though, you don't want to move the punch until you make the second strike."

She felt her cheeks warm as she studied the tools in her hands. She knew better from watching him.

"It's okay," he assured her. To his credit he hid any amusement he might be feeling. "Just place the punch back in the same spot—you should be able to feel the indentation. Then hit it with the hammer again, this time firmly enough to pierce the metal." Again he put action to words to demonstrate.

So how did one gauge exactly how much force was required to pierce the metal? It took experience, she supposed, experience one could only get from doing. Again she took a deep breath and then hit the punch with her hammer, giving it a satisfying whack. She could tell it went through, but had she done it properly? This time when she turned to him she felt a bit more tentative. "How was that?"

"Perfect. But you can take your punch off the metal now."

Sheepishly she relaxed her grip and lifted the punch.

Asher nodded approvingly. "That's all there is to it. You move to the next punch spot on the pattern and repeat the process. The key is to precisely hit the spots indicated on the pattern and to try to hit the punch with the same force to create uniform-sized holes."

She nodded, that made sense.

Then he smiled. "Remember, this is just a practice piece, intended to get you comfortable with using the tools and to help you develop the proper rhythm. You're not doing it for anyone but yourself."

"I'll try to keep that in mind." As she went to work, she was acutely aware of Asher watching her, no doubt to see if she ran into any problems. She understood now why he'd hesitated when she first asked to watch him at work.

But after a few minutes she began to fall into a rhythm of sorts and his presence no longer bothered her. At one point she became aware that he had returned to work on his own piece. Before long she relaxed and forgot everything but the piece she was working on.

She was about a third of the way through the pattern when Rowdy rushed into the work shed, startling her mid-swing. The hammer missed the punch and caught her on the index finger.

Unable to swallow her yelp of pain, Martha dropped the tools and cradled her left hand with her right.

Asher was immediately at her side, his expression one of deep concern. "What happened? Are you hurt?"

She shook her head, trying to force her eyes to stop watering. Crying would only serve to make him feel worse. "I'm sure it's nothing." She pasted what she hoped was a convincing smile on her face. "I shouldn't have let the hammer slip. The finger's throbbing a bit but it'll be okay in just a minute."

"Don't be silly, I can see the pain in your face." He waved his hand in a give-it-here gesture. "Let me have a look."

She tentatively placed her hand in his.

He lightly cradled her hand, studying it with bent-head focus.

His touch was surprisingly gentle as he turned her hand to examine it. His own hands were callused and she saw the scar on his right thumb, the slight crook to his pinkie. These were the hands of a man, not a boy. A man, moreover, who didn't shy away from a hard day's work. But they were also the hands of an artist, a producer of beautiful creations. He was both a creator and a laborer, someone any woman would be lucky to have as her *mann*.

Then she drew herself up short. Her thoughts were headed in a very inappropriate direction—not only was he her employer but he was four years younger than her. Besides, she had agreed to correspond with Laban with an eye toward an eventual courtship. She had no business thinking of another man in that way.

She must have made an inadvertent movement, because Asher looked up quickly. "I'm sorry. Did I hurt you?"

She blinked, trying to collect her flustered thoughts. Then realizing he was waiting for an answer, she quickly shook her head. "*Nee.*"

Hopefully he'd see her warming cheeks and rattled tone as nothing more than a result of her accident.

He studied her face a heartbeat longer, then nodded. "It looks like your index finger took the brunt of it." He met her gaze. "Does any other part of your hand hurt?"

"*Nee.*" The deep concern in his expression was both flattering and concerning. And still he didn't release her hand.

"It doesn't appear the skin is broken anywhere but it's a deep red and there's a welt forming."

"It's not as bad as it looks. I was working on the first, gentle tap, not the firmer one." She mentally winced—babbling was so unlike her.

Apparently he noticed nothing amiss as he nodded toward the workbench. "You've done enough work on that piece for today. I'll walk you back to the house so I can open the door for you."

"Nonsense." She slid her hand from his in a gesture that was more abrupt than she'd intended. "I can open a door one-handed." Realizing she'd sounded less than grateful, she allowed her expression to soften even as she found herself missing the warm protectiveness of his touch. "*Danke* for your concern, but I've kept you from your work long enough." Before he could protest, she added, "I remember when you were in school how you liked to focus on one thing until you finished it—from a teacher's perspective I found it commendable."

With a nod he stepped back and she noted there was a subtle change in his demeanor, though she couldn't quite put her finger on how. But at least he was no longer studying her with the same intensity.

"Of course. I hope your finger feels better soon. Let *Oma* know what happened and she'll help with the *kinner*." And he moved to the workbench, turning his back to her.

Martha stood there a moment longer, then turned and made her exit. As she slowly walked to the house, she cradled her left hand, still imagining the feel of his hand holding hers.

* * *

Asher found his place in the design he'd been working on and methodically continued hammering in the punches. But it took him a while to recapture the soothing rhythm of his actions.

For a while, as he was teaching her the mechanics

of his craft and again when he'd tended to her hand, they'd interacted as equals and had seemed to share a connection.

But then she'd pulled away, both physically and mentally. Her reference to his school days had seemed designed specifically to put distance between them.

Had he imagined the earlier closeness, reading more into their interaction than had been there? And how in the world had he let himself fall back into that same old role of schoolboy with a crush on her?

Just because he wanted to work on mending their relationship didn't mean he should take it beyond friendship.

Especially if she had no interest in doing so.

Chapter 19

By the time Martha returned to the house Lottie had roused from her nap and was in the living room quietly working once more on the puzzle.

Dorcas, who sat nearby doing some mending, frowned when she saw Martha. "What happened?" she asked as she put aside her work.

Martha waved her good hand. "Just a little accident. I'm fine." But Dorcas was having none of that and insisted on fussing over her, leading her back to the kitchen and examining the bright red injury, tsking and holding it up to the light coming in through the door and instructing Martha to take it easy.

Martha was almost relieved when she heard the triplets coming down the hall from their rooms.

With a last admonition for Martha to take it easy, Dorcas let her go.

Martha settled the trio on the living room floor with a long sheet of brown butcher paper and a large box of crayons and asked them to draw and color their favorite animal and favorite bug.

The boys immediately took up the challenge and before long they were on the floor, bellies down, drawing enthusiastically even if not accurately.

"I finished."

Martha turned to Lottie, who was standing next to the card table, beaming at the completed puzzle.

"*Gut* job." She gave the little girl a hug. "What do you say we leave it here until you have a chance to show it to *Grossmammi* Dorcas and your *onkel* and then we can put it away. And after supper you can start work on the other puzzle I brought. Would you like that?"

The little girl nodded vigorously.

"Now, why don't you join your *brieder* and color a picture for us."

With another nod, Lottie joined the boys and found a blank spot where she could work.

Martha sat on a nearby chair, letting her mind wander as she watched them. The throbbing of her finger had eased quite a bit, but the unsettling feelings that had been stirred by the touch of Asher's hand holding hers were still leaving her on edge.

Which was ridiculous, of course. Not only had it signified nothing more than his concern for her injury, but she had no feelings for him other than those of friendship.

Anything else she'd felt or sensed could certainly be laid down to her elation over the bit of success with the tin punching and the sharp pain of the hammer strike.

She should focus her thoughts on Laban. Would his

tooled leatherwork be similar to Asher's pierced tin work? Would he let her observe him at work the way Asher did? Was it something they could connect over?

Martha glanced up as she realized that the background noise she'd been vaguely aware of was the sound of Asher and Dorcas talking in the kitchen.

A moment later Asher stepped in the living room and held out an envelope. "A letter came for you."

Was it from Joan or from Laban? They were the only two who would write to her at this address.

"*Danke.*" A quick glance at the address indicated it was from Laban and she felt a little rush of emotion, though she wasn't sure just how to define it.

Then she glanced back up at Asher with an apologetic smile. "I hope you don't mind. Since I was going to be here for a few weeks I gave this address to James Slabaugh's cousin Laban." She brushed at her skirt. "We have recently become pen pals." She looked back up in time to see something flash in his expression but it was gone so quickly she wasn't sure what.

He turned to study the *kinner*. "*Nee*, that's not a problem. You must consider this your home while you're staying with us." Then he waved a hand. "If you'd like to go ahead and read your letter, I'm sure the *kinner* will be fine for a little while. Especially since *Oma* and I will be nearby."

Martha hesitated a moment. After all, there was really no reason she couldn't sit right here on the sofa and read her letter. Still, a bit of privacy would be nice.

Decision made, she gave him a smile, nodded, then turned and went down the hall with the letter in hand.

Once in her room, Martha sat on the bed and eagerly tore open the envelope. Laban must have penned this response almost as soon as he received her letter. Surely that was a *gut* sign.

She settled down and unfolded the letter.

Martha,

It was gut *to hear from you so soon after our meeting. And* jah, *the trip home was uneventful and I am well recovered from both the festivities and the travel.*

I am wonderful glad to hear how much you enjoy spending time with kinner. *That bodes well for the family you will have in the future, whether it be with me or some other* mann. *And please don't apologize to me for your lack of skills in areas other than homemaking. The woman I marry will have no need to hold an outside job. In fact, I firmly believe the best, most important job for a married woman is to raise her* kinner *and help to maintain a comfortable, well-run household. Which means there is also no need for you to worry about trying to assist me with my leatherwork business. I have apprentices to help with that. It is enough to ask that my future* fraa *provide me with a welcoming and comfortable place to come home to after a day at work.*

As for Fredericksburg, it is indeed a gut *place to live and to raise* kinner. *My* familye *has lived here for several generations and I can't imagine living anywhere else. It is a little bigger than*

Hope's Haven and while I know bigger is not necessarily better, there are a few more shops and some of them are larger and offer more variety than what you have there. The church district I belong to has about thirty-two families, most of them are farmers and workers at the local buggy factory.

The last few days have been eventful for me as well. A merchant in Utah was visiting the area and saw some of my leather goods and wants to carry our product in his stores. It means we will need to expand production and I can hire additional workers. The next few months will be a busy time for me but it will definitely be worth it. And now, more than ever, I need a helpmeet by my side. Perhaps you and I can reach an understanding, one way or the other, in the next couple of weeks.

Sincerely
Laban Slabaugh

Martha slowly refolded the letter and stood, moving to the window. She was disappointed that Laban was so unreceptive to the idea of her showing an interest in his business. But perhaps he was right, perhaps once she had *kinner* of her own to tend to along with a house and garden and livestock, she wouldn't have time for anything else.

Still, Laban's attitude seemed very different from that of Asher, who'd not only been open to her interest in his work but patiently taught her how to actually perform the task herself. Was that because he was younger than Laban? Or maybe because he didn't see her as a potential *fraa*?

Or was it more that he saw a woman's role differently than Laban?

She tried to push aside her feelings of being dismissed, and focused on Laban's other news. His sketchy information about the town of Fredericksburg had been disappointing. It lacked any sort of color or detail but she couldn't blame him—not everyone knew how to be descriptive. She'd just have to ask more specific questions. Or better yet, look to Joan for those sorts of details.

The expansion of his business spoke well of his skills and his business sense. He would indeed be a *gut* provider as James had assured her. And he seemed to value her domestic skills. But his wanting to reach a decision on the matter of their courtship in the next couple of weeks was the big news here.

She'd wanted to move quickly, but perhaps not quite this fast. They'd barely exchanged one letter—hardly enough to get to know each other. Did Laban not think that was important? Of course, there was time for them to exchange at least a few more letters over the next couple of weeks. Perhaps that would be enough.

Which meant she had to give him more information about herself in the next letter she wrote to him and find a way to coax more information from him.

Why was his letter making her feel so unsettled? After all, this was all leading to a *mann* and a *familye* of her own, just what she wanted. And she'd known from the outset this wouldn't be a love match.

She still felt a little torn at the thought of leaving Hope's Haven and all her *familye* behind. On the other hand, Fredericksburg wasn't across the county. It was only forty minutes away if she hired an *Englisch* car to transport her.

Joan had accused her of being averse to change. That's likely all this was.

She'd settle down and write a response to Laban when she retired to her room tonight. Surely by then she would have pulled her thoughts together.

* * *

Asher studied the *kinner*'s artwork, giving them praise and encouragement at frequent intervals.

But his thoughts were on Martha and the letter she'd received. She had eagerly taken him up on his suggestion that she read the contents right away, and in private.

So she had a pen pal. A *gentleman* pen pal. Asher wasn't sure why that surprised him so much. In fact, now that he thought about it, it was more surprising that a woman like Martha Eicher had remained single for so long.

Laban Slabaugh—Asher had a vague memory of a person who'd been introduced as James's cousin, but he couldn't remember many details. He wished now that he'd paid closer attention.

Not that it was really any of his business.

Still, Martha was a member of his household for the time being, which meant in the absence of her *daed* he was technically responsible for her.

That was all this feeling was, a perfectly normal and justified head-of-household responsibility.

Chapter 20

Over the next few days they fell into a routine of sorts.

The mornings were dedicated mostly to chores. As the *kinner* mastered the simple tasks they'd been assigned, Martha worked with them to add a few others, but always working with them until they got the hang of how it should be done.

After lunch, while his niece and nephews napped, she continued to join Asher in his workshop and even continued to practice the techniques he had taught her, though there were no repeats of the accident with the hammer.

Once the *kinner* woke from their naps she would take them outside to play and sometimes Asher and Dorcas would join them, sometimes not.

But the evenings had become Martha's favorite time of day. After the kitchen was cleaned up from supper, the *familye* would gather in the living room and they would either sing, play board games or tell stories. But they always finished the group time with Asher reading from the Bible. And after Martha put her charges down for the night she'd join Asher on the front porch. Sometimes she'd sit quietly on the porch swing while he played his harmonica. Other times they'd discuss the events of the day or the plans for the next day.

Other than Joan, she couldn't remember ever feeling this comfortable with someone who wasn't *familye*.

* * *

On Saturday morning, once the chores were done, Martha and Dorcas went to work planning a menu for the upcoming visit of Noah and his *familye* for Sunday lunch. Once they had agreed on the dishes, Martha decided she wouldn't let Dorcas run her off to take care of everything on her own.

"I'll start peeling the potatoes," she said as if it were already decided.

Dorcas cut her a sideways glance. "What of the *kinner*?"

"I've given the boys some new building blocks to play with and Lottie has a new puzzle to work. They'll be fine. Besides, they're just in the living room so it'll be easy to check on them every once in a while."

To Martha's surprise, Dorcas merely nodded and turned to the cabinet where she kept her large bowls and casserole dishes. The two women worked in companionable silence for a while, only speaking when they needed to consult each other on some aspect of the meal preparation. "Just so you know," Martha said with a grin at one point, "Greta will most likely bring a fruit salad. It's her favorite dish to bring to any gathering."

Dorcas smiled. "That will go well with our menu. And we all have that one dish that we're most comfortable fixing for others, ain't so? For me it's my cherry pie."

Martha nodded. "For me it's candied sweet potatoes. It's my *daed*'s favorite."

Dorcas gave her a sideways look. "We could have put it on tomorrow's menu if you'd said something."

Martha shook her head. "I think the menu is already strong enough." In fact, there would be much more than was needed. But she was certain Dorcas expected to send some of the leftovers home with her guests.

Then Dorcas changed the subject. "Asher told me why you suggested your *shveshtah* and her *familye* come tomorrow. You're doing it for Lottie."

Martha carried the peeled and cubed potatoes to the counter. "*Jah.* But I did it for myself too. It'll be *gut* to see them all again."

Dorcas nodded. "*Familye* is important. It is sad when we lose touch with them."

Dorcas had turned back to the dish she was working on, but Martha studied the wistful expression on her face. "Have you heard from Ephron recently?"

"I received a birthday card from him last month. It included a nice picture of him and his *familye*." Her cheerfulness seemed a bit forced. "His two *dechder* have grown so much since I saw them last—I hardly recognized them."

"So Ephron didn't come visit for Christmas?"

She shook her head. "They'd planned to, but Delores, his wife, fell sick and they had to cancel."

"Perhaps they can reschedule for Easter or Mother's Day."

"Perhaps."

Did Ephron realize how much his *grossmammi* longed to be a part of his and his *familye*'s life? Would it be out of place for her to write him a letter with a nudge of sorts? Of course she'd have to get hold of his address first.

Then Dorcas pulled her attention back to the here and now. "Would you like to see the card and photo? I keep them right here."

Before Martha could respond Dorcas moved to the sideboard. Opening the top drawer, she pulled out a large, well-worn envelope.

Martha accepted it and slid the card out. It was beautifully elaborate with ribbons and glitter. And when she opened it she found the photograph Dorcas had mentioned.

She studied Ephron's image. She'd seen him at his *daed*'s funeral five years ago and again at Shem and Lydia's funeral last year. From his hair to his clothing to his watch and ring, he now had a distinct *Englisch* look about him. It was hard to see the boy she'd taken that trip with twelve years ago in the man pictured here. After a few moments she glanced at the others in the picture. His wife was pretty and his two little girls looked sweet in their frilly dresses.

"His older *dochder* is Priscilla and his younger is Teresa."

Martha handed the card and photo back to Dorcas. "Ephron seems to have a lovely *familye*."

Dorcas nodded. "And he seems to dote on his *dechder*. I always believed he'd be a *gut daed*." That wistful note was back in her voice. Then she cut a sideways glance Martha's way. "You know, there was a time when I thought Ephron might seek to court you."

There was a time Martha had thought that as well. "Ephron and I were only ever *gut* friends. We wanted very different things for our lives."

"Someday you'll need to tell me what happened that summer when the two of you set off for your big adventure." Then she turned and put the card away. "But enough of that for now. Today we have a lot of cooking to do."

Martha held her peace as she turned to peel some carrots. Was that trip down memory lane one she wanted to take with Dorcas? She'd never truly spoken of it with anyone—too many other things happened at that time, the death of her mother being the most significant, that had overshadowed her problem with Ephron.

Nee, there was no point bringing up old hurts. It wouldn't serve any purpose and would only bring hurt to Dorcas.

* * *

Later that evening, Asher sat on the porch, playing his harmonica and waiting for Martha to appear. It was strange how much their nightly chats had begun to feel a comfortable part of his routine. Just like her appearance in his workshop every afternoon while the *kinner* napped. Not just a part of his routine, but something he looked forward to.

And every day he had the same thought—would

she come or had she grown tired of spending time with her former student?

A moment later the door opened, answering his question for tonight at least.

While he finished playing the final verse she moved to the porch swing. When he was done he set the harmonica aside and moved to lean against the porch rail nearby. "From the amount of cooking you and *Oma* did today it appears you're expecting a dozen adults with hearty appetites to descend on us rather than just one *familye*."

She smiled. "Your *grossmammi* shares my philosophy that it's better to have too much food than not enough when company comes calling."

"That sounds like her."

Martha sobered and her gaze didn't quite meet his. "Your *grossmammi* and I did a great deal of talking while we cooked, mostly of recipes and adjustments to the menu. But we discussed more personal things as well."

"Oh?" Something in her tone and demeanor had him bracing himself for her next words.

"One of the things we talked about was Ephron."

Well, that was certainly unexpected. And quite a loaded subject.

Thankfully, she didn't give him time to respond before she continued. "It made me realize it had been quite some time since I spoke to him." She waved a hand. "I saw him at the funeral of course, but I didn't have a chance to speak to him."

Did she *still* have feelings for Ephron after all this time? "If you're looking for another opportunity I'm afraid I can't say with any certainty when he'll be back." He mentally winced as he heard the sharpness in his tone.

But Martha didn't seem to notice. "Actually I was thinking about writing him a letter." She finally met his gaze. "If I did, I'd need to have his mailing address. I'd ask your *grossmammi*, but I think she might not understand."

He wasn't sure he understood either. But he nodded. "I'll get it for you in the morning."

"*Danke*." Then she changed the subject. "Your *grossmammi* insisted on including what she called a Reuben casserole because it's your favorite dish."

"It's wonderful tasty, for sure and for certain."

"I managed to sneak a taste and I have to admit I agree with you. I'll have to add that recipe to my collection."

They chatted for another fifteen minutes or so over inconsequential things before Martha decided to retire for the evening.

As Asher climbed the stairs to his own room he couldn't help but wonder about Martha's request for Ephron's mailing address. She knew his *bruder* was married so it couldn't be that she had any kind of romantic motive. Especially given that she apparently had an interest in this Laban fellow.

Was that it? Was there some kind of unfinished business between her and Ephron she wanted to settle before she moved forward with this new relationship?

Whatever the case, it really wasn't any of his business.

But that was becoming more and more difficult to remember.

Chapter 21

Sunday morning Asher took over keeping up with the *kinner* while Martha helped *Oma* get things ready for their company, including some last-minute baking.

By the time Noah and his *familye* arrived everything was ready. The meal itself was a success. The addition of five extra people—Greta, Noah and their three *kinner*—made for a pleasant and lively gathering. Martha teased her *shveshtah* about the predictability of her bringing fruit salad, and how fortunate that it was so tasty.

Greta, in turn, teased Martha for how painstakingly perfect the table layout was, down to the napkins being folded to exact specifications, guessing correctly that Martha had handled that task.

Noah and his family had arrived about thirty minutes earlier and it had taken several minutes before the children had warmed up to each other. But by the time they'd gathered around the table everyone seemed to have relaxed.

Asher sat at the head of the table but as the meal progressed he felt something of a fraud. He might be the man of the house but not only was he the youngest adult here, unlike Noah he was also still clean-shaven, visible proof that he'd never been married.

He shook off those less-than-happy thoughts and turned his attention back to enjoying his guests.

Noah turned to him. "While I'm here I'd like to see your workshop if that's okay." He gave Asher a grin. "After all, you've already seen where I work, ain't so?"

"*Jah*, we can walk out there later." Asher felt pleased Noah seemed interested in his work rather than just the end product.

"That's enough work talk," Greta said as she took a napkin to wipe the face of her fifteen-month-old son Peter. "This is Sunday and we are guests here." Then she turned to ask Lottie whether she had enjoyed the puzzles Martha had borrowed.

The conversation flowed easily from there and all too soon the meal was over.

The three women shooed him and Noah, along with the *kinner*, out of the house while they cleaned the kitchen.

Asher had taken out the horseshoe game, cornhole board, and soccer ball earlier, and the little ones were all too happy to make use of them.

David and Anna, Noah's two oldest, were playing horseshoes with Lottie. The triplets were running around with a soccer ball, though whatever game they were playing looked nothing like soccer. Peter was toddling around, chasing the boys and giggling in that way toddlers his age had that was so infectious.

Asher and Noah stood by the front porch, watching them play.

"Greta and I were right glad to get your invitation to join you for lunch today." Noah kept a close eye on his youngest as he spoke. "Before Shem and Lydia moved in here we visited many times at their other house."

Asher tried not to show his surprise. "I'm sorry we didn't keep up the practice between the families."

Noah shook his head dismissively. "No need for apologies. You were busy trying to knit a new family together for Shem and Lydia's *kinner*." He waved a hand toward the youngsters at play. "And it seems to me you've done a *gut* job of it, for sure and for certain."

"*Danke*." Asher quickly changed the subject. "And were the *kinner* friends back then?"

Noah stroked his beard thoughtfully. "They were younger then, but *jah*, they got along fine." He tilted his head slightly. "Why?"

"Martha is worried Lottie is too shy and keeps to herself too much."

"So Greta told me." He nodded toward the *kinner* again. "But she seems to be doing fine right now."

Asher grinned. "That's Martha's doing. This morning before you arrived she told Lottie that it was her job to help make your *kinner* feel at home here."

Noah chuckled. "Greta's *shveshtah* is almost as crafty as she is." He turned serious. "So Martha is doing well with the *kinner*."

"For sure and for certain. Her previous experience as an assistant teacher really comes through here. And the *kinner* have already grown to love her."

"And perhaps not only the *kinner*."

Asher cut him a startled glance. "I don't—"

"No point trying to deny it. I've seen the way you look at her when you think no one's watching."

Asher rubbed the back of his neck, not sure what to say. "It's just a foolish crush," he finally mumbled.

"Why foolish?"

"Well, for one thing, I'm four years younger than Martha." As she wasn't inclined to let him forget.

"That's not an insurmountable obstacle."

Why wouldn't Noah drop the subject? "But she still sees me as Ephron's little *bruder*, as one of her scholars, not as a man in my own right."

"And have you done anything to make her see you differently?"

That took Asher aback for a moment. Had he?

Instead of answering he revealed what he considered a clincher. "Besides, she's corresponding with James Slabaugh's cousin Laban."

Noah raised a brow. "A correspondence is not an engagement."

"*Nee*, but it's a first step."

Noah seemed prepared to keep pressing, but Peter took a tumble just then and started crying. Noah immediately strode forward and scooped up the little boy, soothing his tears and then making him laugh.

Asher had always seen the astute-businessman side of Noah. This was the first time he had an up-close look at the doting-*daed* side of him.

Asher looked at his niece and nephews and felt that same fierce protectiveness. Was that what it meant to be a *daed*?

* * *

Martha accepted a freshly washed platter from Greta and went to work drying it. She and her *shveshtah* were taking care of the dishes while Dorcas cleaned the table and stove.

Greta pulled a bowl from the sudsy water. "Hannah and I were talking yesterday about the fact that *Daed*'s fifty-fifth birthday is next Saturday and we want to make sure we celebrate properly."

Martha paused a heartbeat. How could she have forgotten *Daed*'s birthday was coming up? This had never happened before—she was always the one to remind her *shveshtra*. But Greta was still talking.

"Anyway, I know you're the one who usually plans and organizes these things but since you're busy here, Hannah and I decided we'd step up and take care of it for once. Hannah is going to speak to Leah about all of us getting together at their house for lunch. We'll all prepare a portion of the meal. Hannah's bringing the cake and a couple of pies, of course, and I thought I'd bring the pot roast that *Daed* likes so much." Her smile was almost apologetic. "I know it's your specialty but I've had more practice cooking since I've gotten married so I think I can do okay."

Had they left anything for her to do?

"Leah will likely want to cook something and of course you can bring one or two sides if you like. Whatever you feel you have time for will be fine." Greta cut a quick glance Dorcas's way. "Assuming you can use the kitchen here and you can even get away to come to lunch."

Before Martha could respond, Dorcas spoke up.

"Of course she can use my kitchen—it's hers also for as long as she's here. And Asher and I can take care of the *kinner* long enough for her to spend Isaac's birthday with him."

"*Gut!*" Greta turned to Martha with a triumphant smile. "It's settled then. You just cook some kind of side dish and Hannah and I will take care of everything else. We're even planning to get our *kinner* together to have them practice a little program to put on for *Daed*." She rolled her eyes. "Sometimes I think he enjoys his *kins-kinnah* more than his own *kinner*."

Dorcas gave a loud harrumph. "That's one of the joys of getting old—enjoying our *kins-kinnah*."

Martha tried to keep a smile on her face while the talk was going on around her. She also tried telling herself that just because her *shveshtra* had done the planning without her, and Greta was cooking the meal's main dish and she herself had been relegated to bringing "some kind of side," it didn't mean they were moving on without her. But somehow she didn't quite convince herself. Even the fact that Greta and Hannah were getting their little ones together to plan a program for *Daed* only underscored the fact that she herself was unmarried and childless.

That might change by next year, but if she married Laban it also meant she wouldn't be close by to help plan these sorts of events.

This just underscored the fact that she needed to get married so she could establish a family of her own— it was the best way to ensure she remained relevant to someone.

It had been three days since she'd received Laban's letter and she still hadn't written a response, even though last night she'd found the time to pen a short letter to Ephron. What was holding her back? Whatever the case, it was past time she sat down and wrote that letter.

A few moments later Dorcas excused herself, saying she'd be right back. Greta turned to Martha with an eagerness that seemed to indicate she'd been waiting for just such an opportunity. "I hear you're corresponding with Laban Slabaugh."

It was almost as if she'd read Martha's thoughts.

Martha cut her younger *shveshtah* a raised-brow glance. "Word sure does get around, doesn't it?" she asked drily.

Greta flipped a hand dismissively. "You know there are few secrets in Hope's Haven." Then she shook her finger. "But don't change the subject. Tell me about this correspondence."

"We've only exchanged one letter each so we're still getting to know each other." Yes, it was definitely time to write that letter. Tonight for sure.

Greta's gaze was speculative. "But you do like him, ain't so? Otherwise you wouldn't have agreed to this correspondence."

"Of course."

"*Gut.* You need a little romance in your life."

What she had with Laban was hardly a romance. But she felt strangely reluctant to admit as much to her *shveshtah*.

Greta handed her the final dish then hung the washrag over the sink. "Speaking of matches, it occurred to me today that Asher is in serious need of a *fraa*."

The unexpectedness of the comment almost caused Martha to drop the plate. "What?"

Greta dried her hands. "Think about it. He's a twenty-four-year-old man who's responsible for the care of four preschool *kinner*, his *grossmammi* and a farm. I can hardly imagine anyone more in need of a helpmeet, can you?"

Martha turned away as she put the stack of now-dry plates in the cabinet. "I would think such a personal decision would be best left to Asher himself."

Greta waved that suggestion aside as if it were inconsequential. "If asked he would probably say he doesn't have time for courting." She lifted her chin. "That's where someone like me comes in."

"I thought you gave up that type of thing when you married Noah." Before she married, Greta had fancied herself something of a matchmaker. And her belief had been bolstered by the fact that several of her efforts in that department had resulted in marriages. That was, in fact, how she'd begun her relationship with Noah— she'd agreed to help him find a *fraa*.

"*Ach*, I did. But I'd be willing to give it one more attempt for such a worthy cause."

"I'm not sure Asher would thank you for your sacrifice."

"Oh, it wouldn't be a sacrifice. In fact, I think Noah's *shveshtah* Maisie would be an excellent match for Asher."

Maisie? Martha couldn't see her and Asher together at all. "I thought she and Hiram Detweiler were courting."

Greta shrugged. "The two are *gut* friends but I'm not sure they are really courting."

"Still, I don't think she's right for Asher."

Her *shveshtah* frowned. "Why not?"

"She's only eighteen for one thing. You just said Asher needs someone to help him carry his already heavy load. To me that implies a more mature woman."

Greta tapped her chin. "Maisie is very mature for her age. But perhaps you're right. That just means I need to expand my search." She snapped her fingers. "There's Noah's cousin Mary Rose. Oh, or Margaret Bixler. *Jah*, Margaret would be a *gut* fit."

"I still think you're getting ahead of yourself. You don't even know if Asher wants your help finding a *fraa*. For all we know he may already have his sights set on someone."

"Do you think so? Is there someone you've noticed him singling out?"

"*Nee.* But that doesn't mean it's not so."

Greta tilted her head inquisitively. "Is there some reason you don't want me to find a match for Asher?"

Martha saw the knowing gleam in her *shveshtah*'s eye and realized this whole line of conversation had been leading up to this question. She'd very likely had no intention of playing matchmaker for Asher. Greta apparently thought she had seen something between her and Asher. It was preposterous of course. Asher didn't even think of her that way.

So rather than take the bait her *shveshtah* had very cleverly laid out for her, she shrugged. "Not at all. I'm merely saying you should probably speak to Asher before you start talking to potential girlfriends."

And before she could say anything else, Dorcas returned, effectively ending that topic of conversation.

But not Martha's thoughts, which were a jumble of hurt feelings over being left out of the party planning and an unsettling confusion over why her *shveshtah* had tried teasing her about Asher.

* * *

The *kinner* were playing a game of tag in the yard—all except Peter, who was asleep on Martha's lap as she sat in the gently swaying porch swing. Asher sat on a bench nearby and though he wasn't facing her, thanks to Noah's earlier comments he was acutely aware of her presence.

Greta and *Oma* sat on the porch chairs, which had been turned to face the swing, while Noah had a hip braced against the porch rail. There was a general sense of languid post-meal repletion among them as the conversation ebbed and flowed.

After one of the long pauses where the only sound came from the much more energetic little ones, Asher turned to Noah. "This seems a *gut* time to take a walk out to the workshop if you're still interested."

Noah stood. "*Jah*, lead the way."

"Greta, why don't you join them?" Martha suggested. "Asher has some lovely pieces I know you'll appreciate, and Dorcas and I can keep an eye on the *kinner*."

Greta stood. "Well, if you're sure and Asher doesn't mind me tagging along…"

The men both professed to have no objections so Greta happily joined them as Asher led the way to his workshop.

Once inside, Noah studied the examples of Asher's work that were stored on shelves, hung on the walls and strung from the ceiling throughout. "You've been holding out on me. I didn't realize you worked with copper as well as tin."

Asher shrugged self-consciously. "It's something I've just started recently."

Noah moved closer to one of the copper panels. "We need to talk when you come by next week. I think I may have a market for these."

Greta moved to another set of shelves that held some of the ornamental items he'd made. "Martha was right, these are lovely." Then she paused in front of a lamp he'd made, an exclamation springing from her lips. "Noah, look at this, it's beautiful. Wouldn't it make a great gift for your *grossmammi*'s birthday?"

Noah joined her and picked up the lantern, examining it from every side. "*Jah*. The workmanship is excellent." He turned to Asher. "Do you have a vendor you sell these through?"

The question reminded Asher of the conversation he'd had with Martha earlier in the week. "Not yet. But lately I've been thinking about finding someone locally I could partner with to sell the more intricate pieces on a consignment basis."

He knew his words had hit their mark when he saw the considering gleam in Noah's eye as he stroked his beard and turned to study the lamp again.

"Perhaps that's one more thing we can discuss when you come by on Wednesday. And if you don't mind, bring some of those copper panels and a few favorites from what you call your more intricate pieces."

That certainly lightened his mood. Having Noah put his items in his showroom would be a big boost to his sales.

While he and Noah had talked, Greta had moved on to study some of his other pieces.

"How long have you been creating these?" she asked.

"I started that summer Ephron followed Martha to Columbus to keep her company."

"Don't you have that backward? Martha followed Ephron, ain't so?" Her tone was offhand, her attention still focused on one of the more intricately patterned panels.

But it brought him up short. "What do you mean?"

She waved a hand. "I'm sure leaving Hope's Haven was your *bruder*'s idea, not Martha's. She went with him because he asked her to share his adventure." Greta's nose wrinkled thoughtfully as she glanced at him over her shoulder. "In fact, she didn't say so, but I got the impression Ephron had to do a little persuading to convince her to go."

She had that wrong, she must have misunderstood. After all, it had been nearly twelve years ago and she would have been a child—

He grimaced. She would have been two years older than him.

Asher let the conversation between Greta and Noah flow around him as he tried to fit this new piece of information into the story of that summer as he'd always believed it to be. Could he really have gotten it all so wrong?

He'd learned years ago that his middle *bruder* had no intention of ever coming back to Hope's Haven to live his life among the Plain Folk. But he figured the change had come on him gradually, had been the result of living too long in the *Englisch* world. But perhaps it went back further than that.

Knowing what he now knew of his *bruder* and what he'd always known deep down about Martha, which story made more sense?

Oh, yes, he definitely owed Martha an apology.

Chapter 22

That evening, after the *kinner* had been put down for the night and Martha had joined him on the porch, Asher tried to decide how he'd broach the subject that had been on his mind since Greta's revelation.

But Martha was the first to break the silence. "I think today was a success." She gave him a pleased smile. "The *kinner* seemed to have a *gut* time. And Lottie really came out of her shell. Thinking about playing hostess to Anna and David kept her from worrying about her own shyness."

"I agree. It was wonderful *gut* to see the front yard full of people—both *kinner* and adults—having fun. I'd forgotten what that was like."

"I think we should do this again soon. Though Greta did say next time she'd like to have all of us over to their home."

So she thought of such things in terms of *we*, not *you*. Interesting. "I agree."

"*Gut.* I'll let Greta know." She set the swing in motion and looked out into the night. The shuttered expression on her face had him curious about what was on her mind. Should he wait to bring up his own questions and concerns, or was that just a cowardly excuse?

"Is everything okay?"

Her gaze swiveled to meet his, her eyes widening. Then she raised her brows, a small smile teasing at her lips. "Is it ever possible for *everything* to be okay?"

"That's not an answer. But it's okay if you don't want to share."

She hesitated, then shrugged. "It was just something Greta said that hit me wrong. I'll be fine."

And with that, the subject was obviously closed. Asher decided he'd put things off long enough. "There's something I wanted to speak to you about," he said abruptly.

She straightened, obviously startled by his sudden change of subject. "Of course. Is it something about the *kinner*?"

"*Nee.*" He took a deep breath. "Actually, your *shveshtah* said something this afternoon that makes me feel like I owe you an apology."

Martha brushed at her skirt. "Oh? What did she say?"

Was it his imagination or did she suddenly seem wary? "Greta seems to believe that, rather than you talking Ephron into going to Columbus with you all those years ago, he persuaded you."

She didn't meet his gaze as she traced circles on the swing beside her.

When she held her peace he tried a bit of prompting. "Well, is it true?"

She finally looked up. "*Jah.* He didn't want to go alone and I was ready for a little adventure so he really didn't have to twist my arm very hard. I'm sorry."

He frowned. "Why are you apologizing to me?"

Her expression turned soft, sympathetic. "Because I know how much you admire and love your *bruder.* I would never want to do anything to take that away from you."

If possible he felt even worse for the way he'd acted back then. "I learned the truth of Ephron's ambitions many years ago. That Christmas when he brought his future *fraa* here to meet all of us I accidentally overheard some things that gave me a true picture of the kind of life he wanted." He felt his jaw tighten and forced it to relax. "It took me a bit longer to realize it was what he'd always wanted."

She reached across the table and touched his arm briefly. "I didn't realize it either until we were already in Columbus and settled in with your cousin. It's why I came home without him."

He frowned. "But I thought you came home because of your *mamm*'s stroke."

She shook her head. "I didn't hear about that until I got back home."

Yet another lie Ephron had told him and their family. And just like that another small piece of his childhood was trampled underfoot. But none of that was Martha's fault. "Again, I owe you a big apology. I still remember how rude and insulting I was when I confronted you before you left, accused you of luring Ephron away from Hope's Haven and asked you to reconsider." It still had the power to make him wince when he thought about the things he'd said.

She smiled sweetly. "I didn't really blame you. You were young and you didn't want your *bruder* to leave."

Why was she always bringing up the age difference between them? But that wasn't what he needed to focus on right now. "Why didn't you set me straight?"

"I told you, I didn't want to cloud your opinion of Ephron." She shrugged and gave him a more direct look. "Besides, would you have believed me?"

He grimaced. "Probably not."

She spread her hands. "So there you have it. Ephron fooled me too—he was determined to leave the community so he could become a veterinarian. But all of that is in the past. I'd like to put it behind us and move ahead as friends."

"I'd like that too."

"*Gut.*" She stood. "It's been a long day so I think I'll head off to bed now."

Asher remained on the porch awhile longer. Strange how his whole perception of that summer and all that had happened had changed. No wonder she thought of him as a child, he'd certainly behaved as one back then.

But could he ever erase that image in her mind, replace it with that of the man he'd become now?

* * *

As Martha brushed out her hair, her mind was a jumble of emotions. So many things had happened today that it was difficult to sort through it all.

So rather than try, she decided to take action. It was time she replied to Laban's letter.

She pulled out a piece of paper and a pen. Rather than planning out what she wanted to say, she just started writing.

Laban,

I hope this letter finds you well. It was gut *to hear from you this week.*

My days have been very full since I began work here at the Lantz home. I discovered early on that Lottie, the oldest child, was painfully shy. I've been working with her, trying to prepare her for when she starts school in the fall. And I think I'm finally making progress.

Her brieder, *three-year-old triplets, are a handful, but just because there are three of them and they are so active. All four of the* kinner *are a joy to work with and I can already tell that I'm going to miss them when it's time for me to move on.*

Asher and his grossmammi *Dorcas, the* kinner*'s guardians, have been very welcoming to me. In addition to working his farm, Asher also does punched tin work. His work is quite beautiful. I haven't yet seen examples of your work, but I suspect that quality would be something the two of you have in common. In fact the two of you would probably become* gut *friends if the opportunity ever arose.*

My shveshtah *Greta and her family came here to visit with us today. For once Dorcas let me help with the cooking and preparations. It was* wunderbaar *to have so many friends and* familye *under one roof.*

And I was wonderful glad to hear about your new business opportunities. It speaks well of your artisan and business skills as well as the quality of your product. And your willingness to put in the effort to expand your business speaks well of your industriousness. I'm certain sure, too, that expanding your business will be gut not only for you but for the community as well.

Martha paused and chewed on the cap of her pen. She realized she'd been rambling up to this point. That was because she was avoiding replying to the last line of his letter. Truth to tell, it was what had kept her from writing before now. She still wasn't quite sure what she wanted to say.

She sighed. Yes she was. It just wasn't going to be easy to say it.

As to your comment that you would like us to reach an understanding in the next few weeks, I'm assuming you are referring to whether or not we are to consider ourselves courting. To be completely honest I'm concerned that such a deadline won't give us adequate time to get to know each other, but I am willing to try to work on that. So here is some personal information about me.

I've been told I'm too task-focused and that I don't know how to relax and have fun. I suppose that's true to a certain extent, but I've been trying to work on that. Being here with the four little ones has been a help—it's hard to be all work when you're trying to keep up with kinner.

*I've also been told I can come across as some-
thing of a know-it-all. That's hard to hear but it
was said by someone who loves me so it must be
true. So that is also something I will work on.*

*And there is one other thing you need to know
about me. I know you said it isn't necessary
for me to learn anything about your business,
that my role in the home will keep me too busy
for outside concerns. But the truth is, I want to
know as much about your work as I can so that
I can be a true helpmeet to you. I don't feel the
need to work outside the home but I do want to
understand what you do, because it is a way to
understand who you are and what you deal with
on a daily basis.*

*I look forward to learning more about you
in your next letter. But whatever we decide, I
did make a commitment to look after the Lantz
kinner for six weeks and I plan to stand by that.
The little ones deserve to have a caretaker with
them and I am that person until their actual
nanny heals enough to return to them.*

*Sincerely
Martha*

How would he react to what amounted to demands?
Would he decide she wasn't the kind of girl he wanted
for a wife after all? Had she just ruined the last chance
she had of having a family of her own?

Perhaps she should have suggested Greta try to find
her a match instead of Asher.

Afterward, Martha lay awake in her bed for quite

some time. Deciding what she needed was a nice cup of warm milk to settle her down, or better yet hot cocoa, she got up, donned her robe and padded down the hall to the kitchen. She'd just reached into the cupboard for a saucepan when she heard a cry. At first she thought it was coming from the boys' room and quickly headed down the hall to check on them. But before she reached their door she heard it again and realized it was coming from upstairs.

Lottie.

Chapter 23

Martha turned on her heel and quickly headed for the staircase. Before she'd stepped on the first tread, however, she saw Asher enter Lottie's room.

She hesitated a moment. She was the nanny, so technically it was her job to take care of the *kinner*. But Asher was their *onkel* and she'd been telling him he needed to take a more active role with them. Still, if Lottie was having a nightmare, she felt a woman's touch might be better.

Martha climbed the stairs. She could hear the murmur of Asher's voice as she neared the top. Though she couldn't make out the words, she heard the gentle soothing of his tone.

Lottie's doorway was open and Martha paused just outside, wanting to assess the situation before intruding.

"What was it about this time, Lottie *lamm*? Were bees swarming you again?"

"*Nee*." The little girl's response was so soft it barely carried to Martha.

"Then what was it?"

There was a long pause and Martha almost intervened, wanting to tell Lottie she didn't need to speak about it if it upset her too much. But before she could decide to act, Lottie spoke up again.

"I dreamed Acorn was hurt real bad and there was no one around to take care of her."

"Ah Lottie *lamm*, I'm so sorry. Martha told me how much you miss your *mamm*'s horse. I never would have sold her if I'd known. But I assure you Obed Miller, the man I sold Acorn to, is taking very *gut* care of her. We can go visit her if you'd like to see for yourself."

The squeak of moving bedsprings covered whatever response she made, but Martha assumed it was assent based on Asher's next words.

"Then I'll arrange for us to go sometime in the next few days." He shifted again. "Now, I know bad dreams can be upsetting, even for a grown-up. But you do know they're not real, don't you?"

"Grown-ups have bad dreams too?"

"Of course we do."

"Even you?"

"Yes, even me."

Was that a hint of humor in Asher's tone?

"Who takes care of you when you have a bad dream?"

Martha's heart melted a little at the obvious concern in the little girl's voice.

"Well, when I wake up from a bad dream, once I'm awake enough to realize it was only a dream, the first thing I do is say a little prayer and thank *Gotte* that it wasn't real and that He always watches over me, even in the bad times. And that makes me feel better so I can go back to sleep."

"Oh." There was a long pause, then, "If you want, next time you have a bad dream I can come keep you company until you feel better."

"Oh, Lottie *lamm*, that is a wonderful generous offer. I'd be right glad to have you keep me company next time."

From the undercurrent of emotion in Asher's voice she could tell he was as touched as she was by his niece's offer.

"Now," he said, his voice more collected, "are you going to be okay to go back to sleep on your own, or would you like me to sit with you awhile?"

"I'm okay now."

"*Gut* girl. And remember, I'm close by if you need me again."

A moment later he stepped out into the hall. He raised a brow when he saw her standing there but put a finger to his lips to indicate silence. Then he waved a hand toward the stairs and with a nod she started down.

As they descended the stairs, Asher wondered just how much Martha had overheard.

It wasn't until they were in the kitchen that he broke the silence. "It's been several months since she had a nightmare," he said as he raked a hand through his hair. "I'd hoped she was over it."

"You handled that very well."

He gave her a crooked grin. "I'd say *danke* if you didn't sound so surprised."

Her cheeks turned a becoming shade of pink. "I'm sorry. That's not what I meant. I—"

He rescued her from her obvious embarrassment. "That's all right. I know I don't seem to be much of a *daed* to the *kinner*. But the truth is I love them and would do anything to spare them pain."

"Of course you would. They're *familye*."

He felt a touch of irritation at her condescending tone. Was she still looking on him as a *youngie*? "*Jah*, but they're not just *familye* to me, they are my responsibility. They depend on me not just for their physical needs but for protection, for training, for love. For all intents and purposes I am their *daed*, and one who doesn't have a *fraa* to share in their care. So *nee*, it's not a responsibility I take lightly."

"I apologize if I left you with the impression that I thought otherwise." She waved a hand in the general direction of the staircase. "Even if I'd thought that before, after witnessing you with Lottie just now there's no denying that you are more than capable of caring for them and giving them the kind of home and surroundings they need to grow and thrive."

So she was finally ready to see him as a proper head of this household. That was something, he supposed.

Was it possible she would ever see him as more?

* * *

Martha didn't sleep well that night. The interaction between Asher and Lottie as well as the conversation she'd had with Asher in the kitchen afterward had left her feeling unsettled. And she'd forgotten to get her glass of warm milk.

How could she have been so wrong about Asher's commitment to be the kind of guardian these *kinner* needed? She wasn't certain she could have handled the aftermath of Lottie's nightmare any better than he had, and possibly not nearly as well.

He'd been right to take her to task for her lack of confidence in him. It was every bit as distorted as his assumptions about what was going on that summer twelve years ago.

As she dressed her gaze snagged on the letter she'd written last night. She still had some qualms over how it would be received but she couldn't let that keep her from sending it. She wasn't used to having so much uncertainty in her life. Now more than ever she was ready to determine her status with Laban.

Squaring her shoulders she snatched it up, as well as the one she'd written to Ephron Saturday evening, and headed for the kitchen. The sooner she sent the letter to Laban on its way the sooner she would learn his response.

When she reached the kitchen she found Dorcas there but not Asher. Had she finally managed to start her morning before him? Had he had as much trouble getting to sleep last night as she had?

"*Gut matin*," Dorcas said with a smile. "Would you like some coffee before the *kinner* wake up?"

"*Jah*, that sounds *gut*." Perhaps the coffee would help calm some of this unsettled feeling.

Dorcas nodded toward the missives in Martha's hand. "What's that you have there?"

"It's a couple of letters I need to mail. I was going to see if you or Asher had some stamps I could purchase."

"I have some." Asher's voice came from behind her. "But there's no need for you to purchase them. Just give your letters to me and I'll stamp them and put them in the mailbox when I go outside after breakfast."

Martha hesitated for just a heartbeat, strangely reluctant to hand him the letter intended for Laban. But then she gave her head a mental shake. He already knew she was corresponding with Laban and that she'd planned to write to Ephron. And even if he hadn't, there was no need to hide it from him.

She smiled and handed them over. "*Danke.*"

* * *

Asher plodded down the driveway, headed for the mailbox. Given all that had passed between them yesterday he'd wondered if he'd have any trouble facing Martha this morning. But she'd greeted him as if nothing had changed, making it easy to do the same.

He wasn't sure if that was a *gut* thing or not.

When he'd left the house a few minutes ago Martha had put the *kinner* to work on the laundry again. She had also convinced *Oma* to let her and the *kinner* take over dusting the furniture in the living room. Little by little she was finding ways to help with the housework under the guise of teaching the *kinner*.

No doubt by the time Debra Lynn returned the *kinner* would be well trained in handling a number of household chores. Martha was very *gut* at teaching *kinner*. She was also very *gut* at getting things done. When she saw a need she rolled up her sleeves and made certain it was handled.

He fingered the letters in his hand. He was curious about why she was writing to Ephron but that wasn't the letter that occupied his thoughts. It seemed she was still corresponding with this Laban fellow. It was for sure and for certain that she didn't see her pen pal as a *youngie* or as merely a friend. Laban had the advantage of never having been a scholar in her classroom or the younger *bruder* of her friend so she didn't have that image stuck in her mind. In fact Laban was a year or two older than Martha. As if that mattered.

Had the two of them grown close? Did this letter contain sweet nothings and personal secrets?

By the time he reached the foot of the drive Asher had an almost overwhelming impulse to crumple it. He managed to restrain himself and instead shoved both letters in the mailbox, slammed it closed and raised the flag.

It seemed that first day when she'd shown up here he had predicted correctly in thinking having her around would be a distraction.

He'd just been wrong about what kind of distraction she'd be.

Chapter 24

After lunch the weather turned overcast. *Oma* along with Martha and the *kinner* managed to get the laundry inside before the rain started in earnest. Again he was glad she had Martha around to help her.

Asher spent most of the afternoon in his workshop. Noah had asked for some additional pieces, these to be done in copper. Asher had wondered if Martha would join him while the *kinner* napped. When she showed up, sprinting under cover of a dripping umbrella, he felt his spirits lighten.

"So, are you ready to tackle something a little more ambitious today?"

Martha cut him a surprised look as she set her umbrella aside. "Do you think I'm ready?"

He shrugged. "You'll never know until you try." He opened the pattern binder and turned to one that depicted a small bouquet tied with a ribbon and circled by a braided border of dots. Then the whole thing was bordered by a rectangular frame formed by evenly spaced X's. "I thought this might be a good one for you to try. It's a little more complex and it'll require you to use two types of punches."

Martha studied it. "This is nice," she said without looking up. "But I don't remember seeing it when I looked in the book before."

"I just added it this morning."

She met his gaze, her eyes widening. "You designed this?"

He nodded. He'd actually designed it with her in mind, looking for something more challenging than the simple pieces she'd already mastered but not so advanced that she'd be overwhelmed.

Instead of looking for something out of the scrap pile he pulled a blank panel from the stack on his supply shelf. "Here you go. I'll let you tape the pattern on yourself."

He returned to his own work, but watched her peripherally.

She held the pattern as if not sure what to do with it. Then she glanced his way and squared her shoulders. She placed the paper on the metal, fussily rearranging it several times until it appeared perfectly centered. Then she carefully taped it down, and picked up her hammer and punch. He watched as she took a deep breath and then struck the punch with confidence.

Before long she'd settled into a working rhythm. Relaxing, he settled into a rhythm of his own.

Martha leaned back and studied the progress she'd made. She thought it looked *gut* even if such thoughts were prideful. The pattern was simple but lovely—had Asher drawn it up just for her?

She would miss this when she left here.

Truth be told, she'd miss Asher as well. She'd come to think of him as a very *gut* friend.

She cut a sideways glance his way. His head was bent over his work, his brow furrowed in concentration. He had a youthful face, that was for sure and for certain.

But why had she never noticed what a strong profile he had, how firm his jaw was, how his thick hair had a slight wave to it?

Martha blinked, trying to recapture that boyish image. But it was impossible.

She abruptly set her tools down and stood. When Asher glanced up, she turned and reached for her umbrella. "I should get back to the house. Lottie and the boys will be up from their naps soon."

"You did *gut* work today. Once you're finished, I think it might be a piece to place in Charity Umble's shop."

She turned back, her previous concerns forgotten. "Do you really think so?"

He nodded. "I can make a frame for it and it will do well there."

Then he met her gaze. "I forgot to tell you, when Noah looked at my pieces yesterday we discussed the possibility of placing the more elaborate of my pieces in his showroom. We'll work out the details when I see him Wednesday."

She closed the short distance between them and placed a hand on his arm. "Oh, Asher, that's perfect. I don't know why I didn't think of him to start with.

When customers come in to look at his furniture they'll see your pieces as well."

Something flickered in his eyes and she was aware her hand was still on his arm. Feeling her cheeks heat, she snatched her hand away and turned again to grab her umbrella.

Opening it, she stepped out and sprinted to the house without saying another word.

* * *

Tuesday and Wednesday proved to be overcast with on and off light rain throughout the day. The *kinner* had their chores to occupy them in the mornings and Martha did her best to keep Lottie and her *brieder* entertained in the afternoons. They did arts and crafts, including making homemade puzzles. She also told them stories, helped them make up their own stories and taught them songs so they could better participate when they had music in the evenings. She even drew a hopscotch grid for them on the cement floor of the basement.

Martha was relieved when Thursday morning dawned bright and sunny. It wasn't only the *kinner* who were feeling a touch of cabin fever.

Once everyone had settled down for breakfast, Asher turned to Lottie. "I was thinking that later, once the morning chores are taken care of, we could make a visit to Obed Miller's place and see how Acorn is doing. Would you like that?"

Martha smiled as Lottie perked up immediately and gave an enthusiastic nod. "*Jah.*"

"Can we go too?" Zach asked.

"Of course. If you get all of your chores done." He looked around. "In fact, we can all go."

But Dorcas shook her head. "The rest of you go. I want to organize my pantry today. I've let it get a bit jumbled."

Martha swallowed her own desire to join the outing. "I'll stay and help you."

"Nonsense. It's a one-person job." She pointed her fork toward the head of the table. "And I think Asher may need your help more than I will."

Martha looked around the table at the *kinner* and nodded. "Of course." She was the nanny, after all.

After breakfast, the *kinner* rushed through their chores and by ten thirty they were seated with Martha and Asher in the buggy, headed down the lane. Lottie sat on the edge of her seat, as if trying to reach their destination more quickly.

The boys, on the other hand, chattered away about anything and everything, just happy to be outdoors after being stuck inside for two days.

Martha was in a *gut* mood as well. Not only was she happy to have an outing, she also admired Asher for taking this step on Lottie's behalf.

"Does Obed know we're coming?" she asked.

"Not specifically today, but I bumped into him in town yesterday and asked if it would be okay if we dropped by soon."

Martha nodded. At least the explanations would already have been taken care of.

When Asher finally pulled the buggy up in front of the Miller home, Rahab, Obed's *fraa*, stepped out of the side door followed by a preschooler who looked to be Lottie's age.

"*Wilkom*," she greeted with a warm smile. "Obed told me you would be stopping by."

She turned to the youngster at her heels. "Peter, let your *daed* know we have visitors."

With a nod the boy headed off at a trot toward the barn.

"Please, *kum* in while you wait. I have peanut butter cookies I just took out of the oven that I would be wonderful happy to share with you."

"You all go on ahead," Asher said. "I need to tend to the buggy."

Martha, who suspected he wanted to speak to Obed privately, took her cue and ushered the *kinner* ahead of her as they followed Rahab to the house.

A few minutes later Peter rushed back inside, no doubt afraid the cookies would be all gone if he delayed his return.

Martha and Rahab chatted easily, the older woman doing most of the talking. By the time Asher and Obed came inside, Martha felt as if she were all caught up on the latest news around town.

Though Lottie didn't say anything, it was clear from the way her eyes locked on Asher and she seemed poised to spring from her seat that she was eager to get on with her reason for being here.

And Asher didn't make her wait long. "Lottie, if you're ready Obed has Acorn in the paddock."

The little girl quickly slid from her seat and moved around the table to stand beside him. Asher put his hand on her shoulder and looked uncertainly from the boys to Martha.

Martha quickly turned to Rahab. "Didn't you tell me you have some goats? Would you mind showing them to me? Zach, Zeb, Zeke—wouldn't you like to see them too?"

The boys scrambled down from the table, ready for whatever adventure was offered. And as simple as that, they split into two groups.

Thirty minutes later Martha and the Lantzes were headed back down the road. Lottie turned around in her seat to talk to Martha. "You should have seen Acorn. She came right to me like she remembered me."

Martha returned the girl's smile. "I'm sure she did."

"Her coat was so shiny and she looked wonderful happy."

"That's *gut*."

"I think so." She paused thoughtfully. "I think *Mamm* would be happy that Acorn found a *gut* home."

Martha felt her throat choke up and all she could do was nod.

Lottie turned back around and plopped down in her seat. "*Danke*," she said to Asher. "I'm glad I got to see her."

"You're welcome."

Was there a touch of emotion in Asher's tone as well?

Why had she ever thought he wasn't a *gut daed*?

* * *

Friday evening Martha stirred the pot of green beans simmering on the stove. She'd added ham and baby potatoes to it, just the way *Daed* liked it. She also had candied sweet potatoes and baked beans cooking in the oven. She'd been at it since she'd put her charges to bed. She'd even skipped spending time out on the porch with Asher, and by now the rest of the household was no doubt sound asleep. But since her *shveshtra* had relegated her to taking care of the side dishes, she was going to make sure her contribution had a chance to shine.

She opened the oven door and basted the sweet potatoes with the cooking liquid and gave a happy sigh when she inhaled the delicious aroma. The recipe was her own, one she'd perfected over the years. It included maple syrup and a touch of bacon, which always brought an appreciative smile to *Daed*'s face. During the last fifteen minutes of cooking she'd also add some pecans as a finishing touch. The baked beans had been in the oven long enough so she pulled the bowl out and set it on a trivet on the counter to cool.

Closing the oven door, she turned to the eggs she'd boiled earlier. They should be cool enough to peel now. She made quick work of that then combined them with the potatoes she'd cooked earlier. Adding the rest of the ingredients necessary for a potato salad, including a touch of the smoked paprika she'd heard about from Dorcas, she stirred it together then tasted. Deciding it needed just a touch more mustard and a bit more pickle juice, she made the adjustment and decided it was perfect.

She covered the bowl with plastic wrap and placed it in the refrigerator.

Greta had sent word that the Lantz family was invited to the party as well—she said her *kinner* had had a great time visiting on Sunday and would be disappointed if their friends weren't there. Dorcas, of course, had wanted to contribute to the meal, so she'd made baked corn. Martha had assured her that this would not only be acceptable but it would be greatly appreciated.

She closed the refrigerator, then checked on the green beans. With a satisfied nod to herself, she took the pot from the stove and set it aside with the baked beans to cool.

She glanced at the clock. Time to add the pecans to the sweet potatoes, baste and then bake for fifteen more minutes and she'd be done. The other dishes she'd cooked were *gut*, but this one would be the star of the show. It was a favorite with everyone in her family and usually only showed up at Thanksgiving and Christmas because it was so time consuming to make.

With a satisfied nod, she began to clean up the stove and the dishes she'd dirtied to this point. Potato salad, green beans, baked beans and candied sweet potatoes—not a bad night's work. She might not have a little one to participate in the program with her nieces and nephews, and she might not be responsible for the main dish or dessert, but she could show up at the party tomorrow knowing she'd done her fair share to help feed everyone.

A little later Martha wiped a hand across her forehead. She was so tired but it had been worth it. It was time to take the sweet potatoes from the oven. Once this dish cooled off and she could safely store it in the refrigerator she could go on to bed. Just another fifteen minutes.

Martha turned the oven off and opened the door. The sweet, spicy aroma hit her like a caress. The color was perfect and the syrupy liquid looked to be the right consistency. She imagined the delighted look on her family's faces as she set this on the table tomorrow.

She caught herself humming for the next fifteen minutes as she cleaned up the kitchen and then put away the green beans and baked beans. Then she moved to the oven. Once she pulled her sweet potatoes out and gave them time to cool she'd finally be able to turn in. She'd certainly sleep well tonight.

* * *

Asher sat in a chair by his bed, reading his Bible. His door was slightly ajar and he could hear the occasional muffled clatter from the kitchen downstairs, letting him know Martha was still up and cooking. For some reason he didn't want to turn in until she went to bed herself.

A sudden crash had him out of his chair and out the door in a flash. As he rushed down the stairs he strained his ears for any clue as to what had happened. At first he didn't hear anything, then just as he made it to the bottom tread he heard what sounded like a sob.

Truly concerned now, he changed stride to something close to a sprint. As soon as he reached the threshold to the kitchen, however, he paused to take in the scene before him.

Martha sat on the floor next to a large casserole dish and a splattered puddle of what looked like candied sweet potatoes. There was a defeated slump to her shoulders and tears were trickling down her cheeks.

Chapter 25

Asher moved forward almost immediately but when Martha spotted him she buried her face in her hands.

He stooped down and put a hand on her shoulder. "Martha, what happened? Are you hurt?"

"I'm fine. Go away."

Asher blinked. He must have misunderstood. "I know you're upset and possibly hurt, but please lower your hands so your voice isn't so muffled."

She did as he bid and lifted her chin defiantly. "I said I'm fine and to please go away."

At least the tears seemed to have stopped. But why did she now seem so upset with him? Then he saw some of the syrup from the sweet potato dish on her hand and what looked like an angry red blotch beneath it. "You've burned your hand!"

Martha looked at her hand as if it belonged to someone else. "Oh, I suppose I did."

"*Kum*," he said, moving his hand to her elbow,

"let's clean it in some cool water." Had she really not realized she'd burned herself? Had she registered the pain subconsciously and was that why she'd been crying?

She allowed him to help her up and almost list-lessly let him lead her to the kitchen basin. She stood passively as he squeezed a wet towel over her hand several times until the sticky substance washed away.

When he dabbed the red area with the rag she jerked her hand and winced but didn't make a sound. He studied it, not liking the look of it. "Stay here." He went to the pantry and came back with a mason jar and some gauze. And then, because she didn't seem capable of making decisions at the moment, he led her to the table and asked her to sit.

"This is a salve *Oma* mixed up specifically for burns. I'll try to go easy." Using his fingers, he scooped up a generous amount and slathered it on her burn. Then he took the clean gauze and wrapped it loosely around her hand. All the while he kept talking, trying to keep her distracted.

Finally he looked at her face, though she kept her gaze downcast. "Now, why don't you go to bed and try to get some sleep. I can clean this up."

That seemed to finally get through to her and she snapped to attention. "*Nee*, don't be ridiculous. I made this mess, I'll clean it up. And I need to get started redoing this dish."

She couldn't be thinking straight. "It's you who are being ridiculous. It's almost midnight. The other dishes you made are surely enough for the party. Everyone will be focused on the people and the reason for the gathering. One side dish more or less won't make a difference."

That seemed to agitate her even further. "You don't understand. The sweet potatoes were my special offering. Everything else is just ordinary. I can do this—I'm pretty sure there are enough of the ingredients left."

"Martha, you're down to one hand, the hour is late and this looks like something that isn't a quick cook." Her lips were still set in a stubborn line so he tried again. "I'm sure your family will understand. There's nothing wrong with ordinary."

"They've done everything else without me." Her tone bordered on a wail. "I wanted—" She halted abruptly.

But she'd said enough for him to get an inkling of what was driving her. "You want your contribution to be noted and appreciated."

She leaned back heavily. "*Jah.*" She cut him a sideways look. "I suppose that makes me guilty of being prideful."

He took the seat beside her and turned his chair so they were face-to-face. "You don't have to bring a special dish or do anything other than be yourself. Your *familye* loves you for who you are, not for the things you do or produce. Surely you know that."

"*Jah.*"

That didn't sound like she believed what she was saying. "Martha, look at me." He waited until she complied. "What is it you're trying to prove?"

She shifted uncomfortably but didn't respond.

He pressed on. "I remember when you were younger, before your *mamm* died, you weren't so concerned with everything being proper and perfect.

In the classroom you challenged your scholars to try new things even when they felt they weren't up to it—especially when they felt they weren't up to it. And you helped the shyer students feel seen, just as you're doing for Lottie now. Perhaps having to step up and not only take on the role of lady of the house but also help raise your younger *shveshtra* who were still in school was what robbed you of your joy."

She lifted a hand in protest. "No, you're wrong. I never resented doing what I did after *Mamm* died. It was the least I could do after—" Her mouth abruptly snapped closed and her demeanor was that of a person who thought they'd said too much.

Something told him it was important that he press her to complete that thought. "After what?"

She shook her head.

"Martha, whatever it is, it can't be as bad as you think. Just tell me."

Her lips set in a stubborn line and for a minute he thought she'd refuse. But a moment later her expression crumbled and she looked away again. "I don't resent all I did because it was my fault *Mamm* died."

He straightened in surprise. "Your *mamm* had a stroke, ain't so? How could that be your fault?"

She shrank into herself, looking absolutely miserable. "When I left home that summer, I knew *Mamm* didn't want me to go even though she'd never actually try to stop me. And I also knew she'd worry about me a great deal while I was gone. But I selfishly thought it would all be okay, that her worry was just misplaced fretting on her part. But even Greta knew better. She wrote to tell me how sad and distracted *Mamm* was, though I didn't get the letter until after I returned."

She was definitely taking too much on her shoulders. "Worrying about their *kinner* is part of a parent's life, there's nothing unusual in that." Having a parent worry overmuch about you was something he knew quite a bit about.

"But I *knew* she would worry and that she'd be hurt. Before I agreed to make the trip with Ephron we'd planned to work on a special project for *Grossmammi* that summer, just the two of us. But instead of sticking with our original plans and doing what I knew would make my *mamm* happy I was selfish and told her we'd just put the project off for a couple of months. And because I did, *Mamm* died. She died before I could get home to say goodbye. To say how much I loved her. And in those first terrible hours *Daed* was left to contend alone with getting *Mamm* to the hospital while trying to keep my little *shveshtra* calm."

He took her unbandaged hand. "Martha, none of that was your fault."

She didn't appear to have heard him. "It was her worry over me that contributed at least in part to the stress that brought on her stroke."

Had she been carrying this burden for the past twelve years? "Listen to me. It was not your fault. Your *mamm* was a strong woman who had a deep, abiding faith. She knew *Gotte*'s will would be done for you—and for her—regardless of where you were. So no, I am absolutely certain your being away for the summer had no impact on her having that stroke. In fact, by thinking it was your fault you risk being overly prideful."

He sandwiched her *gut* hand with both of his. "Your *mamm* wouldn't want you to take this burden on your shoulders, neither would any of your *familye*. I'm sorry you didn't get to say goodbye to your *mamm*, but you need to stop trying to be perfect and just be the warm, loving *dochder* and *shveshtah* your *familye* needs."

Was that how he saw her—warm and loving? For some reason that made Martha feel better. But not about her negligent past. "I don't know how to stop."

He gave her hand another squeeze and then let it go. She immediately felt the loss of the warmth and comfort it had provided.

But he was responding to her unasked question. "Well, as a first step you should forget about trying to cook anything else to bring to the party tomorrow and be satisfied that you will have only 'ordinary' side dishes to bring."

Easier said than done. But she managed a crooked smile. "All right, I'll try." She waved a hand toward the sticky remains of the sweet potatoes. "But I insist on cleaning up my own mess here."

Asher tilted his head slightly as he studied her. "Why don't we tackle it together?"

She started to protest but he held up a hand to stop her. "Your second lesson will be to learn how to ask for and accept help when you need it."

She shook her head. "You're a much tougher task-master than I would have thought. I certainly hope there's not a third lesson to be learned tonight."

He stroked his chin, his stern frown contradicted by the amused glint in his eye. "I think two lessons are all you can manage tonight. The rest will have to wait."

* * *

The next morning Martha wasn't sure how to face Asher after what had happened the night before. But she was spared any awkwardness when the boys woke up earlier than usual, stopping and redirecting her steps before she reached the kitchen. By the time she helped them get ready for the morning's activities everyone else was in the kitchen, ready to eat breakfast.

The *kinner* were eagerly anticipating the upcoming trip to her home, especially since Martha had mentioned Lady's puppies to them. The table conversation centered on their excitement over the puppies as well as getting to see Greta's *kinner* again. Even Asher seemed to be in a remarkably *gut* mood. He smiled a lot and joined in the conversation with gusto. Whenever his gaze happened to touch hers there was a certain something there she couldn't quite put her finger on. But whatever it was, it made her think of last night. Of his gentle, sympathetic chiding. Of his playful teasing. But mostly of the warmth of his hand on hers.

After one such instance Martha caught Dorcas looking at the two of them with a knowing expression on her face. What was that all about? Dorcas couldn't possibly think there was something going on between her and Asher.

Could she?

It was almost a relief when breakfast was over and everyone scattered to take care of morning chores.

If Martha had had her way she would have arrived at her *daed*'s right after breakfast to help get everything set up and ready. But she tried to be patient while the morning chores were taken care of and the Lantz family got ready to leave.

As Asher took care of loading the food into the back

of the family buggy Martha had a momentary pang about the absence of her sweet potato dish. Then she met his gaze and saw the sympathetic look in his eyes. She felt the heat rise in her cheeks and determinedly squared her shoulders. Though she did still regret last night's accident, she would not let it spoil her day.

Before she could get the *kinner* safely seated in the buggy, Zeke tripped and hurt his elbow. Martha immediately knelt by the tearful boy's side. "Let's have a look at that, pumpkin." She gently examined the scraped appendage. "*Ach*, it definitely needs some attention. Let's take you inside and clean it up so we can have a *gut* look."

She scooped the little boy up and settled him on her hip. "You are being wonderful brave right now."

He sniffled but the trickle of tears stopped. "I am?"

"For sure and for certain," she said solemnly. "Why, you hardly cried at all." By this time they were back in the house and Martha snagged one of Dorcas's oatmeal raisin cookies. "Such a brave little man definitely deserves one of these."

Martha took a wet rag and gently cleaned the scraped elbow while Zeke happily munched on his cookie. As she worked her mind went back to the way Asher had tended to her in a similar fashion, not just last night but the other day when she'd injured her finger with the hammer. He had such a capacity for tenderness that in no way took away from his masculinity.

Giving her head a mental shake, she focused back on the scrape that was now clean and no longer bleeding. Fetching the largest Band-Aid she could find in Dorcas's medicine cabinet, she applied it with a flourish to Zeke's elbow. "Now I think you'll be just fine."

With a nod Zeke raced from the house and she could hear him showing off his bandage to his *brieder*.

Between Zeke's fall and Rowdy picking up a thorn in his paw, they were thirty minutes later leaving than Martha had planned. She tried to rein in her impatience but it wasn't easy.

Sure enough, when they arrived she saw that both her *shveshtra* were there ahead of her.

Noah, Micah and her *daed* were near the horse barn, talking and keeping an eye on Noah and Greta's *kinner*. She didn't see Micah and Hannah's little girl Grace. She must be in the house with Hannah.

The men approached as Asher pulled the horse to a stop and helped them step down. Hannah immediately embraced her *daed*. "Happy birthday."

"*Danke, dochder.*" He waved toward the house. "Leah and your *shveshtra* are in the kitchen getting things ready for lunch."

"Then I'd better get all these dishes in there and join them."

Asher was already pulling a casserole carrier out of the back of the buggy.

"Here, let me help with that," Micah said, taking the food items from Asher. "I was going back to the house anyway."

Daed waved a hand. "You all go on to the house. Noah and I will take care of the horse and buggy."

Martha looked from one of the men to the other. There was an expectant look about them, as if they knew something she didn't, something they expected her to find out shortly. What was going on? Had she missed out on something else?

But she took the bowl of potato salad from Asher and followed Micah into the house.

Once inside she saw Hannah, Greta, Leah and Grace along with a freckled, redheaded boy she didn't recognize. He appeared to be about six years old and he was wearing a brace on his left leg.

Hannah put her hands on the little boy's shoulders, a broad smile on her face. "Martha, Asher, Dorcas, I'd like you to meet Liam, our foster son."

Foster son? When had that happened? But Martha pushed her questions aside for now. This was a *gut* thing. Hannah was unable to have *kinner* of her own and she'd told the family when she and Micah first planned to marry that they hoped to adopt.

She smiled down at the little boy. "*Gutentag*, Liam. Welcome to the *familye*. I'm your *aenti* Martha, Hannah's oldest *shveshtah*."

Liam stared at her in confusion.

"Liam came from an *Englisch* home," Hannah said. "He's not used to our language and customs just yet." She gave her foster son a loving glance. "But he's wonderful clever and is already picking up on some things." She gently squeezed his shoulders. "He's especially learning to ask questions if there's something he doesn't understand, because that's the best way to learn, ain't so?"

Liam nodded shyly.

Hannah turned to Asher. "I take it you brought the *kinner* with you and they're outside?"

Asher nodded. "They were excited to see everyone again."

Then Hannah turned to Grace and Liam. "Why

don't you two go on outside and see what the other *kinner* are up to?"

Grace nodded eagerly but Liam held back.

Hannah exchanged a look with Micah, and he stepped forward.

"Come along. We can go have a look at the new puppies out in the milk barn."

"I think I'll join you," Asher said. "We can gather up Lottie and the boys and take them along to see the puppies as well. They've been talking of little else since Martha mentioned them this morning."

Leah turned to Dorcas. "Would you mind helping me put the cloth on the table and fold the napkins? Everything is set up in the living room."

Once the others had made their exit in a not-too-subtle attempt to leave the *shveshtra* alone, Martha gave Hannah an enthusiastic hug. "I'm so happy for you and Micah. When did this all come about?"

"It happened very quickly, we've only had Liam since Wednesday." The happy glow in her younger *shveshtah*'s face was a joy to behold.

Three days. And no one had thought to tell her. "You said foster son. Will you be able to adopt him?"

"It's not definite yet but Vivian says our chances are very high. We'll know one way or the other in about six weeks."

Vivian Littman was the case worker who had bent over backward to try to help Hannah adopt Grace after Grace's mother abandoned her in their barn two years ago. "And his leg?"

"There is a problem with the way the bones in his left leg formed. The doctors are hopeful he'll outgrow the need for the brace over time."

Martha refrained from asking more. Hannah would tell her in her own time. And those details weren't really important. "He seems a sweet boy and he'll be fortunate to have you and Micah for parents."

"We'll be the fortunate ones. He's already acting like a big *bruder* to Grace. You should see how sweet and protective he is with her."

"He's wonderful smart too," Greta added. "He's practiced with the other *kinner* for the program they're doing for *Daed* later today and even though he isn't familiar with the language he was able to memorize a few lines for his part."

She saw the look her *shveshtra* exchanged, as if they shared a bond she wasn't part of, the bond of motherhood. She tried not to let it bother her, they hadn't intended to hurt her, probably weren't even aware they'd done it.

It was time for her to stop taking things so personally and offer others the grace of assuming they were well intentioned.

* * *

As the men took the excited *kinner* out to the barn to have a look at the puppies, Asher thought of Ephron. He'd always had such a love of animals. It was why he'd wanted to leave them and attend university—to become a veterinarian.

Why had Martha chosen now of all times to write to him? Did it have something to do with her planning to move on with Laban?

He thought about the way he and Martha had worked side by side to clean up the mess on the kitchen floor the night before. He'd managed to get a couple more smiles out of her with some teasing. All in all she'd seemed much calmer and more relaxed by the time they'd finished up. And the shy, sweet smile she'd given him just before she headed for her room had made his efforts feel worthwhile.

He'd never seen the hurt, vulnerable side of Martha that he'd stumbled on last night. It had touched something deep inside him, made him want to hold her and cherish her and make sure nothing ever hurt her like that again.

If what he'd been feeling for her before were remnants of a schoolboy crush, that was no more. What he felt now had nothing of the adolescent schoolboy about it.

The question now was, should he declare himself?

But what about this Laban fellow? How serious was their relationship and did he have any right to get in the middle of it?

And would she welcome it if he did?

Chapter 26

The party itself was a festive affair. The meal was delicious and there was no lack of food—no one missed her sweet potatoes. Martha wasn't sure if that made her feel better or worse.

Much was made over the cake Hannah had made—it was beautifully decorated and tasted delicious. Then the little ones performed for her *daed*'s birthday—even the Lantz *kinner*. Before lunch Greta had taught them one of the songs the others were planning to sing so they wouldn't feel left out. The resultant program was precious, flubs and all. *Daed* was well pleased with the performance, declaring that having such a fine crop of *kinner* to celebrate with him was worth more than any wrapped present they could have given him.

After the meal Dorcas and Leah sent the *shveshtra* away while they cleaned the kitchen, declaring that they welcomed the time to catch up with each other. Martha hadn't realized that the two had been *gut* friends in their younger years.

The three Eicher girls drifted outside and took a seat on the roomy porch swing.

Greta spoke first. "Have you enjoyed yourself today?"

Had her *shveshtah* sensed some of her petty thoughts earlier? "I did." She put all the positive emphasis she could muster into those words. Because whenever she'd forgotten her self-pity, she *had* enjoyed herself. Then, because they deserved the praise, she added, "You and Hannah did a wonderful *gut* job planning this party. But it's *Daed*'s day, shouldn't you be asking him?"

"Of course we hope *Daed* had a *gut* time. But we did this for you as well as him."

That took her aback. "For me?"

Hannah waved a hand. "You always work so hard planning *familye* gatherings. We knew if we didn't take charge you'd do all in your power to plan the party and still do your work at the Lantzes. We wanted to let you take it easy for once."

Greta chimed in. "I hate to admit that it took both of us to handle what you usually manage with such ease on your own. It gives me a whole new appreciation for how you manage all that you do and have done for so many years."

Martha felt even more guilty for her earlier thoughts. She'd never imagined her *shveshtra* gave much thought to the things she did. It seemed she'd been wrong about quite a bit lately. "The only reason it took two of you," she said, "is because you both have growing families of your own. I only had our own house and *familye* to tend to."

The three girls hugged and then the conversation turned to lighter matters.

Twenty minutes later Martha sat alone on the porch swing. Hannah had joined the *kinner* playing in the yard and Greta had gone back inside.

She closed her eyes for a moment, enjoying the sound of the *kinner*'s laughter and chatter—it was like sweet music to her ears.

Would it be so terrible if after getting her last letter Laban decided the two of them weren't so compatible after all? True, she would miss what might be her last opportunity to have a family of her own. And she would miss being close to Joan again, who she missed terribly.

But staying here would give her an opportunity to see her nieces and nephews grow up. Even if it seemed her *familye* could get along without having her close by, how did she feel about getting along without them?

Perhaps she could even look into the possibility of staying on as nanny to the Lantz *kinner*, who she had grown to love dearly. She opened her eyes and glanced toward the water pump where the men had gathered. How would Asher feel about having her around full-time?

"Do you have a minute? There's something I'd like to speak to you about."

Martha looked up to see her youngest *shveshtah* studying her with an uncertain expression. It was the same expression she'd worn back in the days after their *mamm* had died and she needed advice on something troubling her.

Martha slid over and patted the space beside her. "Of course. What is it?"

Instead of answering her right away, Hannah sat

and looked over at the children playing in the front yard. "Liam is such a sweet, precious little one."

"That he is. And he gets on well with the other little ones."

Hannah nodded but didn't say anything else for a few moments. Finally she turned back to Martha. "As I mentioned earlier, Liam is six years old. He's already started first grade, but of course he went to an *Englisch* school over in Millersburg. I'd like to send him to our Amish school but, even though they begin to speak the *Englisch* language once they start school, I don't know if that's fair to him right now. He's already facing so many changes."

"Did you speak to teacher Sara?" Sara Kauffmann was the teacher at the Amish school.

Hannah shook her head. "Not yet. I hope to speak to her after the church service tomorrow." She gave Martha a questioning look. "Does that mean you think he should go to the Amish school?"

"Not necessarily. What did Vivian have to say about Liam's schooling?"

"She left it up to us whether we put him in an *Englisch* school or an Amish one." Hannah drummed her fingers on the arm of the swing. "It's such a big decision."

Martha squeezed her *shveshtah*'s hand. "But not a life-or-death one. Whatever you decide will work out. Little ones are very resilient, so he will adapt." She raised a brow. "But if you're worried about easing him into this, have you considered homeschooling?"

"Homeschooling?"

"*Jah*. At least for the rest of this school year. It would give you the chance to observe how he's doing and where you think he needs the most help in learning our ways." She gave Hannah's hand a squeeze. "I know you have your bakery business, but since you're working mostly from home now—"

Hannah quickly dismissed that objection. "That's not it. I'd put all of it on hold for Liam's sake if that's what was required. I'm just not sure I'd know how to go about it." She gave her a wistful look. "I just wish you were available. You'd do such a wonderful *gut* job of it."

Martha's heart went out to her *shveshtah*. "I only have four more weeks with the Lantz family—after that I'd be happy to work with Liam. In the meantime I can help you figure out how to get started."

"But—" Hannah looked confused. "I mean, aren't you and Laban Slabaugh corresponding? I assumed once you left the Lantzes you'd be busy planning your future..."

Martha mentally winced. She'd mailed her letter to Laban on Monday. It was now Saturday and she hadn't received a response yet. She wasn't sure what to make of it. Was he still mulling her terms over? Had he been too busy to respond—after all, he'd said he needed to quickly expand his production. Or had he decided the two of them weren't a *gut* match after all and he was simply trying to find a kind way to tell her so?

There was no way of knowing so she merely shrugged. "Laban and I are simply pen pals right now. It remains to be seen if we will ever be more than that." Or even if they'd maintain that relationship beyond his next letter.

Hannah sighed. "Martha, you're always so hard to read when it comes to personal matters."

Martha sat up straighter. "What do you mean by that?"

"Please don't take offense, but you don't share your feelings easily. Like now for instance. I can't tell if you think the state of your relationship is a *gut* thing or a bad thing. I mean, I think you want to find a *mann*, and when I heard about Laban I was wonderful happy for you. But now you speak of the relationship between you, or lack of one, as if you were discussing what you were cooking for dinner."

"I just don't think I need to burden anyone else with my personal troubles or concerns." She mentally winced as she heard the defensiveness in her tone.

But Hannah didn't seem to notice. "After *Mamm* died you worked hard to take her place. You ran the household and took wonderful *gut* care of all of us, *Daed* included. And I don't think any of us ever truly thanked you. And for that I'm sorry."

She took Martha's hand between hers. "But we're all grown up now and you played a big part in seeing that we were ready to move on with our lives. Now you deserve to find your own life and love. If Laban Slabaugh isn't the right man for you, then you need to go out and find the one who is. You deserve to have a home and *familye* of your own." She gave her hand a squeeze. "You deserve to be happy."

Martha felt a lump form in her throat. She was too overwhelmed to say anything but "*Danke*."

Hannah grinned. "Now, all that being said, if you're still available when your time at the Lantzes is up, I will most happily and gratefully accept your help getting Liam ready for school."

"I'd be honored. And in the meantime I'll give you some tips on how to get started on your own."

It was getting more and more difficult to picture herself moving away from Hope's Haven.

* * *

When it was time to leave, Martha went in search of Lottie. She finally found her in the barn with Lady and her puppies. Lottie looked up when she entered but didn't say anything so Martha stooped down beside her. "They're a wriggly bunch, ain't so?"

Lottie nodded. "*Jah*. And they're wonderful cute."

"Do you have a favorite?"

Lottie didn't hesitate. "That one." She pointed to a cream-colored pup with three brown stockings and a brown spot on the tip of its tail. "I call him Trip because he keeps tripping over things."

Was that supposed to be an endearing trait? "How do you know it's a he?"

"He just looks like a boy." She frowned up at Martha. "Do you think it's a girl?"

"Hard to tell from this angle." She stood. "But you need to tell Trip and the others goodbye. It's time for us to head home." And just when had the Lantz place begun to feel more like home than this place?

Lottie stood reluctantly. "Do you think we could come back and visit the puppies again soon?"

"I will certainly speak to your *onkel* Asher and see if we can make that happen." She'd also talk to him about taking one of the pups, preferably Trip, home with them when they were ready to be adopted out. But there was no point in getting Lottie's hopes up just yet.

Chapter 27

That evening, when they were alone on the porch, Asher set his harmonica aside. "The party went well today, ain't so?"

Martha nodded. "It did. *Daed* seemed to really enjoy himself."

"And you? Did you enjoy yourself?"

She gave him a knowing look. "I did. But I had to remind myself a time or two of the lessons you tried to teach me last night."

He grinned. "Then I'm very proud of you for trying. There was so much there to find joy in."

"*Jah.* The program the *kinner* put on was so precious. And having Liam with us was a special blessing."

Asher nodded. "It was *gut* of your *shveshtra* to see that Lottie and the boys were included." Then he crossed his arms. "And the meal was wonderful *gut*."

Martha rolled her eyes. "*Jah, jah*, no one noticed the sweet potatoes were missing." Then her expression softened into a sweet smile. "Hannah and Greta spoke to me separately and made me feel included and needed regardless of my very small contribution to the day's festivities."

"I told you—it's not what you physically contribute, it's your presence and participation that matters to them."

"*Jah*. But I sometimes have trouble remembering that."

He grinned. "I'll be glad to keep reminding you."

She rolled her eyes again, but he saw the way her lips turned up. Rather than responding, however, she changed the subject. "The *kinner* really enjoyed playing with the puppies today, especially Lottie."

He nodded. "*Kinner* and puppies just naturally take to each other, ain't so?"

"In a few weeks, *Daed* and Leah will be looking for new homes for the puppies. I was wondering how you felt about maybe taking one for the *kinner*."

Her question caught him by surprise. "I already have a dog."

"*Jah*, but as you say, Rowdy's your dog. This puppy would be for the *kinner*."

Asher rubbed his chin, not at all convinced. "A puppy is a big responsibility."

"*Jah*. But the best way for them to learn responsibility is for them to be given responsibility, ain't so? And what better way to teach those lessons than with the care of a puppy?"

"You truly think they're ready for all that comes with taking care of a pup?"

"They may need a little guidance and patience, but

I think Lottie is ready and the boys can help and learn from watching her."

He knew when he was beat. "Very well. I just hope you're right. Especially since you won't be around to help with any messes they create."

That statement brought Martha up short.

Lately, whenever she thought of the future she pictured herself here, with the *kinner*. With Asher and Dorcas.

Apparently Asher didn't share that vision.

And why should he? Debra Lynn was the *kinner's* real nanny and would be back soon. And once she returned there was no place for her here.

* * *

The church service the next morning was held at the home of Dorothy and Andrew Wagler, which was a twenty-minute buggy ride from the Lantz home. Which meant getting everyone ready and out the door extra early.

This time there were no falls or other accidents to delay them and they managed to arrive at the Wagler home before everyone lined up to enter.

Once Martha stepped down from the buggy she turned to help the boys climb out. Zach and Zeke were on the ground and she'd just swung Zeb down when she heard herself being hailed.

"Hello, Martha."

She turned and then froze. "Laban." What was he doing here? She tried to collect her scattered thoughts. "*Gut matin.* When did you arrive in Hope's Haven?" She noticed Dorcas gathering the *kinner* and moving away, while Asher studied them a moment then moved off himself.

"Yesterday evening. I'd like to speak to you when you have a moment, but I see everyone is beginning to line up for the service. Perhaps after the lunch?"

"Of course."

What did he have to say to her that would have brought him here in person? She couldn't tell from his tone or demeanor whether it was *gut* news or bad. And now she'd have to wait through the three-hour service and the lunch afterward before she could find out.

Once inside, Martha did her best to focus on the church service but she couldn't help sliding her gaze toward the area across the room where Laban was seated with the other single men of the community. Was it merely chance that had Asher seated next to him? For some reason that left her feeling even more uncomfortable. Not that there was any opportunity for casual conversation between them during the service. And as far as she could tell the two men didn't so much as glance each other's way.

Of course there wasn't any real reason for her to be concerned if they did.

As for her own circumstances, she'd felt herself on the receiving end of more than one curious glance, not the least obvious of which came from her *shveshtra*. For once she was glad they sat with the married women while she sat with the *maidals*. As the service progressed she could feel the stirrings of curiosity in the air. She wasn't sure what was causing more interest—Laban's presence or Hannah and Micah showing up with Liam.

After the service, Martha decided she could be of most use working in the kitchen and letting the other women serve those eating at the tables. She wasn't certain she could endure seeing Laban and not speaking of whatever brought him here. Better to wait until they could speak more or less privately.

But that didn't save her from the other women's curiosity.

Greta was the first to corner her, her expression determined. "What's Laban doing here? Does this mean you two are going to move forward with your courtship?"

Before Martha could form an answer, Hannah was there with her own questions. "Did you know Laban was coming when we saw you yesterday? Why didn't you tell us?"

Martha answered Hannah first. "*Nee*, I didn't know Laban had plans to travel to Hope's Haven until I saw him here this morning."

"But did he say why he's here?" Greta asked impatiently.

"There wasn't time before the service. We're going to speak after lunch." Had the contents of her last letter spurred his impromptu visit? Was he here to break it off with her?

Hannah, however, had a different take on things. "Well, I think he must be here to declare himself. Why else would he come all this way? Oh, this is so romantic."

Martha's stomach was still doing weird flip-flops. She wasn't sure how she felt about his appearance here. Or about the possibility of his declaring himself. If that's what this was.

"How does Asher feel about all this?" Greta eyed her speculatively.

"Why should Asher feel one way or the other?" Hannah looked from one to the other of them in confusion.

Greta waved a hand. "Because he and Martha like each other, of course."

Hannah's eyes widened. "They what?"

Martha gave Greta an exasperated look. "Greta is exaggerating. Asher and I have merely moved past our earlier misunderstandings and are friends now, nothing more." She turned away to refill a lemonade pitcher. "As for why Laban's here, speculation isn't very productive." She handed Greta the pitcher then pointed Hannah to a basket of rolls. "Now, make your-selves useful, please."

After a bit of good-natured grumbling about bossy big *shveshtra*, her younger siblings did as she'd in-structed. At one point during the next hour Martha took the opportunity to speak to Leah about reserving one of the puppies for the Lantz *kinner*. Anything to keep her mind off the upcoming conversation with Laban.

Leah smiled in response. "Of course. Is there a particular one they'd like to have?"

Martha described the one Lottie had dubbed Trip.

"I know just which one you mean. He'll be a good puppy for them to raise." Then Leah sobered. "Are you all right?"

Martha frowned. "Of course. Why would you ask?"

"I'm not blind. I know Laban is here and I'm pretty sure you weren't expecting him. And I see how nervous you are, how you're hiding out here in the kitchen. Do you need someone to talk to?"

She hadn't expected such grace from her *shteef-mamm*. "*Danke.* I'm only nervous because I'm not sure why he came. But I'll be fine once we talk."

Leah patted her arm. "I'm certain you can handle whatever comes. But if you need anything let me know." And with that she moved on.

Martha wasn't sure how much longer it was before everyone had been fed and the kitchen cleaned. But finally it was done. She dried her hands on her apron, then hung it up on a nearby hook. Taking a deep breath, she did her best to control the trembling of her hands as she went in search of Laban.

She didn't have to look far. Laban had apparently been keeping a lookout for her because he was at her side almost immediately. "Would you care to take a stroll with me?"

With a nod from her the two of them set off in the general direction of the open field where the buggies had been parked. Martha allowed Laban to set the pace of their walk and tried to keep her self-consciousness at bay. It didn't help that she felt as if the eyes of every adult present were on them, including Asher's. Especially Asher's.

To forestall whatever Laban had to say as well as break the silence she started talking first. "I hope you had a pleasant trip here yesterday."

"*Jah.* The driver I hired is one I've used before and he's quite professional and safety-conscious."

"And you've found a comfortable place to stay?"

"Joan recommended I stay at the Graber Farm Bed and Breakfast. I've found it quite comfortable."

She missed Joan. In fact she wished her best friend

were here today so they could share their thoughts and concerns, the way they always had before.

But things changed, whether you wanted them to or not.

Then Laban took charge of the conversation, pulling her focus sharply back to the here and now. "I got your letter and I must say it took me back a bit."

Martha immediately forgot about who might be watching. Was he here to admonish her? "Laban, I—"

He held up a hand to stop her, which was just as well because she wasn't certain how she was going to finish that sentence.

"Please, let me finish. After I had a chance to think it over I came to the conclusion that I owed you an apology, one that deserved to be delivered face-to-face. I'm sure I came across as pompous and insufferable."

His apology caught her by surprise.

But he wasn't done. "You were quite right. If you want to learn about my work, either the craft side or the business side or both, I should be accepting, not dismissive."

What had caused this complete about-face from him?

"After all, even Prudence Miller, the young widow who does any cloth work I require, is curious about my work. Why should I answer her questions and not yours?"

Young widow? Martha pushed aside the little pin-prick of curiosity and tried to focus on what he was saying.

"From everything Joan has told me, and what I've learned from what you've told me about yourself, you're exactly the kind of woman I want for a *fraa*.

Not only are you a sensible person, a meticulous housekeeper, and *gut* with *kinner*, but like me you value a relationship built on mutual respect and friendship rather than emotion. Too many other ladies are looking for romantic nonsense." He nodded in satisfaction. "I think the two of us will deal wonderfully *gut* together."

Martha's thoughts were jumbled. What if she wanted just a touch of romantic nonsense after all? Not flowery speeches and over-the-top gestures, of course, but just an acknowledgment that there was a place for love between an engaged couple.

When had her feeling about all this changed? And did that mean she and Laban were not as compatible as she'd thought?

He seemed to be waiting for a response from her but she had no idea what she wanted to say. So while she tried to gather her thoughts she took the conversation off on a tangent. "I appreciate your taking the effort to come all this way to have this discussion."

There was a brief flash of surprise in his eyes. That was obviously not the response he'd been expecting. But to do him credit he quickly schooled his expression into something more polite. "Of course." Then he straightened his shoulders and gave her a direct look. "May I be so bold as to ask what your feelings are toward me at the moment? I obviously don't want to put time into pursuing a relationship with you if you don't desire one with me."

It was a fair question. "To be honest, Laban, I'm not entirely sure. But truthfully, I don't think I love you."

He gave her a what-a-strange-thing-to-say look.

"That's to be expected. We've only been acquainted a few weeks and have only been together in person a couple of hours. I thought we were agreed that what we were looking for was a mutual respect and friendship. Love can grow over time." He furrowed his brow. "Isn't that the kind of arrangement Joan and James have?"

"*Jah.*" She and Joan had had long conversations about the merits of that kind of arrangement over those of a love match so she knew Joan's feelings on the subject. And she thought she'd known hers as well.

"What's caused this sudden change in you? Is it the importance of the step we're about to take?"

About to take? In her mind there was still time to consider. "I'd say the change was more gradual than sudden." She cut him a sidelong glance. "How long do you plan to stay in Hope's Haven? As you say, we haven't spent much time in each other's company. Perhaps if we had more time together it would help clarify things in my mind."

"I can only stay until tomorrow afternoon. After that I need to return to take care of my business. But I have a better idea. Why don't you come to Fredericksburg? You've expressed some curiosity about the town and my business. If you came I could show both to you and you could meet some of my family and friends as well?"

Travel to Fredericksburg?

Why didn't the idea appeal to her more?

Chapter 28

Martha paused for a long moment. To be honest, right now she didn't think seeing the place where Laban lived was likely to change how she felt about this match. The more she thought about it, the more her heart was telling her to end this now.

As if to stem off any objection from her, Laban spoke up again, this time more earnestly. "Don't you owe it to yourself, and to me, to fully explore what your life could be like if we were married? And you could stay with Joan while you were there."

Perhaps he had a point about owing it to the two of them to go this one step further. Before she firmly shut the door on Laban and the life he was offering her, shouldn't she give him the chance to show her his world? Her current feelings could just be a momentary resistance to change.

And the chance to spend time with Joan was an

almost overwhelming temptation. But there were also her obligations here to consider.

She met his gaze. "I can't leave the Lantz *familye* in the lurch, not after I promised to stay the full six weeks. I'll have to help them find someone who could take care of the *kinner* for a few days."

The flash of relief that crossed his expression surprised her. "I'm sure there's someone here who could do that."

Martha nodded. "I already have someone in mind."

Laban smiled. "*Gut.* In the meantime, should we start this getting-better-acquainted business now? I'm ready to answer any questions you have for me."

He made it sound like a task to check off a list. Then again, perhaps it was. Where to start? "You mentioned *familye* and friends. Perhaps you could start by telling me about them. Do you have any *brieder* or *shveshtra*? Are your parents still around?"

"I'm the fourth of seven siblings. Two of my *brieder* and one *shveshtah* are older and two *shveshtra* and one *bruder* are younger. My parents are most definitely still around and Nell and Luke, my youngest *bruder* and *shveshtah,* still live at home with them."

A nice-sized *familye.* "Were any of them at the wedding?"

"*Nee. Mamm* has an eye disease that's caused her to lose most of her vision so she doesn't like to travel very far from home. And of course *Daed* won't leave her. Two of my siblings have new *bopplin* and two others moved to Montana when a new church district was started there."

"It sounds like you are all very close."

"For sure and for certain. *Familye* is important,

ain't so? It's one of the reasons I'd like to start one of my own."

She shied away from responding directly to that statement. "What about your business? How many people do you employ?" That should be a safer topic.

"Right now I have one experienced leatherworker and two apprentices, then there's Prudence, the seamstress I mentioned who does work for me."

She remembered, the young widow.

"But as I said in my letter," he continued, "I need to expand right away. Henry and David, the two apprentices, will be able to step into full-time duties almost immediately. I'll take on two new apprentices and at least one more full-time craftsman if I can find one who's qualified. I think Prudence will be able to handle the increased seamstress workload for now— she's been asking for expanded hours anyway."

Quite impressive plans.

He spread his hands. "And as for the work itself, I'll be very happy to give you a tour of the workshop when you come to Fredericksburg and, if time permits, demonstrate any part of it that catches your interest."

He really was going above and beyond to please her. For just a moment Martha wondered why he wasn't married already. Was it his attitude about "romantic nonsense"? But she brushed that aside and met his gaze. "Do you have any questions for me?"

He rubbed his jaw. "I know you have two younger *shveshtra* who are married and that your *daed* is a widower who recently remarried. What I don't know is why you took this job caring for someone else's *kinner*."

For some reason that question irritated her. "I

thought I explained that in my letter. The nanny broke her arm and the Lantz *familye* needed someone to take her place until she heals."

"*Jah.*" He waved a hand. "But why you?"

What was he trying to get at? "I happened to be the one who brought them the news of Debra Lynn's accident and I offered to help out for a day or two. Then after staying with the *kinner* for a couple of days it just seemed natural that I volunteer to stay until Debra Lynn is able to return to work. After all, I'd just returned from a three-month visit to my cousin, so *Daed* and Leah were used to getting on without me. And it was the neighborly thing to do."

"Commendable."

Something in his tone seemed to indicate otherwise. Or was it just that she felt guilty for not being completely honest about her motives? That she'd taken it on partly to get away from a home that suddenly felt foreign to her.

Laban cleared his throat. "It appears some people are beginning to leave. Perhaps we should return to the group."

With a nod she turned and they started back.

"I'm sorry I won't be able to drive you home this afternoon," he said, "but I arrived here with the Grabers in their buggy. I'll look into renting my own buggy for tomorrow." He kept his gaze focused straight ahead. "Since the goal is for us to get better acquainted, it makes sense for us to actually spend time together while I'm here. Perhaps I can take you out for lunch tomorrow?"

"I can hardly leave my charges for the three hours such an outing would likely take." He had a point, though. And she *had* agreed to give it a good-faith effort. "The *kinner* do go down for a nap right after lunch and I have free time that I can stretch into about an hour and a half. Perhaps you could come by the Lantz home then."

Laban nodded. "*Jah*, I'll be there, for sure and for certain."

She nodded. "The Grabers can provide you with directions."

But would going down this path truly change anything? And what was holding her back? Hadn't Laban just promised to give her exactly what she'd said she wanted? A house and *familye* of her own, the ability to be a part of his work, to be a true helpmeet?

Were her *shveshtra* right—was her desire for certainty keeping her from experiencing true happiness?

Speaking of her *shveshtra*, as soon as she and Laban parted ways a few moments later they were both there, questions coming on top of each other.

"What did he want?"

"Why didn't he tell you he was coming?"

"How long is he staying?"

"Did you make any decisions?"

Martha held up her hands. "Please, enough questions. He's staying until tomorrow afternoon but other than that, our discussion was between Laban and me and it's not something I'm ready to talk about yet. Laban and I still need to learn more about each other and we have some things to work out."

Hannah met Greta's gaze. "It sounds like they haven't ruled out a courtship."

Greta nodded. "So there's still a chance." She glanced Martha's way before returning her gaze to

Hannah. "Unless Martha's decided she wants something different from what Laban has to offer."

Martha had had enough of being spoken of instead of to. "I'm right here, but not for long. I need to check on my charges and see if the Lantzes are ready to return home yet." And lifting her chin she strode away without a backward glance.

Now, to see if her idea for a stand-in while she was away had merit.

* * *

Asher brushed Axel down, hoping the familiar rhythmic motions would help clear his thoughts. Martha and his family had gone inside as soon as they arrived home, leaving him to tend to the horse and buggy. Not that he minded. In fact he was grateful for the chance to be alone with his thoughts.

Laban's arrival had caught him off guard, and he was pretty sure Martha had been taken by surprise as well. But he hadn't been able to tell whether she considered it a *gut* surprise or a bad one.

He'd tried not to stare as Martha walked off with that Laban fellow but he hadn't been able to resist a quick glance or two. Whatever they'd been discussing had left both of them looking quite serious. Interestingly enough, when they parted ways there was no happy glow or triumphant smiles that one would expect if a courtship agreement had been reached. But what else could they possibly have been discussing?

Unfortunately he had no right—or valid reason—to ask her about that discussion so he was still in the dark.

And he didn't like that feeling at all.

Later, when he stepped in the kitchen he saw Martha helping *Oma* get supper ready. He could hear the sound of the *kinner* playing in the living room.

As soon as Martha realized he was there she turned and faced him with an almost defiant look. "As you know, Laban Slabaugh is here in town and he and I have been corresponding since Joan's wedding. He asked to spend time with me tomorrow and I told him he could come over during my free time while the *kinner* are napping. If you prefer, we can go out for a ride in his buggy so as not to disturb anyone here." She relayed the information all in a rush, as if she were worried about interruptions.

Asher tried to read her expression, tried to figure out if her obvious agitation was because she was excited about Laban's upcoming visit or because she was worried about his reaction to it. Did this mean the two of them were ready to commit to each other? Had he already missed his chance?

And why had she picked the *kinner*'s naptime? He'd come to think of it as their time, an hour or so where they could work side by side in his workshop. And she was making progress—she had a real talent, she just needed to allow her creativity to flow a bit more.

Pushing aside those thoughts, he offered what he hoped was a polite smile. "He's welcome to visit you here, for sure and for certain." The words tasted sour as he spoke them.

"*Danke.*" She took a deep breath, her expression giving nothing away. "There's something else. Laban asked me to visit Fredericksburg for a few days. Joan already invited me to come stay with her anytime I want to visit so accommodations wouldn't be a problem."

Asher held himself very still. This had gone much farther than he'd realized if she was planning a visit to Laban's hometown. "I suppose *Oma* and I can handle things here for a few days."

Martha gave him a relieved smile. "Actually, I think I found a solution for that."

Already? Had she been planning this trip for a while? "I'm listening."

"Debra Lynn's younger *shveshtah*, Faith, is available for the four days I plan to be gone."

Four days? That was more than a quick visit.

Martha brushed at her skirt. "I know Faith is young and inexperienced, but she's a *gut* girl and a hard worker. Debra Lynn is also willing to come here with Faith to lend her the direction she'll need. Between the two of them, they should be able to manage quite well."

She *had* been busy. Apparently this trip was very important to her. "That sounds workable but let me think on it."

"Of course. But you understand that I'll need a little time to make arrangements."

He frowned. "What days were you planning to be gone?"

"Debra Lynn and Faith won't be available until Thursday so I thought I'd leave on Thursday morning and return sometime Sunday."

And would she be an engaged woman when she returned?

There was a long pause and it was *Oma* who finally

broke it. "I'm sure Joan will be wonderful happy to see you."

Martha turned to *Oma* with what looked suspiciously like relief. "And I'll enjoy seeing her as well."

Finally Asher nodded. "If those days work for *Oma* then I don't see a reason you shouldn't go ahead and make your plans."

"*Danke.* I'll let Laban know when I see him tomorrow."

With a nod Asher left the kitchen and joined the *kinner* in the living room. How would they take it when Martha left? Had he made a mistake by letting them get so close to her while Debra Lynn was healing?

By letting himself get so close?

Chapter 29

Almost as soon as she'd finished settling the *kinner* down for their naps on Monday, Martha heard the sound of a buggy coming up the drive. She'd tossed and turned all night, still not certain if going to Fredericksburg was the right thing to do. Perhaps this time spent with Laban would help settle her thoughts on the matter.

When she passed through the living room she could hear Asher in the kitchen talking to Dorcas. Why hadn't he gone out to his workshop after lunch as usual?

To her surprise, when she stepped outside to greet Laban, Asher was right behind her. In fact, before Martha could so much as say *gutentag*, Asher stepped forward.

"*Wilkom.* I don't think we've formally met yet." He held out his hand. "I'm Asher Lantz and this is my home."

Was it her imagination or was there something almost territorial in his tone?

Laban accepted the proffered hand and gave it a firm shake, his gaze calculating.

The two men seemed to size each other up for a few moments, then they unclasped hands and Laban turned to Martha. "*Gutentag.* I hope the timing of my arrival is appropriate."

She returned his smile with an added warmth to make up for Asher's brusqueness. "*Jah.* The *kinner* just settled down for their naps."

Asher moved to the horse's head. "I'll lead your horse over to the water trough and then tether her to the fence."

Laban frowned. "I thought Martha and I might go for a drive."

Asher gave an I've-got-this grin. "That's not necessary. You're welcome to visit here. I assure you, you won't be bothered."

Martha decided to speak up before Laban could protest. "I baked some cookies this morning. I thought we could take a platter of those and a pitcher of lemonade out on the front porch where we can talk. If that's okay with you?"

Laban's expression turned indulgent. "*Jah*, that sounds wonderful nice."

Then he turned to Asher. "Before you lead the horse away, let me just get something." He reached back into the buggy and pulled out a large leather-and-fabric satchel, then nodded a dismissal Asher's way.

Firmly turning his back on his host, Laban smiled at Martha.

Martha caught the scowl Asher gave him before she turned her focus back on Laban, who was speaking to her.

"You said in your letter you'd never seen an example of my work so I brought this for you."

She held up her hands in protest. "*Ach*, Laban, I didn't intend—"

He shook his head with an indulgent expression. "Of course you didn't. It's my gift to you." Then, as she took it, "It's intended to be a travel bag but it has other uses as well."

While he watched expectantly she studied the gift. The honey-colored leather was unbelievably soft and the stitchwork impeccable. The fabric portion was a pliable canvas with an embroidered crosshatch pattern. There was a patch of tool work on the leather flap in the outline of a delicate flower. "It's lovely," she said as she brushed her hand across the leather. "Did you create this yourself?"

His chest visibly expanded. "*Danke.* And *jah*, this is my work." Then he waved a hand. "Except for the fabric work, which was done by Prudence."

"You're wonderfully talented." She traced the tool work with her finger. "In a way this is quite similar to what Asher does with his punched tin work."

There was a quick flash of something in Laban's expression but it was there and gone so quickly she wasn't sure it hadn't been her imagination. They walked to the house and when they stepped inside the kitchen, Dorcas was nowhere to be seen. Apparently she and Asher had decided to give her and Laban some semblance of privacy.

"I'll get these," Martha said as she moved to

the platter of cookies on the counter. "Would you mind getting the pitcher of lemonade and those two glasses."

A few minutes later they were both sitting on the porch, a small table between them.

Laban reached for one of the cookies. "Have you decided about visiting Fredericksburg yet?"

"Arrangements have been made for someone to take my place here for four days starting on Thursday," she temporized. "But the more I think about it the more I've come to believe it's unfair to you for me to go through with this trip. I don't think a change of scene will make a difference to how I feel."

He pointed his cookie at her. "I do understand that your coming to Fredericksburg doesn't signify any sort of commitment on your part so there's no chance of any misunderstanding." He gave her a probing look. "That being said, I still think you should go ahead with the trip. It's the only way for you to give our possible future together a fair chance."

Martha smothered a sigh. He seemed so determined. "Then I'll make the trip. But it will be as much to visit Joan as to see your world." She poured them each a glass of the lemonade. "You can let Joan know when I'll arrive."

Laban's expression held a note of relief. Had he actually been worried beneath his calm, determined exterior? "That's *gut*. I can show you around both the town and my workshop while you're there. And when I can't be with you, you can have the nice visit with Joan you want."

"I look forward to seeing Fredericksburg." And that was true. "Both you and Joan have described it as a fine place to live." She leaned forward. "But I want to be clear one more time that I'm just doing this to prove to both of us I made every effort."

Laban seemed to ignore all but the first part of her statement. "I think you'll like what you see." He took another cookie. "If you'll allow me, I can make arrangements with my driver to pick you up here Thursday morning so you know you're riding with someone who knows me and knows Fredericksburg."

Taking a deep breath, she nodded. She was making this trip primarily to visit Joan, she told herself again. Talking through her jumbled feelings with her best friend would help her untangle them.

* * *

For Martha, the next three days were filled with a feeling of hurry up and wait.

She still joined Asher in his workshop while the *kinner* napped and on the front porch before retiring in the evenings. But the closeness she'd felt before seemed to have evaporated. Their interactions were still friendly enough, but there was something missing, something it was difficult to pinpoint but that was real all the same.

Tuesday afternoon she finished the piece Asher had designed the pattern for. It wasn't as *gut* as his work of course, but she was happy with the results all the same.

Asher, too, seemed pleased with it. "This is very *gut*. I'll make a frame for it when I come back from town tomorrow and place it with Charity on my trip next week if you like."

"*Danke*, I'd like to have it framed. But I haven't decided if I want to sell it or not. I may want to keep it for myself."

The smile he gave her had a touch of the old warmth to it. "Of course. You want it as a memento."

"Perhaps. I haven't decided yet."

"Then I'll set it aside until you make up your mind. It'll be here for you when you return." And then his expression shuttered as if he'd remembered something.

When she told the *kinner* she was taking a trip they were upset, even after she reassured them that she'd only be gone for four days.

"But four days is a long time," Lottie complained while her *brieder* nodded emphatically. "What will we do until then?"

"Debra Lynn and her *shveshtah* Faith will be here to take care of you. You all remember Debra Lynn, don't you?"

"*Jah.* But she doesn't tell us stories or tuck us in at night the way you do."

"But I'm sure there are lots of things she does better than me. And remember I said her *shveshtah* was coming too. That means you'll have two nannies instead of just one."

The *kinner* didn't seem appeased by that and Martha had to assure them several more times that she would only be gone for four days before they finally settled down.

When Thursday morning finally arrived she still wasn't sure she was doing the right thing in making this trip. But feeling she was committed, she climbed into the car Laban had arranged for her and settled back for the forty-or-so-minute ride to Joan's house.

Chapter 30

A ch, Martha, it's wonderful *gut* to see you again."
Joan had rushed out to greet her almost before the car
came to a stop.

"And you too." Martha gave her friend an enthusiastic hug. She hadn't realized just how much she
missed Joan until she saw her smiling face again.

"I know it's only been a few weeks but it feels like
so much longer since we had a *gut* visit." Joan led the
way into the house. "James is in town picking up some
horse feed and he took Hilda with him so we could
have a nice visit."

"That was wonderful considerate of him."

Joan smiled fondly. "He's a *gut* man." Then she
waved toward the staircase. "Let me show you to your
room so you can unpack your things and then we can
have a nice long chat."

Joan led her to a room at the top of the stairs and
then left her there to unpack and freshen up.

As Martha put her things away she wondered just how much she should tell her friend. Would Joan be upset to learn she didn't want to court James's cousin?

Ten minutes later she was back in the kitchen, sitting at the table across from Joan. They each had a cup of hot tea and a slice of pie Joan had baked this morning.

"This is wonderful *gut* cherry pie, for sure and for certain."

"*Danke.* I remembered cherry is your favorite."

"I like your home. It has a comfortable, lovingly kept feel to it."

"It was built by James's *onkel* and has been in his family for thirty years." She forked up another bite of pie. "Later I'll give you a tour of the outside. There's a nice garden area and the outbuildings are all well maintained."

There was an understandable pride in Joan's voice.

"By the way, Laban told James he wanted to give you time to settle in and for the two of us to catch up so you won't see him until he joins us for supper tonight. But I understand he plans to spend the day with you tomorrow."

Martha nodded. "That's very considerate of him." Then she waved toward the sideboard. "That's a lovely pierced tin lamp. Did Asher make it for you?"

Joan looked over her shoulder. "*Jah.* Has he showed you his work?"

"*Jah.* I didn't know he did such special work until I started as the *kinner*'s nanny."

"You didn't know because he's so modest about his work. I don't think he realizes how talented he is."

Martha nodded. "He is that, for sure and for certain."

Joan leaned forward. "But enough about Asher. How's your correspondence with Laban going? I know he visited Hope's Haven last weekend and you're here now." She gave her a sly look. "Does that mean things are going well?"

Martha didn't respond for a moment, then she met her friend's gaze. "Are you happy with your new life here?"

Joan's brows rose at the abrupt change of subject, but she nodded. "I am. There are times when I miss my *familye* and friends back in Hope's Haven, of course. But I like Fredericksburg and James's *familye* and friends have been very welcoming and accepting."

"That's *gut*. But what I meant was, are you happy with your *married* life?"

Martha winced when she saw Joan's frown. "I'm sorry. I had no right to ask such a personal question." She stood up. "Why don't we take a walk outside so you can show me around like you offered earlier."

Joan stood as well. "Of course."

As they stepped outside Martha mentally took herself to task. There was a limit to how far you should pry, even with your best friend.

Joan cleared her throat. "I'm sorry, I didn't mean to push back that way, you just caught me by surprise. I can understand why you'd want to ask such questions if you're thinking about taking such a step yourself."

Martha rushed to reassure her. "You don't have to—"

But Joan ignored the interruption. "We are best friends, we've always felt free to ask and tell each other anything. That shouldn't change now. So *jah*, I do like my life as James's *fraa*. I finally have my own home, I have a sweet little girl to raise and someday, if *Gotte* is willing, I'll have several more *kinner* to love and raise alongside her." Her smile was open and warm. "It's the kind of life I've always hoped to have."

Encouraged by Joan's openness, Martha pressed on. "But you and James are not in love."

Her friend shrugged. "You know I've never been much of a romantic. James and I are both satisfied with our arrangement and we get along well together."

"Still, do you sometimes wonder if you should have held out for a love match?"

Joan waved a hand. "I'm not sure it would have made me any happier than I am now. And who knows, in time what James and I have could grow into something more than friendship." She eyed Martha curiously. "Why? Are you having second thoughts about Laban?"

Martha hesitated for a long moment. But Joan had been open with her and she *had* come here to talk to her friend, so she gathered her courage and nodded. "I can't continue with this courtship, if that's even what this is."

Joan stopped in her tracks and turned to face her. "So, it turns out you're not willing to settle for a merely practical arrangement after all."

"Apparently not." Martha felt almost apologetic making that admission.

Then Joan's eyes narrowed. "Martha Eicher, have you actually fallen in love with someone else?"

That was something she was definitely not ready to talk about, not even with her best friend. "It doesn't matter." She waved a hand. "That's not what this is about. It just means I've discovered I can't marry without love, even if it means I become a spinster."

"Oh, I disagree, it absolutely does matter. Who is he? And when did you find time to meet someone? Haven't you been working as nanny to *Aenti* Dorcas's *kins-kinnah*?"

Martha brushed at her skirt and looked off in the distance. "Is that the garden plot you mentioned? I agree, it's ideally situated."

But Joan refused to be distracted. "Why won't you—" Then her eyes widened. "*Ach du lieva*, is it Asher?" Her expression changed to one of certainty. "You've fallen in love with my cousin."

Martha groaned. Apparently she wasn't as good at hiding her feelings as she'd hoped. "I told you it didn't matter. A match between me and Asher would be inappropriate."

Joan crossed her arms. "Why would it be inappropriate?"

Was Joan really so oblivious? "He's four years younger than I am. And I was also his teacher for two years."

"I don't see why his age should stop you. And being his teacher might have mattered back then but it hardly has any bearing now." She gave Martha a pointed look. "Those are just excuses you're using because you're scared to face your feelings."

"All that may be true, but he doesn't feel the same for me."

"You're sure of that? Have you told him how you feel, given him a chance to tell you how he feels in return?"

"Of course not." Just the idea of confessing such a thing to Asher made her stomach flutter.

But Joan was shaking her head in disapproval. "*Ach,*

Martha, when are you going to learn to take chances? You weren't like that when we were scholars. Remember how adventurous we were?"

"We're not *kinner* any longer. Today we have responsibilities and know that taking chances carries consequences."

"But that doesn't mean some chances aren't worth taking all the same." Joan touched Martha's arm briefly. "Ever since your *mamm* died you've been playing it safe. Doing so might make you feel more in control, but think of all you miss out on."

Was that how Joan saw her? More troubling was the thought that she might be right.

Joan surprised her by embracing her in a bear hug. "You and Asher. I think it's *wunderbaar*! You two will make each other so happy."

Hadn't Joan paid attention to anything she said? "I told you, Asher doesn't—"

"Don't be *verrict*. Of course he loves you—how could he not?" She tapped her chin. "Now we must get you back to Hope's Haven so the two of you can declare yourselves to each other."

Martha rolled her eyes. "I thought you weren't a romantic."

Joan waved a hand dismissively. "I said I didn't need romance in my life. That doesn't mean I don't enjoy experiencing it vicariously in someone else's life." She started walking again. "But first we have to figure out what to do about Laban."

" 'We'?"

"Of course. I feel partly responsible for getting you into this situation, so now I shall help you get out of it."

Martha rubbed her upper arms. "*Danke.* But I've already told him that I don't think a match between us will work out. It was he who insisted I come here so that I would get a true picture of what I'd be giving up."

"*Gut*—that means the hard part is over. So you allow him to show you around tomorrow and if nothing you see changes your mind, then you tell him, in no uncertain terms, that you still feel the two of you won't work together and you'd like to return home. And don't worry, James will make sure you have a driver."

"How will James feel about all this? Laban is his cousin after all."

"You leave James to me. And trust me, he'll be okay."

Martha already felt better after only twenty minutes in her friend's company. But was Joan correct—was there truly a future for her and Asher together?

* * *

That evening at supper Laban and James spent a great deal of time speaking to each other. But he was solicitous with Martha and she felt his eyes on her often.

At the end of the meal, Martha walked Laban out as far as the front porch.

"Is there anything specific you'd like to see or visit tomorrow?" he asked "Or will you allow me to set our itinerary?"

Martha had decided she owed it to Laban to make a good-faith effort to learn all she could about him and his life. "At some point I would like to see your workshop and perhaps some of your favorite places."

Laban's smile was confident. "*Jah*, we can definitely do that. And my *mamm* would like for you to have lunch with us tomorrow as well."

Martha felt a stab of conscience. "Do you think that's a *gut* idea? Considering what I told you back in Hope's Haven about me feeling this match won't go forward, I mean? I don't want her to assume anything other than friendship between us."

"She knows you're here and that we've been corresponding. I haven't told her anything beyond that. But it would be rude to refuse her invitation, ain't so?"

"Of course. I just didn't want to set any false expectations."

"Let me worry about that." And with that he turned and headed for his buggy.

The next day was very full. Laban pulled out all the stops in showing her everything there was to love about his life in Fredericksburg.

They visited his workshop, where he showed her all aspects of his business. She met the other workers there and was very impressed with the size of his operation and the efficiency of his setup. He answered every question she asked and even demonstrated some of the techniques that went into making his most popular offerings.

The workshop was in an outbuilding on his place so Laban also showed her his home, a comfortable-looking two-story with a wraparound porch and a large kitchen. If she'd been looking to find fault with it she was disappointed.

When they finally left he drove by a field to show her his favorite "thinking spot," a fallen tree trunk near a grouping of black raspberry bushes.

Lunch with his parents and two younger siblings would have been nice if she hadn't felt they were all evaluating her as a potential spouse for Laban.

By the time Laban had given her a tour of the countryside and turned the buggy to take her back to Joan's, Martha knew without a doubt that, nice as this was, her future lay elsewhere.

"Tomorrow I have some business to take care of first thing in the morning," Laban said. "But then I thought I'd take you into town for lunch and afterward we can visit some of the shops and craft stores if you like."

"*Nee.*"

Laban looked taken aback at that. "If you'd prefer to see or do something else, just tell me what it is."

Martha took a deep breath. "Laban, you're a *gut* man, you've agreed to all of my requests and you've been nothing but patient and kind since I arrived yesterday. You've been wonderful patient with me today. Joan was right when she said you were exactly the kind of man I described when she asked me what I wanted in a *mann.*"

His expression had taken on a resigned, defeated look. "But it's still not enough."

"I'm so sorry. I can't explain my reasons, even to myself, but it would be unfair to you if we were to continue pursuing any kind of relationship beyond friendship."

Laban sighed. "I'm disappointed, but I can't say I'm surprised."

"Oh?"

"It was obvious when I saw you back in Hope's Haven, as was the reason, even if I didn't want to believe it."

"I tried to tell you."

"*Jah.* Even though you said you weren't looking for a romantic relationship, that wasn't true, was it? Your heart already belongs to someone else."

Was she so transparent that even Laban, a near stranger despite their correspondence, could see what was in her heart?

"Laban, do you mind if I ask you a question?"

"It depends on the question," he said with a wary look.

"Why were you so set on me seeing this through? I mean, why didn't you just give up and look elsewhere when I told you I didn't think we would work together?"

He flicked the reins and looked straight ahead, not responding immediately. The silence drew out so long she tried to withdraw the question. "I'm sorry. You don't have to—"

"I don't like to admit I failed at anything," he said abruptly. He cut her a miserable look. "And your rejecting me felt like a failure."

"Oh, Laban, it wasn't your failure, it was mine. And I think once you accept that, you'll find someone who deserves you more than I do. And that someone could be right under your nose." She hadn't missed the looks the "young widow Prudence Miller" had given the two of them in the workshop this morning. Or the fact that every time he'd mentioned her earlier his face had taken on an appreciative light.

He frowned. "What do you mean?"

"It's just a feeling I have."

By this time they'd arrived back at Joan's house.

"I assume you'll be returning to Hope's Haven tomorrow."

"*Jah.*"

"Then I suppose this is goodbye."

"Goodbye, Laban." Martha stepped down from the buggy then smiled back up at him. "I wish you well, wherever life leads you. And please thank your *mamm* again for the lovely meal she prepared today and for making me feel so welcome."

Then she turned and headed into the house. Now to figure out what she'd say to Asher when she returned tomorrow.

Chapter 31

If anything, the forty-minute drive to Hope's Haven the next morning was even more anxiety-filled than the drive to Fredericksburg on Thursday. Joan had been insistent that she absolutely must tell Asher how she felt as soon as she got back, and last night it had made sense. But now, in the light of day and with the moment of truth fast approaching, she was no longer certain it was a *gut* idea.

What if he didn't feel the same? That would make the three weeks she had left on her time as nanny awkward for sure and for certain. Perhaps it would just be best to wait until her time here was up to say anything. If even then.

Much too soon the car was turning into the Lantzes' drive.

When the car pulled to a stop, Rowdy was the only one who came out to greet her. She paid the driver then carried her bag into the house.

When she stepped inside she found Dorcas at the stove.

"*Ach*, Martha, *wilkom* back. I'm sorry I didn't come out to greet you but I had to keep stirring this gravy so it wouldn't burn." Then she gave her a concerned look. "You're back a day early. I hope you didn't run into problems."

"*Nee.* I just finished my business there sooner than expected." She looked around. "Where are the *kinner*? It's not nap time yet."

"Debra Lynn and Faith took them out for a buggy ride." She gave Martha a knowing look. "And Asher is out in his workshop. Perhaps you should let him know you're home."

Martha nodded. "As soon as I put my things away."

Five minutes later Martha headed for Asher's workshop, still not sure what she'd say to him.

She paused in the workshop doorway, watching him work, waiting for him to notice her, enjoying the sight of his broad back, the way his hair curled at the nape of his neck, the sure movements of his arms as he swung the hammer.

But when he didn't turn around after a few minutes, she frowned uncertainly. Where was that sixth sense he'd always seemed to have before? Finally she cleared her throat. "*Gutentag*, Asher."

"You're back a day early," he said without turning.

Was something wrong? "*Jah.* I'd accomplished what I went there for so there was no reason to stay longer."

"Then I assume you and Laban settled matters between you."

Of course he'd know why she went. "We did."

She smiled, feeling a sense of satisfaction that she'd finally brought things to an end in as unconfrontational manner as possible.

"That's *gut*. And I have some news as well."

Why did he sound so formal? Was the news bad?

He finally turned and faced her with his arms crossed. "I've noticed the *kinner* have begun to form an attachment to you, a much faster and much stronger attachment than what I'd anticipated when you first arrived."

So far it didn't sound like bad news. She gave him a warm look. "I've grown to love them dearly as well. In fact I missed them quite a bit while I was away."

He frowned. "Surely you can see that when you finally leave us that attachment will be a problem for all involved."

How did she tell him she didn't want to leave? "I—"

He didn't let her finish. "So I've decided it's best we don't draw this out."

His tone was giving her an unsettled feeling. "What do you mean?"

He turned his gaze away, focusing back on his work. "Forgive me if I keep working on this panel but this order is due to Noah on Wednesday and it's intricate, time-consuming work."

She managed to utter a fairly calm "of course" before he continued.

"I spoke to Debra Lynn yesterday. And even though she's not yet healed enough to take care of the *kinner* on her own, she and Faith have been working well together. They've agreed to continue this way until Debra Lynn is fully healed and can handle things on her own."

Martha felt as if she'd been kicked by a mule.
"You're letting me go?"

He waved a hand. "It was always the plan for
you to leave us in six weeks. I'm just seeing that it
happens sooner rather than later. And this seems a *gut*
time. You were gone for three days so the *kinner* are
already growing used to you being absent from their
lives. They can go back to looking to Debra Lynn for
their day-to-day care, and you can get on with your
own life and plans."

Martha held herself together by sheer force of
will. Joan had obviously been wrong—Asher had no
feelings for her besides gratitude and a neighborly
goodwill. "And this is what you want?"

"*Jah.*" He gave her a challenging look. "Don't you?"

Apparently her crumbling heart wasn't obvious to
him. So she gave a short nod and lifted her chin. "I'll
pack up and be ready to leave within the hour." She
paused a moment. "If it's all right with you, I'd like to
be the one to tell the *kinner.*"

He nodded.

Feeling there was nothing left to say to him, Martha
turned and headed back to the house.

Pausing only long enough to nod to Dorcas, she
headed straight for her room—she supposed Asher
would turn it back into his office now—and quickly
packed up her things. The puzzles and books that
belonged to her *shveshtra*'s *kinner* were in the living
room—she'd retrieve them later.

When she returned to the kitchen, the *kinner*, as well
as their two caretakers, had joined Dorcas there.

"Martha!" Lottie jumped up from her seat and ran
to hug Martha around the legs. "You're back."

The boys were right behind, adding their own greetings and raising their arms for hugs.

"It seems you were missed," Debra Lynn said with a smile. Then she cocked her head to one side. "Have you talked to Asher yet?"

"I have, and don't worry, the job is all yours and Faith's."

"So you're leaving us." Dorcas's brows drew down in disapproval.

"*Jah*." Martha sat at the table and drew the *kinner* to her. "There's no reason for me to stay now."

"You're leaving again?" Lottie's voice reflected dismay. "But you just got back. And you promised."

"I know, *liebchen*, but I only promised that I'd be back. It's time for me to return to my own home now."

"Don't you like being with us anymore?" The forlorn note in Zeb's voice nearly broke her heart.

"Of course I do. I love all of you very, very much. But you have Debra Lynn and Faith to look out for you now and I'd just be in the way here. Besides, I'll see you at church services and other gatherings for sure and for certain. In fact, I expect each of you to come find me when it's church Sunday. Do you promise?"

When they all nodded, she stood. "Now, I need to hitch Cinders to the buggy. Who wants to help me with that?"

Before they could respond Asher stepped inside. "I was just coming to tell you that I have your buggy all hitched up for you."

He was obviously in a hurry for her to leave.

He turned to his niece and nephews. "Martha brought a few puzzles and books with her when she came that are still in the living room, ain't so? Why don't you fetch them for her?"

And he obviously didn't want to leave her with an excuse to return. Which was okay by her.

As Martha directed Cinders down the drive a few minutes later she felt numb. Not only was she going back to the life she'd left at home a few short weeks ago, but she had the added burden of having fallen in love with a man who seemed to want nothing to do with her.

She couldn't return to her *daed*'s house, not right away. She needed some time to think, a place where she could be alone while she tried to figure out what now.

She finally pulled the buggy to a stop next to a wooded patch that bordered the lane. She tied the reins to a sapling then walked a short way until she felt hidden from the road.

Then she slid down to sit with her back against a tree and let loose the sobs that had been clogging her throat since she left the Lantz place.

Chapter 32

Asher watched Martha's buggy as it moved down the drive, away from his home. Away from him.

When it turned onto the country lane and out of sight he headed back to his workshop. Sending her away had been one of the hardest things he'd ever had to do. But better he do it than have her here while she made plans to wed another man. The smile he'd heard in her voice when she talked of settling matters with Laban had hit him like a knife.

But her feelings for Laban obviously hadn't lessened her affection for the *kinner.* He'd overheard what she told them there in the kitchen. It had been sweet and kind.

Of course she'd had no such words for him. Why would she when her future was intertwined with Laban's now?

He stepped inside the workshop and then paused.

He wasn't in the right frame of mind to focus on his work.

Turning on his heel, he headed for the toolshed. There were several fence posts near the hayfield that could use replacing. That was just the kind of labor-intensive, mindless activity he needed right now.

* * *

On Wednesday Asher made a detour on his way into town. He'd left before lunch today so he could take care of some long-delayed business.

There was still a deep ache inside when he thought of Martha marrying Laban, a sliver of his heart that he felt would always feel the pain. But he wasn't going to let it cripple him. There were lessons he'd learned these past few weeks, truths she'd helped him see, and it was time he acted on them. Starting right now.

He pulled his buggy up in front of the home he'd leased to Daniel Mast.

Twenty minutes later he and Daniel were shaking hands while Marylou looked on with a broad smile.

"We'll hammer out all the details in the next few days," Asher said. "But for now I just wanted you two to know I'm ready to sell the place and I can't think of a better *familye* to sell it to."

"You've made us wonderful happy," Marylou said. "We really love this place."

Asher noticed that as she spoke she placed her hand over her stomach in what was almost certainly an unconscious gesture. Was the couple expecting? Was that why they were eager to purchase a home of their own?

As he set the buggy in motion again his thoughts turned back to Martha, not that she was very far from his thoughts these days. She would appreciate the gesture he'd made today and understand what it meant. It was a shame he'd never have the chance to tell her himself.

Yesterday *Oma* had received a long newsy letter from Ephron, the first they'd heard from him since the Christmas card they'd received back in December. Among other things he'd declared his intention to come visit for Mother's Day. He now suspected he knew just why Martha had written to him.

He'd dismissed her four long days ago and he hadn't seen or spoken to her since. It was even longer since they'd had any kind of meaningful interaction because she'd been in Fredericksburg three days before that. Missing her left him with an almost physical ache.

Strange now to think that before she started work as the *kinner*'s nanny she hadn't been in his life in twelve years. And now he couldn't get used to the idea that he'd never again see her smiling face in his kitchen in the mornings, never again hear her read stories to the *kinner* in the evenings, never again have her by his side taking a simple joy in her attempts to create punched tin art.

Never again end his day with those moments of warm companionship on the front porch.

When she married Laban and moved to Fredericksburg he wouldn't even see her at Sunday services. Would that make things easier or more difficult?

Would things have turned out differently if he'd spoken up about how he felt before Laban made his surprise visit? Why had he waited?

Then he straightened. Who's to say it was too late? He could speak up now, tell her how he felt. It might not change the outcome but at least he wouldn't have to live with the burden of wondering what-if.

Fifteen minutes later Asher knocked impatiently on the freight entrance to the Stoll Woodworking Shop. Andrew Wagler opened the door and stepped aside to let Asher enter with his work.

"You're early," Andrew said. "Noah's up in his office." He waved to a nearby worktable. "Set your stuff over there and I'll get him."

But Asher tried to stop him. "That's all right, I don't want to interrupt him. I'll leave the panels here and Noah can look at them when he has time. Tell him we'll settle up next week." Now that Asher had decided to talk to Martha, he was impatient to be on his way.

But Andrew merely waved and continued on his way. "He won't mind and I know he wants to see what you brought in." And before Asher could say anything else he was off.

While Asher waited impatiently, he tried to decide if he'd stop at the Eicher place when he left here or if he'd take some time to plan out what he wanted to say. He had a feeling he'd only get one shot at this.

To Asher's relief, it was only a few minutes before Andrew returned with Noah beside him. With a brief greeting for Asher the cabinetmaker turned to study the panels Asher had placed on the worktable.

Asher frowned. Did he detect a stiffness in Noah's attitude? What was wrong? Did it have anything to do with Martha's upcoming nuptials?

Finally Noah leaned back with a nod, recapturing Asher's attention. "These are all acceptable." He signaled to Andrew who came over and collected the panels.

Then Noah turned back to Asher as he pulled a checkbook and pen from a nearby drawer. "I assume these are still at the agreed-upon rate?"

Asher nodded, more sure than ever that something was wrong. No easy smile, no offer of a cup of coffee. Something was definitely off. When Noah handed him his payment, Asher decided to be direct. "Have I done something to offend you?"

Noah drew himself up with a glower. "*Jah.* I find your behavior toward Martha, a very *gut* woman who is also the *shveshtah* of my *fraa*, quite offensive."

Asher felt as if Noah had punched him. "My behavior?"

If anything his glower deepened. "You kicked her out of your home with very little notice and even less explanation, leaving her to feel as if she'd done something wrong. What would you call that if not dishonorable and shameful."

Asher felt himself getting defensive. "I didn't kick Martha out. As I told her, I let her go so she could get on with her life."

"That's certainly not much of an explanation." He crossed his arms. "And did you give her a chance to say whether or not she wanted to 'get on with her life'?"

Asher rubbed the back of his neck, uncomfortable under Noah's hard stare. Had he really hurt Martha's feelings? He'd have an even steeper hill to climb when he spoke to her than he'd imagined.

"I just figured she'd want the time to begin planning her wedding."

He saw something flicker in Noah's eyes but the man was harder to read than any other person he knew.

"You figured?" Noah stood straighter. "Again, did you do Martha the courtesy of discussing it with her?"

"*Nee*, but I intend to correct that. In fact there are a few things I'm planning to discuss with her when I leave here."

"*Gut*." Noah finally seemed to unbend a little. "And I suggest you don't make the mistake of doing all the talking. Give her a chance to speak as well."

"I'll keep that in mind." He straightened. "Now, if we're done here, I have someplace to be."

And without a backward glance Asher headed for the door. Time to speak to Martha.

Chapter 33

Martha smiled down at Liam as he recited the word list she'd given him in their language. One of the benefits of moving back home was that she now had time to work with Hannah's foster son. He was a bright, courteous boy who was somewhat withdrawn. But he worked hard and had already wormed his way into her heart.

She had Hannah working with them as well with the hope that her *shveshtah* could eventually take over. But to be honest, if Liam continued doing as well as he was now, she would recommend that Liam actually go to school with the other *kinner* for the last few weeks of the school year.

As she worked with Liam her thoughts often turned to Lottie. Had Asher made sure to continue to give the little girl opportunities to push herself? She knew Asher was friends with Noah so hopefully he would continue to bring the *familye*s together to give the *kinner* opportunities to get together again. The little ones shouldn't be penalized just because she was no longer part of their lives.

Which reminded her, there was something she owed those four little *lamm*s. And since today was Wednesday, the coast should be clear for her to make the delivery.

Later as she ate lunch with her *daed* and Leah, she conversed easily about Liam's progress, about how Grace was learning new things on an almost daily basis and Leah's plans to make new curtains for the kitchen. Martha had come to terms with her new role in this house and felt totally at peace with how Leah was running things. Now that she'd let go of her sense of outraged lady of the house, she and Leah had formed a close friendship.

Martha didn't linger over the meal. As soon as she finished eating, she turned to Leah. "If you don't mind, I'd like to deliver one of Lady's puppies to the Lantz *kinner* this afternoon."

Leah and her *daed* glanced at each other in concern. She hadn't talked to either of them about what had happened with Laban or with Noah but she had the feeling that they'd guessed at least a portion of it.

Then Leah nodded. "Of course. The puppies have been ready to be weaned for a week or so now. Would you like some company? I wouldn't mind a visit with Dorcas."

Martha gave her a grateful look but shook her head. "*Danke*, but I need to do this myself." She pasted on a reassuring smile. "And don't worry, Asher always goes to town on Wednesday afternoons." Not that she planned to hide from Asher. She just wanted to make things as comfortable as possible for his *familye*.

"If you want to go on now, I can take care of cleaning the kitchen."

"There's no rush. If I arrive too early the *kinner* will still be down for their naps."

An hour later Martha climbed out of her buggy and turned to retrieve the wooden crate that held Trip. She carried the crate to the front porch and set it there while she knocked on the door.

Dorcas opened the door and her expression blossomed into a wide smile. "Martha, *kum* in." She moved aside. "You don't need to knock, you're like *familye*."

Martha stepped inside. "*Gutentag*. I hope you're well."

"Very well, *danke*. It's so *gut* to see you again." Then she gave Martha a direct look. "If you're here to see Asher, he's in town right now."

Martha shook her head. "Actually, I came to see the *kinner*. I brought their puppy. Are they up from their naps yet?"

"Not yet, but they should be up soon. Let's go in the kitchen and have a cup of tea and some pie while we wait."

"That's not necess—"

"I insist. I want to hear all about what you've been doing since you left us."

Dorcas made it sound like leaving had been her idea. But Asher's *grossmammi* had already turned and headed to the kitchen so Martha had no choice but to follow.

There was already a kettle on the stove so Dorcas poured hot water in two cups and added tea. While the brew steeped she retrieved honey and cream then joined Martha at the table.

Before Dorcas could bring Asher up again, Martha spoke. "Where are Debra Lynn and Faith?"

"They like to rest while the little ones are napping. They use a room upstairs."

The two women chatted about a number of inconsequential things for ten minutes before they were interrupted. "Martha! You came back." Lottie rushed into the room and threw her arms around Martha.

Martha encircled the girl in a bear hug, savoring the familiar scent and feel of her. She'd missed this the past several days. "*Gutentag*, sweet *lamm*. I'm happy to see you too."

Lottie looked up to meet her gaze. "Are you going to stay?"

"*Nee*, I'm just here for a visit."

Before either of them could say more there were sounds of the boys stirring.

Martha smiled at Lottie. "Go get your *brieder*. I have a surprise for you all."

With a nod, Lottie raced from the room. Before the *kinner* returned Debra Lynn and Faith came downstairs.

Greetings were exchanged and then all four of Martha's former charges were back in the room.

"Lottie says you brought us a surprise," Zach declared.

"I did. And I left it out on the front porch. Shall we take a look?"

Martha led the way to the porch and as soon as the *kinner* stepped outside, Lottie rushed forward. "Trip! It's Trip." She knelt down by the crate and put her fingers down for the pup to sniff. As her *brieder* crowded round she glanced back at Martha. "Does this mean we can keep him?"

"You can. But only if you promise to take very *gut* care of him, even when it gets messy and he's trouble."

"I promise," the girl said solemnly.

"We promise too," Zach said quickly. And both his *brieder* nodded agreement.

"Can I take him out of the box?"

"*Jah*, but be gentle."

With a nod, Lottie turned and gingerly lifted the dog from his crate.

They let Trip run loose on the porch and Martha smiled as the *kinner* enjoyed the animal's antics. She also noticed that Lottie kept a close eye that the pup didn't get too close to the edge of the porch.

Rowdy came up to check things out, and Martha kept a close watch on the older dog.

At the sound of a buggy, though, Martha looked up and froze. What was Asher doing home so soon? She wasn't ready to face him just yet.

She stood and brushed at her skirt. "I believe it's time for me to be getting back home."

The *kinner* immediately crowded around to try to get her to stay longer. But she smiled down at them as she shook her head. "I really do need to go. You all take *gut* care of Trip and I'll be back for another visit soon."

Dorcas met her gaze. "I never took you for a coward."

Martha's cheeks warmed as she shifted uncomfortably. "He doesn't want me here," she answered in the same quiet tone. Then with a nod she headed for her buggy.

Chapter 34

Asher couldn't believe his luck, Martha was still here. He'd stopped at her *daed*'s place first only to discover she wasn't there. When pressed, Isaac had told him that she'd gone to his place to deliver the puppy. From the man's stone-faced demeanor, he apparently had the same opinion of Asher's actions as Noah had.

He'd pushed Axel to go as fast as safely possible in the hopes he'd arrive home before she left, and from the looks of things he'd barely made it.

Or was she leaving because she'd seen him arrive?

He moved to intercept her and she met his gaze with a defiant look. "There's no need for you to worry. I just came by to drop off the puppy. I'm leaving now."

Not an auspicious start. "Don't go. I'd like to speak to you." He mentally winced. "Actually I'd like to speak *with* you."

"About what?"

If she had hurt feelings he sure couldn't tell it. "First there's the matter of the apology I owe you."

That got her attention. "Apology?"

"*Jah.* When you returned from Fredericksburg I sent you away without taking the time to discuss with you all the reasons I thought it was a *gut* idea or giving you the opportunity to give me your thoughts on the matter." He drew his shoulders back. "And for all of that and any hurt I might have caused you, I sincerely apologize."

She nodded. "Apology accepted." But he couldn't see any softening or warmth in her expression. "Now, if you'll excuse me, I should be getting home."

"Wait, there's more I want to say." He kept his gaze focused on Martha but he was peripherally aware that *Oma* had gathered the *kinner* and was ushering them back inside.

Martha didn't say anything, but neither did she make a move to leave. Taking some heart from that, he waved a hand toward the open field past the barn. "Would you mind if we walked while we talk?" What he had to say might come easier if they weren't standing in this face-to-face standoff.

She hesitated and he held his breath until at last she nodded and stepped forward. He let her set the direction and pace. For a few moments neither said anything and after a while he felt a subtle shift in mood, more of a companionable air than an adversarial one.

He wasn't quite sure how to start but apparently she wasn't going to give him unlimited time.

"You said you had something else to say to me," she prompted.

"That day when I let you go, I wasn't completely forthcoming with you about my reasons."

She raised a brow. "You lied?"

"*Nee*, of course not. I really was concerned about the *kinner* getting too attached. And I really did want to give you the time you would need to, well, to plan your wedding to Laban." Those words were like sour milk in his mouth.

"To plan my wedding?"

Was that surprise in her voice? Did she truly think him so slow that he hadn't figured it out? "I know it hasn't been announced yet. But it was no secret that you went to Fredericksburg at Laban's invitation to view the community and meet his *familye* and friends." He let his gaze slide away from hers. "And when you came back and said matters were settled between you it was clear to me that you were engaged, or all but."

She nodded. "I see. And you didn't think that if and when I'd need time off to plan was something we should discuss."

"I know now that was a mistake and I've already apologized for it, but let me say again that I'm sorry."

"I made a promise when I came here to stay for six weeks and I had intended to fulfill that regardless of whatever else came up."

Was that why she was upset? "That's commendable, for sure and for certain. I just figured since we had another option, I could release you from that obligation so you wouldn't have all the distractions that came with being here."

She stopped in her tracks and turned with a ready-for-battle look in her eyes. "Distractions? Those sweet *lamm*s are not distractions to me. Don't you know how much I've grown to love them?"

Did that affection extend only to them?

Then she lifted her chin. "Besides, you should know by now that I'm outspoken enough to ask for time off if I need it. Just like I did when I wanted to go to Fredericksburg."

How had this conversation gotten so far off track? "For sure and for certain. But as I said earlier, all of that wasn't the whole reason I let you go. I'm ashamed to admit it wasn't even the main reason."

"Which was?"

"The true reason I was in such a hurry to send you away was that I couldn't bear the thought of seeing you every day wearing that smile you came home with, and knowing it was because you were planning your life with another man."

There was the slightest hitch in her step, but other than that he couldn't detect a reaction. "And why is that?"

Surely she knew what he was saying? "You're not going to make this easy on me, are you?"

She crossed her arms and held his gaze.

He scrubbed a hand across his chin. "All right, I probably don't deserve an easy out anyway. So here goes." He took a deep breath. "I couldn't bear it because I love you, Martha."

She dropped her arms. "What did you say?" From the intensity of her gaze, it seemed he finally had her full attention.

Encouraged, he continued. "I said I love you." He jutted his chin out. "I know you're engaged to another man and I will always regret that I didn't speak to you before you left for Fredericksburg. But I had to let you know how I felt and hope that perhaps it's not too late."

"You love me?" Her gaze searched his face as if trying to discern the truth.

He took her hands, determined to convince her. "I have always loved you. Even when I was angry with you, I still loved you."

Was that a flash of disappointment in her expression? She slipped her hands from his and took a step back, her expression hardening. "I would have thought you'd have outgrown schoolboy crushes on the teacher by now."

The words cut him. Did she still see him as a schoolboy, after everything they'd been through these past weeks? "It's no childish crush." Hearing the anger in his tone, he tried to moderate it before he continued. "*Jah*, perhaps it started off that way all those years ago when you were a teacher. But I haven't been a scholar in a very long time and a crush is most definitely *not* what I feel for you now. When I say I love you that's exactly what I mean."

She didn't seem convinced. "And you would probably have said the same thing when you were in my classroom." She lifted her hand, turning it palm-up. "Someone who truly loves you doesn't make quick assumptions about you, doesn't send you away before you can discuss what's come between you."

How many times would he have to apologize for that? How long would that mistake haunt him? "If you tell me that you love Laban more than me then I won't say another word and will step aside. But don't push me away because you doubt that I truly love you."

She turned and started walking again. He kept pace with her, waiting for her to say something, anything.

He'd just declared his love, after all. But the silence drew out.

What was she thinking? Was she trying to come up with a way to let him down? Should he say something and then turn back so she could be on her way?

But at last she spoke up, keeping her eyes focused straight ahead. "If you had bothered to let me speak when I returned from Fredericksburg you would know that I broke it off with Laban. It's the reason I came back a day early."

It was his turn to halt in his tracks. She wasn't engaged to Laban? Wasn't even considering his suit? What did this mean?

He focused back on Martha to find her watching him with an expectant, vulnerable look on her face.

"Do you mind if I ask why you two broke it off?"

She hesitated so long he thought she might not answer. Finally she lifted a hand in a gesture that was surprisingly vulnerable. "I didn't love him," she said quietly.

His pulse jumped at that. But he told himself not to leap to conclusions again. "I thought you weren't looking for a love match."

She sighed. "That's what I thought too."

Don't push too hard. "What changed your mind?"

She shrugged but held her peace. He noticed a telltale tinge of pink color in her cheeks.

"You accused me of having nothing more than a schoolboy crush on you, that I don't know the difference between that and true love. Well, let me tell you why you're wrong. I know you're not without your faults, in fact I see your faults quite clearly. You try too hard to be perfect, to control any situation you participate in. You try to hide it but inside you're a tangle of insecurity. Like your biblical namesake you often act as if it's more important to get things done than to look for the joy in any situation."

Martha shifted uncomfortably. He was making her sound like a harridan. She should have left when she first announced her intention to do so.

But Asher wasn't finished. "In addition to all of that, though, you are smart, warm and generous. Yes, you work hard, but that's because, even with your maddening perfectionist tendencies, you care about others and want what's best for them, even at your own expense. You are wonderful *gut* with *kinner*—mine miss you and ask about you every day. You're not afraid to give your opinion but never try to force a response. You hate to disappoint anyone. And above all you are a sweet, *Gotte*-fearing and beautiful woman."

He saw all of that in her?

"When Noah told me my actions had hurt you I felt devastated. I would never want to do anything to cause you pain."

Was this pity? "I don't know exactly what Noah said to you and in what context, but you have nothing to be concerned about. I'm perfectly fine." Physically anyway. "So you can go back to your life and let me go on with mine."

His jaw worked. "So are you saying you *don't* love me?"

Martha felt a whole tide of emotions wash through her. Why couldn't he just let it be? But she couldn't lie to him.

She started walking again. "I didn't want to love

you." She waved a hand. "For any number of reasons. You're four years younger than I am. You were my student for two years. You're Ephron's little *bruder*. And you believed for a very long time that I'd wronged you."

His expression fell. "I see. I'll let—"

She held up a hand to halt his protest. "But in the past few weeks I've learned other, more important things about you. You're artistically talented but never boastful. You're strong enough to provide for your *familye* and hold them securely together but you're not afraid to be tender and understanding with the *kinner* when they're hurting. You've borne all sorts of responsibilities and sorrows on your own without complaint and while quietly standing strong for others to lean on, the way only a mature, honorable, upstanding man would do."

She saw the flash of surprise in his eyes, the way he stood straighter.

"You've also seen me at my worst and rather than turning your back or taking me to task, you challenge me to be better."

He was smiling now. "If that was your worst you have nothing to feel bad about."

She shot him a reproving look, but she wasn't really upset.

"The biggest thing I've learned, however, and the thing that took me the longest to understand, is that love is not something that's logical or practical or even reasonable. Love just is. And once I finally learned what a love like that was, I couldn't picture myself married to anyone I didn't feel that for. Which is why I broke it off with Laban."

"And have you experienced that kind of love for anyone?" He sounded tense and hopeful at the same time.

She considered not answering, just walking away and keeping her feelings secret. Could she trust his declaration of love or would he just push her away again at the next bump in the road? Remembering her talk with Joan, she decided to make the leap.

"The truth is, I've grown to love you, Asher." She raised a hand to brush his cheek and saw the pulse jump in his throat. "Deeply, undeniably, truly love you." She dropped her hand and turned away, infuriated and embarrassed by the tears pooling in her eyes. "I'm afraid I always will."

She felt his hands come to rest gently on her shoulders. "Those words are the sweetest I have ever heard," he said, "even if you did speak them in an accusatory tone."

Was he trying to tease her at a time like this?

But then his tone softened. "Martha Eicher, you are the most infuriating, exacting, beautiful, loving person I know. And learning I caused you even a moment of pain is a heavy burden that will haunt me for a long time to come. But I promise I'll spend the rest of my life trying to make it up to you." He gently turned her to face him. "A life I hope you'll let me share with you."

Then he paused, apparently noticing the moisture in her eyes. "Aw *liebchen*, don't cry."

"I'm not crying," she insisted. "My eyes are just tired."

"Of course they are." He tipped her chin up with a finger. "But you didn't answer my question."

"I didn't hear you ask one."

"Didn't I?" He smiled fondly. "Then let me correct that right now. Martha Eicher, even though I am younger than you and have twice made disastrously wrong assumptions about you, will you do me the great and undeserved honor of becoming my *fraa*?"

She studied his face while he spoke and saw the undeniable honesty and love reflected there. The weight that had lodged itself in her chest ever since he sent her away lifted, to be replaced by joy.

With a heart full to bursting she nodded. "*Jah*, oh *jah*! I would love nothing more than to be your *fraa* and to be a *mamm* to those sweet *kinner* of yours."

He folded her into a gentle hug and she felt her heart swell even more. Why had she ever considered him boyish? This was a man, a man who had declared his love for her.

Asher had held himself very still as he waited the heartbeat it took her to answer him, afraid to hope she would say yes. And now that she'd said it he wanted to let out a yell that could be heard in the next district. She loved him despite all the reasons she shouldn't. Was there ever a man so lucky as he?

He reveled in the feel of her head against his shoulder, of the contented breath that tickled his neck. "You have just made me a very happy man. And I promise to try my best to make you every bit as happy as I am, not just today, but every day for the rest of our lives."

And he couldn't think of a better future to look forward to.

Epilogue

Three and a Half Weeks Later

Martha felt someone slip up behind her and knew without turning that it was Asher. When he placed a hand on her shoulder it was all she could do not to cover it with her own hand. But they weren't alone.

The Mother's Day luncheon was over and the kitchen cleaned. All of the adults—her and Asher, Dorcas, Ephron and his wife—were on the front porch enjoying the spring sunshine and watching the *kinner*, including Ephron's two, playing on the front lawn with Rowdy and Trip. Her term as the fill-in nanny had ended two weeks ago but she'd stayed on. After all, she'd be their *mamm* in another couple of months. They hadn't told anyone yet. They had arranged for both *familye*s to be together the next between Sunday. But it made their engagement all the more special to have it a secret just between the two of them for the time being.

There was a drowsy sort of peace here, enhanced by the warmth all around them. And the warmth didn't just come from the sunshine. It also came from the feeling of contentment that surrounded them.

Asher cleared his throat and then came around to where he could meet Martha's gaze. "Would you like to join me for a walk?"

Smiling, Martha stood. "A bit of exercise sounds *gut*."

As if only now remembering their presence, Asher turned to the other three. "Anyone else care to stretch their legs?"

Dorcas gave him a knowing look and even Ephron's smile seemed a bit smug. "I think we're fine here," Dorcas said indulgently. "You two enjoy your walk."

Asher nodded but Martha hesitated a moment.

"I want to fetch something from my room. I'll meet you out back."

Her response caught Asher by surprise, but he simply nodded and headed down the porch steps. It was as difficult for him to believe Martha had professed to love him as it was to believe Ephron had thrown away his own chance to marry her. He had waited a long time for her to really see him, but it had been worth it. He was truly blessed.

A few moments later Martha stepped out on the back porch, a large sketch pad in hand.

He smiled. "Do you plan to do some sketching this afternoon?"

"Actually, it's something I've been working on and I'd like to see what you think."

There was an endearing vulnerability beneath her matter-of-fact demeanor that made him feel both protective and tender. "Of course. Do you want to show me here or should we take it to the workshop?"

"The workshop would probably be best."

He took her hand to help her down the steps, then released it as she hugged her sketch pad. He already missed the softness of her touch. But he was content to walk beside her. He'd accompany her anywhere. Knowing she would soon be his *fraa* centered him, brought him a joy he'd never thought to experience.

"It was *gut* to see Ephron again and that he's able to spend several days here," Martha said as they strolled toward the workshop. "It's obvious seeing him and his *familye* has made your *grossmammi* wonderful happy."

Asher raised a brow. "I know you played a hand in that."

She brushed at her skirt with her free hand. "What do you mean?"

"The letter you wrote to Ephron, you pushed him to come, ain't so?"

She cut him a sideways glance. "I know it was presumptuous and I really didn't push too hard. I just let him know how much you all missed him and that Dorcas wouldn't be around forever and he'd regret it later. I—"

Asher held up a hand to halt her babbling confession. "There's no need to apologize, Martha. I just wanted to say *danke*."

She seemed to relax at that and a moment later

they'd reached the workshop. "Now, let's see this sketch you wanted to show me."

She placed the sketch pad on the table and took a deep breath before opening it up. She took a step back as he moved in to get a closer look.

He studied the hand-drawn design, which seemed to be based on a patchwork quilt. "You designed this yourself?"

She nodded. "I'll never be as *gut* as you, of course. But this is a project I feel inspired by and would like to attempt." She bit her lip as if self-conscious. "It's supposed to mimic a patchwork quilt, one with a special meaning."

He offered what he hoped was a reassuring smile. "The composition is quite *gut*. And the image is original and eye catching."

Some of her tension eased. "*Danke*. I had a *gut* teacher."

He picked it up to get a better look. There were five quilt "blocks." Two smaller blocks on each end and one larger one in the middle. "So, are you going to tell me what makes the design so special?"

"It represents us."

She seemed quite pleased with herself now. "Us?"

"All of us." She pointed to the top left corner. "This pattern is called Sunbonnet Sue. It represents Lottie." She moved to the top right corner. "This pattern is called Triplets."

He was catching on. "So it represents Zach, Zeb and Zeke."

She nodded. "And this one in the lower left is a Grandmother's Flower Garden pattern—I chose it to represent your *grossmammi*."

"And the one in the lower right? Is that supposed to be me or you?"

"Both of us." Her smile had an air of mischief about it this time. "It's called a Friendship Knot, and I thought it appropriate since our friendship has always been pretty knotty."

He raised a brow at that. "All in the past I hope." Then he pointed to the central image. "And this large pattern in the middle?"

Her expression softened as she touched the piece lightly. "It's called Linked Hearts. And if you'll notice it touches each of the other designs, connecting them all together." She met his gaze. "I know we won't be married for a couple of months, but it may take me a while to finish this. Besides, I already feel part of the *familye*. And this patchwork design is my attempt to represent that." There was the little hesitation again as she bit her lip. "What do you think?"

Martha studied his face closely, wondering if he really understood why she'd created this piece, if he understood how much this *familye* meant to her. How much *he* meant to her.

Rather than answering immediately, however, Asher put an arm around her and gave her a kiss, gentle yet warm and loving. Enough to set her stomach fluttering.

Then he pulled back and caressed her cheek. "What I think," he said with a tender smile, "is that it is almost as beautiful as your heart and spirit."

She leaned into his hand, basking in the warmth of his touch, reveling in the knowledge that she had every right to do so.

"The other thing I think," he continued, "is that the

only question is whether we hang this in the living room or in our room."

Our room. She liked the sound of that even though it brought the heat to her cheeks.

She had finally found the place where she belonged—in the heart of her patchwork family.

About the Author

Winnie Griggs is the multi-published, award-winning author of romances that focus on small towns, big hearts and amazing grace. Her work has won a number of regional and national awards, including the Romantic Times Reviewers' Choice Award. Winnie grew up in southeast Louisiana in an undeveloped area her friends thought of as the back of beyond. Eventually she found her own Prince Charming, and together they built a storybook happily-ever-after, one that includes four now-grown children who are all happily pursuing adventures of their own.

When not busy writing, she enjoys cooking, browsing estate sales and solving puzzles. She is also a list maker, a lover of exotic teas, and the holder of an advanced degree in the art of procrastination.

You can learn more at:
WinnieGriggs.com
Twitter @GriggsWinnie
Facebook.com/WinnieGriggs.Author
Pinterest.com/WDGriggs

Looking for more second chances and small towns? Check out Forever's heartwarming contemporary romances!

THE TRUE LOVE BOOKSHOP
by Annie Rains

For Tess Lane, owning Lakeside Books is a dream come true, but it's the weekly book club she hosts for the women in town that Tess enjoys the most. The gatherings have been her lifeline over the past three years, since she became a widow. But when secrets surrounding her husband's death are revealed, can Tess find it in her heart to forgive the mistakes of the past...and maybe even open herself up to love again?

THE MAGNOLIA SISTERS
by Alys Murray

Harper Anderson has one priority: caring for her family's farm. So when an arrogant tech mogul insists the farm host his sister's wedding, she turns him *and* his money down flat—an event like that would wreck their crops! But then Luke makes an offer she can't refuse: He'll work *for free* if Harper just considers his deal. Neither is prepared for chemistry to bloom between them as they labor side by side...but can Harper trust this city boy to put down country roots?

HER AMISH PATCHWORK FAMILY
by Winnie Griggs

Martha Eicher, formerly a schoolteacher in Hope's Haven, has always put her family first. But now everyone's happily married, and Martha isn't sure where she fits in...until she hears that Asher Lantz needs a nanny. As a single father to his niece and nephews, Asher struggles to be enough for his new family. Although a misunderstanding ended their childhood friendship, he's grateful for Martha's help. Slowly both begin to realize Martha is exactly what his family needs. Could together be where they belong?

FALLING IN LOVE ON SWEETWATER LANE
by Belle Calhoune

Nick Keegan knows all about unexpected, life-altering detours. He lost his wife in the blink of an eye, and he's spent the years since being the best single dad he can be. He's also learned to not take anything for granted, so when sparks start to fly with Harlow, the new veterinarian, Nick is all in. He senses Harlow feels it too, but she insists romance isn't on her agenda. He'll have to pull out all the stops to show her that love is worth changing the best-laid plans.

STARTING OVER ON SUNSHINE CORNER
by Phoebe Mills

Single mom Rebecca Hayes isn't getting her hopes up after she has one unforgettable night with Jackson, a very close—and very attractive—friend. She knows Jackson's unattached bachelor lifestyle too well. But in his heart, Jackson Lowe longs to build a family with Rebecca—his secret crush and the real reason he never settled down. So when Rebecca discovers she's pregnant with his baby, he knows he's got a lot of work to do before he can prove he's ready to be the man she needs.

A TABLE FOR TWO
(MM reissue) by Sheryl Lister

Serenity Wheeler's Supper Club is all about great friends, incredible food, and a whole lot of dishing—not hooking up. So when Serenity invites her friend's brother to one of her dinners, it's just good manners. But the ultra-fine, hazel-eyed Gabriel Cunningham has a gift for saying all the wrong things, causing heated exchanges and even hotter chemistry between them. But Serenity can't let herself fall for Gabriel. Cooking with love is one thing, but trusting it is quite another...